DAD BOD
—SCREWED—

Jasinda Wilder

SCREWED

ONE

It's three o'clock in the morning and I'm sitting at Laurel's dining table swirling the inch or so of Angel's Envy around the bottom of my glass, desperately fighting the urge to toss it back and pour another. I've already had two fingers of this stuff, but as tempting as it is to get black-out drunk, I refuse to do so. I haven't been drunk like that since…well, since Craig. But I refuse to think about that. At least right this moment.

I don't drink like that, and as tempting as it is to want to escape, I know better. It won't help anything, and I'll only wake up feeling like crap; I came to Laurel to talk, not to drink. I need to vent, I need advice, not a buzz. I just…I don't know how to start, or where.

Laurel sits in silence for a moment longer, looking at me expectantly, waiting for me to speak. When I don't say anything right away she stands up, tugs her thick, plush robe tighter, and ambles to the refrigerator.

"What are you doing?" I ask.

She reaches into the freezer and pulls out two pints of ice cream, grabs two spoons from a drawer, and sets them on the table in front of us. I pick one up and examine the ingredient list.

"Hmmm. Looks interesting," I say.

"Sugar-free, dairy-free, low calorie, and delicious. Ice cream unicorn, basically," Laurel says. "And I think for us, ice cream is a more effective coping mechanism than alcohol."

"No kidding," I agree, and dig in. I find it to be delicious, and I'm grateful for a few minutes of quiet as we both eat the ice cream.

And then the pint is empty.

I laugh. "Wow, that goes down fast."

Laurel chuckles and nods. "Sure does. This stuff is a real lifesaver when I'm on my period and want to eat literally everything in sight."

"Good to know," I say, setting the empty pint aside. I leave the last of the whiskey in my glass untouched. I turn to Laurel and say, "I...I don't know where to even start."

Laurel shrugs. "Honestly, Nova, I know very little about you, so if you just need to vent then, by all means, vent. I'll be a sympathetic listener and a shoulder to cry on if you need. But if you happen to want my advice or anything like that, I need a bit of background."

"You guys have all been so great to me, even though nobody knows much about me," I say. "I tend to keep my history to myself."

"Pretty much the only thing I know about you in terms of your personal history is that you were going into politics and then some shit happened. Then you worked as a party planner and a bartender, and then some more shit happened, and then you got your nursing degree."

I'm restless, as evidenced by my bouncing knee. I probably look like teenage boy. I glance at Laurel, sitting comfortably in her robe. "I need to go outside, Laurel. I'm too restless and upset to just sit here."

Laurel nods, and leaves the table. I follow her to the mudroom, where she shoves her feet in Ryder's huge work boots, and then reties her robe more tightly around her waist before leading the way outside.

"You're going out there in a robe?" I ask, amused.

She shrugs, nods, and gestures around us. "Well, yeah. Who's gonna see me?"

About fifty yards away kitty-corner to the house is a classic red barn, the kind you see on the side of the highway in rural areas—this one is clearly old, but has been restored, which is unsurprising, given that

Ryder and the guys are all builders. Around us, there's nothing but rolling hills with a few scattered trees here and there. I don't see another house anywhere in view, and I know from driving here that you can't see this house and barn from the road, as the half-mile-long driveway winds through a stand of trees and then curves behind them before dipping down and winding around the base of a hill.

"So do you often just walk around in nothing but a robe?" I ask.

She snickers. "We often walk around out here in less than just a robe, if you know what I mean." She ducks her head. "The back deck is really nice. There's a built-in couch around the perimeter with outdoor cushions. I have a feeling Ryder designed it with a... *specific*...purpose in mind."

I snort. "Wait, really? Outside, on the deck?"

She shrugs and nods again. "It's a lot of fun. Felt sort of...naughty, I guess, the first couple times. But there are no neighbors anywhere, no way to see any part of the house or barn from anywhere except, like, a satellite, and honestly, if someone is watching Ryder and me have sex from a satellite...? Well, that's a little weird, but I don't care."

"Huh. I like to think I'm pretty adventurous in the sex department—or at least, I used to be—but I can't say I've ever done it outside," I say.

Laurel bumps me with her shoulder. "You should try it sometime. It's a lot of fun."

I huff a laugh. "Assuming I ever have sex again, sure."

Laurel eyes me. "Meaning what? You're in a dry spell?"

"A dry spell? Nah, not really. More like…a self-imposed celibacy."

"For how long?"

I hesitate to answer. "It's going on three years."

Laurel chokes on a gasp. "Are you serious?"

I nod and shrug. "Yeah."

"On purpose?"

"Yeah."

Laurel is silent a while as we stroll slowly across the dew-sparkled grass. "Can I ask why?"

I sigh. "I…I guess for you to really understand that, I'd have to give you the backstory as to why I moved here at all."

"I'm listening."

I let out another long, tense sigh. "Okay, so…the first thing you should probably know is that I'm from a wealthy East Coast family. My great-great-grandparents made a bunch of money in shipping and the railway back in…god, like…the eighteen hundreds? My subsequent great-grandparents and their kids, and then my own parents, all expanded the family holdings through various investments and business enterprises. So, basically, my parents paid for me to go to Brown University with the spare cash they had lying around in a safe. *That* kind of old, old money."

She examines me with new interest. "Really? I'd have never guessed."

I smirk. "That's the point, actually. I'm sort of… estranged from them. They were shitty parents. They gave me every available luxury in life—a Mercedes for my eighteenth birthday, a stable full of horses each worth tens of thousands of dollars, birthday parties that cost more than most people make in a year, a no-limit credit card, yada yada yada. Imagine the most spoiled rich kid from, like, *Clueless* or whatever, and that was me. But money was all they had to offer. They didn't know how to love, probably because they grew up the same way—spoiled but neglected, which is a weird combination that's pretty much guaranteed to fuck you up."

"I can see how that would be."

We reach the barn and Laurel tugs a giant sliding door aside—it slides open silently and easily, revealing the darkened interior of the barn—rafters high overhead, the smell of hay strong in the air, the whicker of a horse, walls, slats, shadows. She reaches to one side and flicks on a light—and with a quickening flicker, fluorescent lights come to life, bathing the barn in light. The floor is strewn with hay and straw, and along one side are several stalls, three of them containing horses—a tail swishes in one, a head peeks over another, and a pair of ears shows from the farthest stall. A loft high above, accessible via a ladder along the wall opposite the horse stalls, is filled to capacity with hay bales. Near the ladder a swing hangs from the rafters via thick chains, a folded blanket on it.

"This is one of Ryder's and my favorite places to come and talk," Laurel says.

"I can see why," I say, plopping down on the swing. "So, that's my background, so to speak. In high school, I was in the popular crowd, more because of my parents' money than any particular merits of my own, but still. I hated them, hated living with them, and couldn't wait to go to college so I could get away on my own. I had plans, you know? I'd been to a couple rallies for some hoity-toity East Coast politicians, and had attended a few debates, and I just sort of fell in love with the energy, the ideas, the sense of being part of shaping the country itself. Granted, I was an idealistic teenager, but still, that's what I fell in love with, and it's what I pursued when I got to college. Back then I was idealistic, naive, full of piss and vinegar and determination, you know? But being innocent and sheltered, I was also…god, so much different than I am now. Believe it or not, I was open, I was passionate, and I made friends with anyone and everyone. Back then, I was the girl who became the center of any party I went to."

Laurel smiles at me, sitting beside me and kicking the swing into motion. "Actually, I can see that pretty easily."

I arch an eyebrow at her. "Really?

She shrugs. "Sure. You put on a pretty convincing show with the aloof tough-girl act, but I see a softie underneath all that."

I snort. "Soft? No, not by a long shot. I grew up neglected and unloved. The closest thing to affection I ever got was an occasional, awkward hug. So, no. Soft is one thing I've never been. Fun, open-minded, easy to talk to? Sure. Soft and nice and sweet? No way."

"My point *is*," Laurel says, rolling her eyes at me, "that I see through the tough -act you put on."

I laugh and smile at Laurel. "Okay, just don't tell anyone," I joke, "I've got a reputation to maintain."

Another knowing smile. "Yeah, hon, about that— we all see through it, you know. We're just waiting for you to get over yourself and trust us a bit." She pats me on the arm. "Anyway. Continue with your story."

"I...um." I sigh. "Well, jumping to the juicy bits, I suppose...I met a guy named Landon Price my sophomore year at Brown. He was a senior. We met at a rally for some bigwig from the DNC, discovered we went to the same school and started hanging out, going to parties together. It started like that, but then we started sleeping together, and that turned into spending the night together, and things just sort of progressed from there without us ever really putting a label on it. We were just together all the time."

"What was he like?" Laurel asks.

I grin. "Six-three, blond hair, blue eyes, fit, beautiful…he was your classic boy next door, All-American, Tommy Hilfiger model specimen of male beauty. He really was a Hilfiger model, too, in high school. As he liked to put it, he 'dabbled' in modeling, but once he got into Brown he put it behind him to focus on politics. By his senior year he was already interning with one of the DNC's rising stars, a young senator from Massachusetts with a lot of controversial views, a shitload of charm and charisma, and big plans for the future. Landon was positioning himself to ride the senator's coattails up the ladder until he was ready to run for senate himself. And let me tell you, that was hot as hell for me. Landon got me an internship with the senator, and by the time I graduated Landon and I were just about running the reelection campaign ourselves. We were definitely the top aides. It was… exciting."

"So how does this lead you to sobbing about a

wedding at my breakfast table at three in the morning?" Laurel asks.

I laugh. "Oh, keep listening. It gets gnarly, I promise." I push away the old emotions and focus on just telling the story, because I haven't spoken of this to anyone...pretty much ever, and I'm ready to unload it. "So, I met Landon sophomore year, and we dated through graduation. He proposed my junior year, I accepted, and we agreed we wanted to wait until after I graduated to get married, and for him to get a bit more settled and established in the political scene in DC. So after graduation, I just sort of started planning the wedding. Coming up with the overall theme, picking the dress with my girlfriends, finding the perfect church and venue for the reception. Only...I could never get Landon to agree on a date. He kept just putting it off. Saying the timing wasn't right, let's get through the midterm elections, blah blah blah."

"Uh-oh. Sounds like a case of commitment-itis."

I laugh. "I wish it had been that simple. I loved him, but I got the sense he was sort of intimidated by me, or jealous of me, or resentful, or something. He started interning for Senator Calhoun before I did, and he got me the job with him, but I sort of stole Calhoun's favor. I was smarter than him—I had better grades, I had better ideas, and Calhoun listened to me more, favored me. Which, in hindsight, was as much because of these"—I cup my boobs—"as this," I say tapping my temple.

"Regardless, Landon was jealous."

"Right." I take a deep breath, hold it, and let it out slowly. "So, this is where things began to change. I always knew the senator was…well, attracted to me, you might say. I never acknowledged it, never did anything about it—I was with Landon, for one thing, and Calhoun was married with kids, for another. So it was just sort of this unspoken thing where I avoided being alone with Calhoun to avoid any weirdness or potential impropriety. I also knew he was somewhat prone to…well…straying, I guess. He had me do some *fixing* for him, if you want the dirty truth. Handing checks to mistresses to keep them quiet about his indiscretions."

"Yuck," Laurel says.

I keep my voice neutral and focus on just relating the facts. "His wife knew about it, to be fair. It was one of those marriages of convenience, appearance, and political maneuvering rather than love, and we all knew she had her own side action going on. It was just another one of those dirty political messes, you know? I just did my job and tried to distance myself from his private life. The truth is Calhoun was going places, and I stood to gain by sticking with him until a better offer came along."

"Let me guess…Senator Calhoun assaulted you?"

I shake my head. "Nope. Again, nothing so simple." I gather my strength to relate the next part. "Landon and I had an argument about getting married. I either wanted a firm wedding date, or to know that he wasn't interested, and he tried his best to weasel his way out of both options." I make my voice deep and gruff, quoting Landon. "'I love you, but it's not the right time yet. You know I love you, we have a good thing, why fix what's not broken.' All that jazz. It got ugly. I was tired of being strung along. I wanted to move in together, or get married, or *something*, but he didn't, and I was sick of it. I got mad."

"Understandable."

"So we fought, I left, and we ignored each other at work the next day. He left for a working lunch, and I stayed at the office to get some stuff done. And then I spilled coffee all over my top and skirt. My apartment was twice as far from the office as Landon's, and I had plenty of clothes at his place. We had keys to each other's places, so me going to his place to change was no big deal."

Laurel closes her eyes slowly and sighs, seeing what is coming. "Shit."

"Yeah. So, I'm on my phone with Calhoun's PA, sorting out the details of a meeting with another senator. Whatever. I'm not really paying attention to what I'm doing as I go up to Landon's apartment and let myself in. I end the call and head for the bedroom, juggling my phone, purse and shoes while trying to undress. I had a bunch of shit to get done, and I really wanted to get back so I wouldn't be at the office till midnight." I pause to breathe a moment, remembering. "I opened the bedroom door, and just stopped in my tracks, my shirt half off, skirt hanging open, shoes, phone, purse all dropping to the ground."

"He was cheating on you."

I laugh bitterly. "Yes, he was. When I walked in, he was on his back on his bed, balls-deep in Senator Calhoun's wife."

"Well, fuck."

"Yeah. But that's not all." I laugh again, even more bitterly. "It wasn't just his wife. One of the other aides, an office assistant—a coffee getter and copy maker. Nineteen if she was a day, and she was riding Landon's face, and he had his hands all over both of them. He was eating out the aide like he was in a porno, and fucking the senator's wife. The whole deal. I was…to say I was shocked would be an understatement. Given his recent behavior, I was expecting him to dump me, or to keep putting off the wedding, but to be cheating on me? No. Dumb of me, maybe, but I never saw it coming. Especially not with our boss's wife, let alone a threesome with her and another aide. It was awful."

Laurel winces. "My god, I can't even imagine. What did you do?"

I can't help laughing. It is almost funny in hindsight. Almost. "They didn't even notice me, at first. I stood there, stunned, watching them fuck for almost two minutes. And let me tell you, Landon *never* fucked me the way he was fucking Presley Calhoun. It cut me to the bone."

"I can imagine it would," Laurel says. "So...what happened?"

I shake my head. "The bastard didn't notice me until after he finished. I guess I showed up right at the end. So he came, and then looked over and saw me and freaked out. Tossed the Calhoun bitch off him one way, the aide another way, and tried to start with excuses and explanations."

"Men," Laurel huffs, laughing. "They think they can apologize and excuse their way out of anything."

"I ignored him. I packed all my shit into a suitcase and some trash bags and left. I didn't say a word to him. I tossed my key to his apartment on the counter, fished his keys out his pants pocket and took mine back, and went to work."

Laurel frowns at me. "So then what?"

I sigh. "This is where it gets a little...ugly. And embarrassing," I say. "I told my—*our*—boss what had happened."

Laurel barks a laugh. "You went in and told your boss, a senator, that his wife was fucking two of his aides?"

I nod. "Yep. What I actually said was, "So, Senator. I just walked in on Presley, your wife, fucking Landon, my fiancée...*and* Eileen."

She sputters a disbelieving laugh. "Wow. So what did he say?"

"Not much, initially. He did the whole stressed and disappointed important guy thing, where he leaned back in his desk chair, took off his glasses, and rubbed the bridge of his nose with a sigh."

"Sounds cliché."

"He was kind of cliché in a lot of ways, actually. Tall, slender, perfectly coiffed blond hair, big smarmy blue eyes, Harvard Law School alumni, put on the fast track to politics by his wealthy, influential father, blah blah blah. Partner at a high-powered law firm by the time he was thirty, senator by thirty-five, all that. Handsome, wealthy, with a beautiful trophy wife and two trophy kids, a bunch of plaques and degrees and bullshit on his office wall. And a total horn dog." I groan, scraping my hands through my hair.

"So, I have to point out a few things, here," I say.

"Like I said, I knew Calhoun was a horn dog who couldn't keep his dick in his pants. I *knew* it. I *knew* his wife was the same—she'd slept with half of the good-looking aides in Washington, and a good many of the law students and interns. She had a thing for younger guys, apparently. But the senator and his wife had an agreement—keep it discreet, no pregnancies, no tabloid or news attention, and don't shit where you eat. Meaning, no sleeping with your own office people. I guess that was a major part of the agreement: neither the senator nor his wife was allowed to sleep with anyone who worked for them. Anyone else was fair game, but not the interns, aides, or office workers."

"And Mrs. Calhoun broke that rule," Laurel says.

I nod. "Yep. Worse yet, she'd done so in the most dramatic way possible—she didn't just sleep with *one* aide, but two. And not just that, but she'd come between me and Landon. Plus, Eileen was married too. Newly wed, the ink still wet on her marriage license, basically. So Presley had ruined not just her own marriage, but my engagement to Landon, *and* Eileen's marriage, all in one fell swoop."

"Wow. Shitty decision making, huh?" Laurel says.

I sigh. "Yep. But it doesn't stop there, and the story doesn't leave me squeaky clean, either, unfortunately."

Laurel blinks at me, and then shakes her head.

"You didn't."

"I did."

"You slept with the senator?"

I groan. "Yeah, I did."

"Wow." Laurel pauses. "Not trying to be judgmental, but…*wow*."

"Not, like, that day. I held out for…shit, like three months? The senator divorced Presley, and that was a quick, quiet, and truly savage deal, too. Being connected the way he was, Calhoun made sure she didn't get shit. He paid her a lump-sum deal and that was it. No alimony, nothing. She didn't get a car, the house, nothing. He got her a halfway decent Georgetown apartment, they split custody in his favor, he paid minimal child support…it was ugly. But that's beside the point. Landon got fired, and went to work for a congresswoman—who I think he also slept with, incidentally, but again, whatever. Eileen left her husband and moved to Norway to be a diplomatic attaché. Which left only me—and he, as far as I'm aware, never did dip into the pool of women who worked for him in terms of his sexual misadventures."

"Except for you."

I nod. "Except for me."

"How'd that happen? I mean, you don't strike me as that type of person, you know?" She rolls a shoulder. "Especially knowing what you did about him."

"I got drunk with him. The day the court finalized his divorce, he and I went out to celebrate. Which wasn't unusual, honestly. We often had working lunches, dinners, cocktail parties that kind of thing. This time, though…it was different. We both got just…obliterated. One of only two times in my entire life I've ever been that drunk. I was lonely and horny since I hadn't been with anyone since Landon, and I think even Calhoun had been holding off until his divorce was done, for whatever reason. And we just…we got drunk and stupid, and ended up in bed together."

Laurel eyes me. "But that's not it, is it?"

"It?" I ask, clarifying.

"That's not all that happened—you getting drunk and sleeping with your boss—and it's not why you're here."

I shake my head. "Nope. Sadly, I was not that smart. I continued to sleep with him. And somehow it snowballed from sleeping together to becoming involved, openly. And then he proposed, and I accepted—"

"What?!" Laurel shoots forward, her feet stopping the swing. "You *didn't*!"

"I did." I shake my head. "Young, dumb, lonely, and naive, I guess. I was still in my early twenties, and delusionally idealistic. I convinced myself I would be the one to change his philandering ways. He'd be faithful to *me* even…though he hadn't been to his wife and kids, blah blah blah." I waved a hand. "So stupid. He wanted to get married right away, so I started planning. And he was…well, he was really good to me. Took me on vacations to Europe and the Caribbean, got me a nicer apartment—even got me a job with a different senator so there wouldn't be office drama in our relationship."

"Let me guess…and then he wasn't faithful."

"Yep. Got it in one." I sigh for the millionth time. "He didn't even try to be sneaky about it. I had a dentist appointment one afternoon, so I took off work in the morning, went to the dentist, and when the appointment was over I thought I'd surprise him with lunch and desk sex."

"And you walked in on him."

"With…get this…my new boss's secretary."

"Wow. Not subtle, was he?"

I laugh. "No, not really. That was the last straw for me. That was when I realized Washington was just…gross. Everyone was lying to and manipulating everyone, working solely for their own ends and using anyone they could, and everyone was sleeping with everyone else. It's a surprisingly small town, in a way. The people who work on Capitol Hill tend to know everyone, and everyone knows everyone's business.

The whole town knew Calhoun was cheating on me, and with whom. That shit goes around, you know? You discuss who's sleeping with whom around the coffee machine."

"So you dumped him?"

"I threw his ring in his face, went back to my office and told my boss I quit, there and then, on the spot. I called a moving company and had them pack my apartment and put all my shit into storage. I packed my clothes and I just...left. Washington, my job, my friends, my apartment, everything. I ended up in Chicago, and at first I got a job at a law firm, clerking. Familiar work, but I hated it." I push the swing back into motion.

"Then I met Craig at a coffee shop. He was the barista. We flirted while he made my coffee. This went on for months. Just flirting. Talking. He asked me out, and I accepted. He was...different. From a shitty background, lots of abuse and stuff, and ran away to the city, and was sort of just surviving on his own. Younger than me, but so, so, *so* amazing. Just absolutely the kindest, sweetest, funniest guy I'd ever met. Genuine to the extreme. He made you feel like you were the only person on earth. We dated for four months and then I moved in with him."

"Oh shit," Laurel says. "I don't like where this is going. There's no way you got bamboozled by him, too. Your taste in men can't be *that* bad."

I hesitate again. "Honestly, I wish that was it." I stand up, pace across the barn to one of the horses and pet its nose. "Craig and I had it good—really good. We were together for five years altogether. During that time I started the party planning business. A friend of ours wanted to throw a party for her graduation but just couldn't make anything work, so I offered to help. I guess I did such a good job, she talked me up to our friends and someone else asked for my help. That snowballed into an event planning business. I loved it. Craig and I were barely making ends meet, but we were happy. He was a barista and a janitor, I was an event planner, and we just sort of scraped by, but we had each other and it was enough."

I have to stop again, gathering myself.

"I've never talked about this before." I scratch the horse on its nose, and it nudges me whenever I stop. "So, um. Craig started acting weird. Not eating much, getting cranky, taking naps—all of that was wildly out of character for him. He shaved his head randomly, and he'd always been sort of vain about his hair. He got cagey, like he was hiding something."

"He was cheating on you?"

"That's what I assumed." I twist my hair up and then let it fall loose again, going back to the swing. "I followed him around one day, thinking I'd get to the bottom of it. Instead of going to work, he went across town, and I thought, aha, got you now, asshole. But instead of a hotel or some chick's apartment, he went to an outpatient medical facility. A...um, cancer center."

Laurel's face falls. "Ohhh. Oh no."

"Yeah. I went in. Found him in a chair, getting chemo." I swallow hard. "He had cancer, and he'd never told me. He was hiding it. Hoping he could beat it. Or maybe hoping it would kill him before he had to tell me he was dying. I don't know. We never discussed why he didn't tell me. I just..." I blink hard. "I stared at him for a minute, and he stared back, and then sat down with him, held his hand, and...that was it. I stayed with him. Went to every round of chemo with him. Went to radiation with him. Sat next to him for every oncologist appointment, sat at his bedside while he died."

"Holy hell, Nova."

"I found out in May, and he was gone by September."

"Jesus."

I wipe at my face. "Yeah." The memories are sad and bitter. "Two weeks after his death, after I'd cleaned out our apartment and donated his stuff and everything, I got a letter. From Craig. He wrote it before he died. It had a ring inside. He had planned on proposing, had the ring, but then he got sick, and he couldn't bring himself to ask me to marry him when he knew he was going to die." I lift my wrist and tap the hospital bracelet. "This is his. From his last hospital stay. He gave up treatment at the end, knew it wasn't going to save him and he didn't want to fight it, so he just came home, and I took care of him. That was…hell. There are no words for it. None."

"Nova, god. I'm so, so sorry."

I nod. "I really truly loved him. Like, so fucking much. I'd been waiting for him to propose. I had our wedding planned, in my head at least. I knew exactly what it would look like, everything."

"But you never got there."

"Nope."

"So then you went into nursing."

I shrug, nod. "Yeah. I couldn't go back to Washington, had no desire to. Planning parties was a thing I'd done because I enjoyed it but somehow, without Craig, it wasn't fun anymore. So I went back to school, at first just sort of taking random classes to see what sparked my interest. An anatomy and physiology class caught my attention, and I ended up in the nursing program."

"That's the class where you met the guy who wanted to churn your butter?"

I laugh. "Yeah, exactly. I decided I wanted to try

something different. I'd always been sort of buttoned up, by the book. I only had sex with guys I was in relationships with, and then only long-term—that oops with Calhoun was an exception, and even that turned into a relationship. I kept to myself for a long, long time after Craig died. But then I was just...I don't know. Lonely? Horny? Tired of being alone, and lonely and horny? I needed sex, but couldn't deal with emotions. So I tried hooking up—casual sex. That guy, the butter churner guy, and a few others. There was about...I don't know exactly...maybe two years while I was in nursing school where I was pretty promiscuous. But I just...I don't know. I gave that up, once I got my MS and got a job out here."

"Gave what up?"

I shrug. "Sex."

"That self-imposed celibacy you mentioned," Laurel says. "So you really haven't had sex in three years?"

"Yep. That lifestyle just stopped being fun. I was always the kind of girl who got more enjoyment from sex when it...I don't know...when it meant something. Even a little bit of something—it didn't have to be love. I just needed some kind of connection. I couldn't do the casual sex thing. I tried—I really did, but I hated it. I felt dirty, like I was using the guys. I always felt more empty afterward than I had beforehand. So eventually, I just stopped pretending and focused on my nursing work."

"And you have no intention of—" Laurel stops, shrugs. "I don't know, of…letting anyone get close again?"

I shake my head. "Nope. After Craig, my heart was just…irreparably broken." I drag my toes on the barn floor as the swing gently creaks, creating parallel scuff marks in the dust. "I loved Landon, but he'd broken my heart and my trust. I can't say I exactly *loved* the senator, but he'd still hurt me. Craig, though—I'd given myself to him heart, mind, body, and soul, and his death just…shattered me. I'm broken by it, and I don't know how to…" I shrug, shake my head, trail off.

Laurel leans her head on my shoulder. "I understand. As well as I can, at least, not having been through that."

I stare at her. " I know you have more to say than that."

She shrugs. "Sure. But you're not here for my advice. You needed to vent."

"You're not going to bring up James?"

She grins. "I don't have to, because you just did."

"Everyone wants me and him to get together, and neither of us are there. He for his reasons, and me for mine."

"They're the same reasons, I think. Or similar."

I groan. "Sure, maybe. But so what? We're both dead to love. Why bother?"

Laurel wraps an arm around me. "Oh, Nova."

I pull away. "What?"

"If you were dead to love, you wouldn't be here."

I glare at her. "Meaning?"

"Meaning, if you were dead to love, it wouldn't be so hard for you to plan Jesse and Imogen's wedding."

"It reminds me of Craig, that's all."

She glares at me. "You're a bad liar."

I growl in annoyance. "I'm not saying I'm, like, without feelings. I'm not some sociopath or whatever. I loved Craig. Planning weddings was something I did frequently when I was with him, and they were my favorite kind of event. I did bachelor and bachelorette parties, kid's parties, graduations, all that, but I loved doing weddings best of all." I swallow hard. "Probably because I was so sure that one day soon I'd be planning my own to Craig. That's what kept me going, what gave me my creativity." I wave a hand. "It has nothing whatsoever to do with James."

"Then why'd you bring him up?" Laurel asks.

"I didn't. I asked if you were going to."

Laurel just smirks. "Sure."

I stand up, annoyed. "God, you're all so smug about this. You're all so certain I'm going to just, what? Fall into bed with James, and end up in love?"

"None of us have said that."

"It's implied."

"You're lonely, Nova. Lonely and bitter. And cranky. You need sex. You need companionship. We all just think there's something there with you and James, and that you should at least give it a look, see what it is and see if it's worth pursuing."

"It won't be." My voice is flat, hard.

"What makes you so sure?"

"Because nothing will ever compare to what I had with Craig, And James is just as closed off as I am, so even if I did want to pursue something, he doesn't."

"How do you know?" Laurel asks.

"Because we talked about it!" I snap. "We both acknowledged things, and we both made it clear we weren't in a place to fuck around with something that would only end up in more heartbreak for both of us. And there are his kids to think about, too. He doesn't want to get them confused, so we agreed to move on without lingering over it. For both our sakes."

Laurel just shakes her head, sighing. "Nova…"

"What?"

She shakes her head again. "Nothing. Never mind." She wraps her arm around me again. "I'm glad you shared this with me, Nova. Thank you."

"I'm sorry to crash like this, I just..." I lean against her. "I was up late after work, trying to come up with creative themes and centerpieces and such, and I just... couldn't. It all came up all at once, and I had to get it out. I've kept it bolted down for so long."

Laurel tugs me to my feet. "Come on. You can sleep in one of our extra rooms."

"You're sure it's okay?" I ask.

She nods. "It's not just okay—I insist."

"All right," I say, "I'm too tired to argue."

I follow her back to the house and she leads me to an extra room at the end of the hallway upstairs. There's a queen-size bed with a cozy flannel quilt and an electric fireplace, and a few cute, kitschy, coun-try-chic decorations that make it feel homey.

I hesitate when Laurel asks if there's anything I need, and when I don't reply right away Laurel just snorts at me. "It's not that hard to just ask for something, Nova. It's really not."

"Maybe not for you," I murmur. "Do you have anything I can sleep in?"

Laurel eyes me—I'm several inches taller than her, and thicker in the butt and thighs as well as bust-ier. "Ummm, maybe? I can't guarantee anything of mine will fit you all that well, though."

She leaves and comes back a few minutes later with a T-shirt.

"This is the best I can do, considering the difference in our builds. An oversized T-shirt…well, oversized for me."

I smile at her, lean in for a hug. "Perfect. Thank you."

She kisses my cheek. "This is what friends are for, Nova."

I change into the shirt—which isn't really oversized, but whatever. I'm too tired from crying, or maybe it was the twenty-hour shift I'd worked followed by three hours of wedding planning; every detail of which made me think more and more of Craig, and the wedding we never got to have.

Regardless, I passed out the second my head hit the pillow.

TWO

I WAKE UP DISORIENTED—I'M NOT IN MY BED; WHAT TIME is it?

I blink slowly, stretching, noticing that the sun is blazing in through the window, high in the sky. Ten? Eleven? Near noon, maybe? I know it's later than I've slept in a long time. I hear voices, smell food being cooked. Grilled cheese? Oh my god, I'm hungry—I skipped both lunch and dinner yesterday, and now I'm famished. I follow my nose down into the kitchen, bleary-eyed, still half asleep, and disoriented and groggy. When I stumble to a halt in the kitchen, I'm still half asleep. I was not thinking about anything except where the coffee pot was, and how I could get my hands on a grilled cheese sandwich. I'm not thinking about what I'm wearing, who's here, or what I look like.

At the same round table where I'd sobbed last night, I see Ryder, Nova, Nate...

And James.

Nate is in Star Wars pajama pants and nothing else, chattering a mile a minute about who knows what, he's just talking for the hell of it. It's too early for that much chipper chatter. Ryder and James are both dressed for work, in faded jeans, hoodies with sleeves pushed up around their thick forearms, Oakleys pushed up on their heads, massive clunky boots under the table.

James has his huge bear paw hands wrapped around a diner-style coffee mug, making it look like a toy teacup. His brown eyes slide across the room and land on me, and flick in slow increments downward—eyes, hair, chest, legs. He coughs, suddenly—as if he literally choked on his coffee.

I remember, groggily, that I'd braided my hair before bed but didn't have a hair tie, so it came loose from the braid, which means my hair must be coming loose in a bombed-out spray of curly ginger. Like a cloud of red around my face, loose and wild.

And then I remember that I never took off my makeup, so I must have raccoon circles and smears.

Furthermore, I remember that I borrowed pj's from Laurel, and that she's four inches shorter than me, and at least one cup size smaller in the chest.

I glance down at myself: a blue Eeyore T-shirt that's probably adorably too big on Laurel, but on me is more than a little tight around the chest and the hem barely covers my butt. My nipples poke against the fabric, tightening under his scrutiny.

James's eyes widen, rake upwards and latch onto my breasts one more time. And then he clears his throat gruffly, yanking his gaze away, staring determinedly into his coffee.

"Mornin', Nova," he mutters.

"Hi," I mumble back. "Is it morning? I have no idea."

Ryder gives me a quick once-over, glances at James, and then at Laurel, not quite hiding a smirk. "It's eleven thirsty—I mean thirty."

James gives Ryder a death glare. "You can just shut the fu—the heck up."

Nate grins widely. "I know what you were going to say. You were gonna say a bad word."

James rolls his eyes. "Got me there, kiddo."

"Mama says I shouldn't repeat pretty much anything any of you guys ever say, because you're all good guys but terrible potty mouths."

James snorts. "I'd say your mama is right." James is studiously avoiding looking at me.

I cross my arms over my chest and take a seat at the table—and, unfortunately for both of us, the only open seat is next to James, between him and Nate.

Laurel is biting her lip to keep from laughing.

"Good morning, Nova. Sleep well?"

I nod. "Yes, I did, thank you. I appreciate the hospitality."

"I'm guessing you wouldn't turn down coffee and breakfast?"

I shake my head. "I certainly would not."

"I have grilled cheese and tomato soup, but I can rustle you up some eggs, or a bagel, or something else if you'd rather." Laurel pours me a cup of coffee into a giant Blackhawks mug.

I accept the coffee and smile at her. "Grilled cheese and tomato soup sounds incredible."

"You're gonna have lunch for breakfast?" Nate asks.

I glance at the kid—I'm not much for children, as a rule, but with James's girls and Laurel's son, I'm learning to deal with them. "Food is food, kiddo. Steak for breakfast, pancakes for dinner, eggs for lunch, it's all just food."

"Mama, can we have steaks for breakfast tomorrow?" Nate asks.

Laurel laughs. "Maybe."

Nate, being a kid and thus lacking in any concept of social convention, is staring at me. He frowns. "Is that my mom's shirt?"

I nod, sipping coffee. "Yeah. I stayed the night and needed something to sleep in that weren't my work clothes."

He frowns a bit harder, his stare unabashedly curious. "It doesn't fit you."

I blink at him, unsure how to respond to that. "I…um. No, I guess not. But when you borrow someone else's clothes, that happens sometimes."

"Is it because your no-no's are so much bigger than Mom's?"

I choke on coffee, spluttering and coughing.

"Nathaniel Paul Madison!" Laurel snaps. "What the hell is wrong with you? You know better than to talk like that! Especially to a guest."

Nate's face falls, and he meets my eyes, abashed. "I'm sorry, Nova."

James looks like he's about to bolt, and Ryder is choking back laughter. Laurel, however, is furious.

"It's fine. I wasn't thinking clearly when I came down dressed like this." I stand up, leave the table. "I'll be right back."

"I mean, the kid *does* have a point," I hear Ryder say.

"*Ryder*," Laurel snaps. "Not helping."

"Sorry, Laurel."

"I…um—I have to go," I hear James say. "I've got, a, um…I've gotta go."

"You've got a…*tit*-uation?" Ryder says, chuckling.

"RYDER MCCANN!" Laurel shouts. "Not okay."

"I swear I'll fire your ass, Ryder, best friend or not," James says. "Now let's go. We have work to do. Early lunch is over."

"I'm still eating, James," Ryder says, "so chill."

I don't hear the rest of James's response as I enter the bedroom and close the door.

God, I don't remember the last time I was this embarrassed.

I suck up what's left of my dignity, change back into my scrubs, head into the bathroom down the hall and find a hairbrush, drag it through my hair, and steal a hair tie from the doorknob. I wash the makeup off my face, dry off, and head back downstairs. Ryder and James are both gone, and Nate is in the living room playing *Mario Kart* on a console, tongue sticking out the corner of his mouth, utterly focused. Laurel is at the stove, stirring tomato soup in a pan, and using a spatula to tip a grilled cheese up to check the doneness on the bottom, scoops it onto a paper plate, ladles a full bowl of soup, pours a fresh mug of coffee for herself and warms up mine, and then sits kitty-corner to me as I take the seat at the table where she placed the plate and bowl.

I eat a few bites of each, groaning in pleasure. "God, grilled cheese and tomato soup are my comfort foods. How did you know?"

Laurel laughs. "It's become a staple in this house.

It's both Nate's and Ryder's favorite thing to eat, so I make it for them pretty much every afternoon. James and the guys all work early, usually, but then take an early lunch, and there's always at least one of the guys here for soup and sandwiches, so I'm always making a lot extra. I wouldn't be surprised if Jesse or Franco breeze in at some point."

"Well, I needed this, so thank you."

She shrugs. "You're welcome."

"I mean thanks for last night, and for breakfast. Lunch, whatever. Everything." I lapse into silence for a few moments, take a few bites of soup. "I haven't cried like that in…god, years. Not since Craig died. I guess I…I've held it in so long I'd almost forgotten how to…" I sigh, unable to articulate it any further.

"How to express emotions?" I nod, and Laurel rests a hand on my forearm. "You once joked that you're a cold-hearted bitch. I don't think you are, Nova, I think you're just pretending to be one because it feels safer after what you've been through."

I dip the sandwich into the soup, and take a bite. "I'm not sure how pretend it is, Laurel. Most of the time I really, truly, genuinely just don't want to connect with anyone, and don't care about much of anything."

"You've trained yourself not to."

I shrug. "You may be right. I needed to vent, and

you were here for me, so thank you. That's my point."

"I'm sorry about Nate's comment. He's not usually that kind of kid. I feel terrible." Laurel winces as she says this. "He definitely knows better."

I chuckle. "I mean, I was essentially naked. The poor kid is probably traumatized for life."

Laurel snickered. "I dunno about that—he walked in on me in the shower more than a few times before I lost weight. If that didn't traumatize him, seeing a beautiful, fit, well-endowed woman in a T-shirt and underwear certainly isn't going to."

I snort. *"You're* well-endowed—*I'm* a freak of nature."

Laurel bit her lower lip, a pained expression crossing her face—as if trying to hold back a comment that was bursting to emerge.

I roll my eyes. "Don't say it, Laurel."

"I'm not."

I glare at her—she's still biting down on her lip as if literally biting down on the joke. "You want to, though."

"So bad." She grimaces. "Sorry."

I set the sandwich down and lean back, crossing my arms over my chest. "Fine. Go ahead. You're clearly about to burst."

"James was walking kinda funny when he left," Laurel says in a rush. "And the only way he could've gotten out any faster is if he'd run."

I laugh. "Yeah, well, I have that effect on men."

She tilts her head toward me with a droll stare. "Not what I meant."

"I know, Laurel."

"I meant he was running because he was worried you'd come back down and see him trying to hide his erection."

I groan. "I *know* what you meant, Laurel. God."

She grins. "Had to be said. The man is wildly attracted to you."

"So is my department head at the hospital, but I don't date him, or sleep with him."

"Probably because he's eighty, bald, and overweight," Laurel says.

"Actually, he's a fit fifty, and a silver fox." I pause for effect. "And an obnoxiously arrogant, self-important, sexist douchebag, but that's beside the point."

Laurel finishes her coffee. "I mean, did you see the look on James's face when you came down?"

"He choked on his coffee."

"Because all the blood in his body ran south, leaving him without enough brainpower to breathe, look at you, and swallow coffee all at the same time, and clearly looking at you won that contest."

"Laurel." I shake my head. "I'm not gonna keep having this discussion, not with you, not with anyone.

James and I are not a thing, and we never will be."

She shakes her head again. "Shame." She eyes me. "So, you're gonna stay celibate the rest of your life, then?"

"Maybe," I say. "I'm a lot more productive this way. Men just get in the way and distract me."

Laurel stares at me thoughtfully for a moment, and then throws up her hands. "I'm obviously not going to change your mind, so I'll stop bugging you about it. But let it be known, my dear Nova, it is my firm belief that you and James are meant for each other, and you're only delaying the inevitable, and depriving yourself of something amazing in the meantime." She holds up her hands and brings them down in an X motion. "And that's my final word on the subject forevermore. I support you regardless of whether or not I think you're being an idiot."

I narrow my eyes at her. "Wow, okay. Delaying the inevitable, depriving myself of something amazing, *and* an idiot. Anything else?"

She shrugs cutely and leans in to hug me—which is awkward for me because I'm not a hugger. At all. Or much for any kind of affection, really.

"Only that I love you," she says.

"Love you too, Laurel." I can't be mad at her— she's too sweet, too well-meaning. I hug her back, briefly, rigidly, and then stand up. "By the way, I have one question for you."

She stands up with me and walks me to the door. "What's that?"

"Why does your son call breasts no-no's?"

Laurel blushes and laughs. "Well, as a little guy just learning to speak and having just been weaned, he was constantly grabbing my chest. So I kept saying no-no to him whenever he grabbed at my boobs. Which led him to call them no-no's, and it just stuck even at an age where he knows what they're called, plus a few other slang terms for them."

I laugh. "Ah. Kid logic."

She nods, laughing. "Yep, kid logic." She shoos me out the door. "Now go on with you. Take your big ol' no-no's and go to work."

"I'm actually off today. I've got some work to do around the house, and I have to talk to Jesse and Imogen about finding someone else to finish planning their wedding." I wince. "That's gonna suck. I hate letting them down, but it's just too hard for me."

"They'll understand, especially if you give them some backstory as to why. The abridged version, at least."

I hesitate on the steps, thinking. "I don't know, but maybe now that I've told the story once, telling it again doesn't seem so insurmountable."

THREE

THE NEXT MORNING, I'M FINISHING UP LAUNDRY AND tidying my bedroom when my phone rings.

I answer it, propping the phone between shoulder and ear. "Hello?"

"Hey, Nova. It's Imogen."

"Hey, Im. How are you?"

"Fine. So, um, I had some thoughts about the centerpieces. Do you have a minute for me to run them by you?"

I stifle a sigh. "I…um…actually, I wanted to talk to you too. Are you home? I could pop over."

"Yeah, I'm home. Come on over."

Imogen's house is an adorable little place, sided with white vinyl, a dark roof, a red front door and red shutters, all recently redone, thanks to Jesse and the guys. I park in the driveway behind Imogen's car and head for the front door. Imogen welcomes me with a hug, and leads me inside. Her house smells like new paint and sawdust. There're power tools everywhere, sheets of drywall stacked near the back door, and a tarp over the kitchen table.

"Wow, more construction, huh?" I say. "Didn't the guys just redo your roof and siding?"

Imogen laughs. "Yeah, but the roof was thirty years old and starting to leak into the attic, and the siding was warped in places, so that had to be done." She gestures at the work being done inside. "This is a different prospect. My kitchen used to be separate from my dining room and living room, and I guess it bugged Jesse. So he decided to knock down the walls and put up a giant beam across the ceiling so I don't need posts to support the roof, and voila, open concept house."

She gestures at a thick, dark wooden beam running the length of the room, with another equally large beam running crossways. The house is now open-concept, and it seems like Jesse isn't just knocking down some interior walls, but pushing the back wall of the kitchen outward to create a few extra feet of space for the kitchen.

I admire the job being done here. I know that Jesse and the guys are builders, but I've never actually seen any of their work. At least, not work in progress. I know they did James's house, and that's beautiful, as well as Ryder's, which is also gorgeous…but seeing

Imogen's house in the process of being torn apart and rebuilt makes it more...real, I guess. The remodel opens the home and makes it feel more breathable and airy.

I'm kind of jealous, actually. I bought a little ranch on a huge lot a few miles from here, and I've been wanting to open it up a little, pretty much exactly like this. I have quite a tidy sum saved for the remodel, but I've just never got around to doing anything about it.

"Can I get you anything—coffee or tea?" Imogen asks.

I shake my head. "No, thanks. I'm good."

Imogen has a folder out and open on her coffee table, and the folder is stuffed to overflowing with magazine pages, printouts from online articles, and Pinterest boards...her vision for the wedding. My gut churns as she excitedly spreads out Pinterest board printouts of various centerpiece ideas.

"So, I know we'd talked about white roses, but I think I like this look better," she says, tapping a printout showing bursts of white lilies with a single brightly colored accent flower in the middle.

I let out a breath. "Imogen, I..."

Her face falls. "You're quitting."

"I thought I could do this, Imogen. I really did. I'm sorry."

She shrugs. "I wondered." Her eyes go to mine. "Can I at least know why?"

I hesitate over how much to say but then, once I start, I end up relating the story in full again, and this time it's easier. Still painful, but not quite as hard to talk about as it was with Laurel last night.

When I'm done, Imogen is quiet for a while. "And planning my wedding just reminds you of Craig."

I nod. "Yeah. I didn't think it would be this hard."

"Did you have wedding plans when he passed away?"

I shrug. "I mean, yeah. Of course. You've known you and Jesse are going to get married for a while now…and I bet you were planning it in your head for months before he ever proposed."

She laughs, nodding. "Yeah, I was." Imogen sobers, then. "I get it, Nova. I really do."

"I'm sorry, Im. I really am. I've been fighting this realization for weeks now, but last night it just…it all came to a head. I was looking at venues for the reception, and one of them was the place I'd picked for Craig's and my reception. And I just…I lost it."

"I understand, I promise." She reaches into her folder, rifles to the very back, where she has a business card for another local event planner tucked into the very bottom of the folder pocket. "I felt you pulling away from this for a while now, and while I was hoping you'd keep going, I figured it couldn't hurt to be prepared in case my intuition was right."

"You're *sure* you're okay with this? I care about you, and our friendship, Imogen. I just—"

Imogen wraps me up in a tight hug. "I promise you, I'm fine. There's plenty of time. And plus, this way, you get to be in the wedding and party with us at the reception."

I grin as I pull away from the hug. "Thanks for understanding."

She shrugs. "We've all got our stuff, you know?" She eyes me sideways, and there's not time to forestall the comment I feel coming. "James has his stuff, too."

"ARGH!" I shout, shooting to my feet. "Not this again."

She bites her lip, hiding a smirk. "Wow, okay. Abrupt reaction."

"I just got the full-court press from Laurel about it. I seriously can't handle anyone else trying to push me and James together."

"No one is trying to push anyone," Imogen says. "It just makes sense, and you guys have obvious chemistry. We just don't know why you both refuse to see it."

"We see it, okay?" I snap, knowing I'm unfairly lashing out at Imogen. "We see it. We've acknowledged it. We just don't want to act on it."

Imogen shakes her head. "That I do *not* comprehend. But it's your life, your business. I just want to see you happy."

I frown. "Who says I'm not?"

Imogen purses her lips to one side. "Ummm, well?"

I huff. "Never mind, I don't want to hear the answer to that."

Imogen snorts a laugh. "In denial?"

"If that's what you want to call it, sure." I stand up and give her a hug. "I have some things I need to get done at home."

Imogen walks me to the door. "Skedaddling just in time, huh?"

I frown at her, pausing on the porch. "What do you mean?"

She gestures at the tools. "The guys are all working here today. They just had to go pick up some supplies. By which I mean they used the excuse of needing more nails as a reason to day-drink, but whatever. I'm getting a pretty remodel done for the cost of materials, so who am I to begrudge them some lunchtime beers on a Saturday?" She points down the road at Jesse's truck, which is approaching with a throaty diesel rumble. "Here they come now."

I groan. "Yeah, I better get going before everyone shows up and I have to go through yet another round of *James* this, and *James* that."

Imogen laughs. "Smart. Jesse and Franco are just as bad about the gossip and drama as the rest of us girls."

"Yeah, I've noticed," I say as I head down the steps. "For a bunch of big, macho construction dudes, they sure do like to yap."

Imogen cackles. "Oh, honey, you have no idea. Jesse's favorite topic for pillow talk is gossip."

I hang in the open door of my car a moment. "Gossip? About what? The rest of you guys are all shacked up and happy, so what is there to gossip about?"

She shakes her head. "You'd think, but no. The whole contractor, construction community around here is very, very small, so all the guys know everyone else. Going to Home Depot for them is like going to the salon for us—they hang out in the power tools and lumber departments gossiping about which guy nailed which girl and in which position. It's funny, actually."

"Jesse told you this?"

She nods, laughing harder. "Oh yeah. I know the names of every carpenter, electrician, plumber, roofer, framer, drywaller, painter, and flooring guy within fifty miles, and who they're hooking up with, divorcing, and cheating with, or cheating on."

I laugh. "Who knew?"

She holds up her hands. "I sure as hell didn't." Right then, Jesse's truck idles to a stop at the curb, and he and Franco hop out. "Hey, babe!" Imogen calls. "How was the beer?"

Jesse pats his belly. "Delicious. I only had seven, though, so don't worry."

Imogen rolls her eyes. "You big ol' fibber."

He jogs up the steps and kisses Imogen, one hand on her cheek and another big paw resting possessively on her very slightly rounded belly. "Can't get anything past you. We each had two, and probably more chili cheese fries than any two humans should be able to eat."

Imogen pats his cheek. "I guess I'll need to make sure we have Pepto for later, huh? You know how those things give you indigestion." She eyes Franco. "I thought you didn't eat that crap, Franco?"

Franco shrugs. "I don't, usually. But I give myself one tasty treat every Saturday afternoon. This week, it was chili cheese fries. Next week, it's gonna be a whole pizza, I'm thinking."

Jesse eyes me. "Whassup, Nova? How you doin'?" He says this in a funny and terrible approximation of a New York accent.

"Going home, that's how I'm doing," I say. "Just had to have a quick chat with Imogen."

Jesse elbows Franco with a meaningful expression exchanged between them. "You quit?" His question is addressed to me.

I blink at him. "What?" Both men hold carefully blank expressions. "What do you mean?"

He arches an eyebrow at me, and then looks at his fiancée, and then back at me. "You did, didn't you?"

I glance quizzically at Imogen, who just shrugs and shakes her head.

"I been thinking you're gonna quit the wedding sometime this week, and Franco says next week. We got a hundred bucks riding on it, so tell me—who won?"

"You guys were betting on whether I'd quit planning your wedding?" I ask, trying to wrap my head around the idea.

He shrugs, nods. "Well, yeah. You've been more uptight than ever lately—and saying this as a friend, babe…that's really saying something. So I figured you'd end up quitting sooner than later, for reasons you don't seem inclined to share."

I blink, hard. I know his words were coming from a teasing, friendly place, but they still hurt, for reasons I don't quite want to examine at that moment.

Imogen frowns up at Jesse. "Jesse, baby—not cool. That was insensitive of you."

I shove down my emotions and paste a smile on my face—years of nursing has taught me how to do that with the best of them. "It's cool, Imogen. He couldn't have known." I click my tongue and shoot a finger gun at Jesse. "You win, bud."

Jesse seems confused. "I…shit. Sorry, Nova. I didn't mean nothin' by it."

I shake my head. "It's fine, honestly. I'm hard to offend." I glance at Imogen, then. "You can fill him in. I've told that story twice in the last twelve hours, and I don't think I've got the energy for it at the moment."

I go out to my car, slide onto the sagging cloth seat of my Explorer, buckle up, and start the engine. Or rather, I try to—it wheezes, rattles, and refuses to turn over. I groan in annoyance, give it a second, and then try again, and fortunately this time it starts. Albeit, the belt squeaks, the pistons rattle, and the gas gauge doesn't work, but it runs, and it gets me from point A to point B.

I grew up driving the newest, slickest, fanciest cars. If I wanted an upgrade, all I had to do was ask. I didn't pay for gas, didn't pay insurance, and I had an unlimited credit card. I got a new Mercedes every year and, on my eighteenth birthday, I got a Ferrari. Which I crashed within a week, and got it replaced with a Range Rover Autobiography a week later because the power of the Ferrari scared me.

So, when I left for college, I sold the year-old Range Rover for cash, bought this Explorer new, and have driven it ever since, and plan to drive it into the ground. I clip coupons, never buy anything that's not on sale, pay cash for everything, and save at least 70 percent of my income. Not because I have to—I make good money at the hospital and have no dependents and very few bills—but because I choose to live a drastically different lifestyle than my parents provided for me growing up.

I'm probably never going to get married or have kids, but if I ever do, I'll do it differently than my parents did, that's for sure.

I'm less than two miles from home, stopped at a red light, and...rattle, rattle, sputter, jerk...silence.

"FUCK."

I just filled the gas tank two days ago, so it's not out of gas; I changed the oil myself a month ago, so it's not that. It's just...dead.

I turn on my emergency flashers, roll down my window, and wave for the people behind me to go around. I shove the shifter into neutral and get out of the car, wait for traffic to clear, and then brace myself in the open door of the car and start pushing. The big bitch is heavy, but I'm a strong girl and I get it moving. I angle across the intersection for a Walgreens parking lot, ignoring the honks and shouts for me to move out of the way.

And then, suddenly, my Explorer becomes a hell of a lot easier to move. I glance backward, and see a shape through the rear window—just a head and shoulders, but I know exactly who it is.

No one else I know has shoulders like that, mountain-wide and bull-heavy.

James.

I'm not about to turn down the help, because he's basically pushing the SUV by himself at this point, and I'm about gassed from pushing it as far as I have.

Together, we get my car off the road and into the Walgreens parking lot, and when it's parked out of the way, I lean in, shove the shifter into park, and collapse against the frame, sweating and panting, hands on my knees.

I hear his feet on the ground, and straighten just in time to see him rest one massive, burly shoulder against the window.

"Nova. Thought this was your car."

"Yep." I pat my now-deceased vehicle on the hood. "Looks like I'm in the market for a new one, huh?"

"She's a goner?" he asks.

I nod. "Yeah. I've been expecting it for a while, now. It's probably something fixable, but it'll cost more than the car is worth, at this point." I kick a tire.

"She's got close to two hundred thousand miles on her, so I'd say she's served me well."

James makes an impressed face. "Wow. You bought her new and have driven her ever since?"

I nod. "Yes, sir. Drove her off the lot, paid her off, and drove her into the ground." I can't help but brag a little. "I did pretty much all the routine maintenance myself, actually. Oil changes, stuff like that."

"Huh. That's impressive. Renée didn't even like to put gas in her car herself." He rubs the back of his neck. "Course, I couldn't boil water, so it all evened out."

He seems embarrassed to have mentioned his dead wife, and scuffs his big brown Red Wing boot against the ground.

"There was a period of time I was too broke to be able to afford oil changes, so I taught myself, and now I actually kind of enjoy it, so I kept doing it myself even after I could afford to have someone else do it." I hunt for something else to say, to cut through the awkwardness.

"Impressive," James says again.

I thump the back of my foot against the dead SUV's tire again. "So, I guess, I uh...I have to get a tow truck and a cab home. So...thanks for the help. I appreciate it."

James's brow furrows for a moment, and then he

slides a first-generation iPhone out of his pocket—
the device is encased in a battered, scratched, paint-
stained OtterBox. He scrolls through his contacts,
taps one, brings the phone to his ear.

"Hey, Bill. Got your flatbed? Friend of mine has
a dead car. Walgreens at…Fourth and Washington.
Nah, man, it's a goner." He gives me a look. "It's a
ninety-six?"

I nod. "Yeah. But I don't need you to—"

"Ninety-six Explorer. Two hundred thousand
miles."

"James—"

He holds up a finger to stall me. "Nah, man. It's
worth more than that just in parts and you know it."
James pauses, listens. "Seven-fifty?…fine. Five hundred—got yourself a deal. Great. Thanks, Bill. See
you shortly."

I blink. "James."

He grins, a rare and brilliant sight. "My buddy
owns a wrecking service and parts yard. He's gonna
come get your girl, and he'll give you five hundred in
cash for it."

I shake my head. "James, that thing is *dead*. It's
not worth five hundred dollars."

He just lifts a bull-like shoulder. "Sure it is. The
body is in great condition, very little rust, no big dents
or scratches. The interior looks like it's in similarly

good shape. I'm guessing your pistons are shot, and you've probably got an internal oil leak, meaning it's leaking somewhere inside and burning up so you never see spots on your garage floor or whatever." He gestures at the Explorer. "Between the body, interior, transmissions, axles, suspension, all that, yeah, it's worth five hundred easy. He'll make that in parts plus a profit. Trust me. You're still getting a decent chunk of cash for a dead car. Take it and run, I say."

I sigh. "Fine." I eye him. "I owe you more thanks, then. I'd have had it towed to a junkyard and paid money to get rid of it."

He juts his chin at the road—I see his massive truck idling with the flashers blinking toward the back of the right turn lane. "Come on. I'll give you a lift."

I hesitate. "I half live out of my car. So, if your friend is towing it away, I'll need to clean it out."

He nods. "Oh, right. Okay, well I'll grab my truck and run it over here."

I frown. "I'm fine, James. Thanks."

He frowns back. "Why would I let you take a cab when I'm here? Besides, good luck getting a cab around here. Tried that once, after the boys and I tied on a few too many. Took almost an hour to get anyone to show up at Billy Bar, and the asshole charged us fifty bucks for a twenty-minute ride. So no, you're not taking a cab."

He's right and I know it. It just galls me to accept help from anyone, but especially him. Plus, the prospect of being alone with him in his truck scares me. Just standing here with him has my head, heart, and body all at odds.

I huff in annoyance. "Fine. You're right." I wipe my face with both hands, and then run them through my hair. "Okay. Grab your truck."

When I said I live out of my car, I wasn't kidding. It's not trashed inside, but there's twenty-two years' worth of detritus in it—dirty scrubs, clean scrubs, sports bras, running shoes, work shoes, ankle socks, old partially empty purses, various charger cords for various brands and generations of cell phones, a tape-deck adapter for an MP3 player that's also floating around here somewhere, a cigarette lighter charger cord for my phone, a case of CDs, lots of trash, Tupperware containers that once contained leftovers and which now contain their own ecology, a pair of kettlebells, a tennis racket, an emergency kit containing a gallon of water, a thick wool blanket, a winter hat and gloves, thick wool socks, a crank-powered flashlight, some protein bars, a spare car battery, and a collapsible trenching shovel.

While James goes to get his truck, I run into Walgreens and buy a couple of storage bins, and toss all the random, still-useful items into it, and then throw out all the trash. I empty out the console and glove box, and then the trunk, and then check under all the seats. Once the vehicle is empty of all my belongings, I figure I may as well toss the random crap I no longer want or need, and go through the bins, trashing the cords, adapters, and other stuff I haven't used in years. James has his truck over here by now, and he's idling in the parking spot next to me; his window is down, a burly, hairy arm hanging out, fingers tapping to the rhythm of the jazz wafting through the speakers.

A long flatbed truck pulls into the parking lot and stops, backing up near my SUV. A short, portly, dirty, bushy-bearded man with messy graying black hair hops down, wearing blue mechanic's coveralls, a pair of cloth work gloves clutched in one hand. He ambles over to me, smiling a chewing tobacco-stained grin at me.

"Bill Moynihan," he says, in a fast, gruff, friendly voice. "You the proud owner of this very nice piece o'shit?"

I laugh. "Yes, I am. Nova Benson."

He gestures at the Explorer. "Mind if I give'er a quick once-over?"

I shrug. "Be my guest."

I lean against the warm hood of James's truck, the diesel vibrating through me. Bill pops the hood first, sticks his head in, twists and pokes and rattles and peers, tries the ignition, listening carefully, and then does a much quicker look around the outside— he even flops to his back and pokes his head underneath, and then hops to his feet and shuffles over to me.

He reaches into the open front of his coveralls and withdraws a greasy fingerprint-stained envelope. "She's in great shape, aside from bein' dead as a doornail. I think you've got an internal oil leak, and some fucked-up pistons. Won't know until I take her apart, but I'd say you're making the right decision, junking her." He hands me the envelope. "Five hundred, as agreed."

I hand him the title and take the envelope. "Thank you, Bill."

He stuffs the title inside his coveralls. "My pleasure." He hands me a business card. "If you ever need a tow again, gimme a call. Any friend of Jimbo's is a friend of mine. I can do minor roadside repairs too, I should mention."

I take the card and extend my hand. "Thank you, that's good to know."

He slides his work glove off and shakes my hand. "My pleasure, my pleasure." He jerks a thumb at the Explorer. "All right, well…I'm gonna load her up and get her to the yard. Now's the time to say goodbye, if you're the sentimental type."

I'm not, usually, but I've been driving that Explorer since I was eighteen. It's the first thing I ever bought on my own. I've put thousands of dollars into keeping it running, spent countless hours changing oil and washing and vacuuming and cleaning. I've had some memorable sex in the back seat—Craig was… adventurous, and spontaneous, until he got sick.

I remove the license plate, pat the hood, give my beloved Explorer one last look, and then turn away. I climb into the passenger seat of James's truck, buckle up, and watch out the window as Bill lowers the flatbed and hooks the chain onto the car. And then James is pulling out of the Walgreens parking lot, my car is out of sight, and I'm alone with James for the first time in months.

FOUR

IT'S EASY TO FORGET EXACTLY HOW HUGE JAMES REALLY IS, sometimes. I'm not a small girl, not in any way, but James makes me feel small and dainty. Everything about him is just...*huge*. His arms are the size of my thighs, his shoulders are so broad you could serve dinner on each of them, his chest barrel-like and bulging with muscle, his legs are the size of my waist, his hands are like dinner plates. His eyes are wide and deep and molten brown, reserved and shuttered most of the time, hard to read. His hair is chestnut brown, shot through with streaks of silver. He wears a beard, short and neatly trimmed and brushed, rounded off, as streaked with silver as his hair. He's wearing a black short sleeve T-shirt, ripped here and there, dotted with paint and clumps of caulk and who knows what else, printed with the logo of a local lumber supply company. The sleeves are stretched nearly to ripping around his biceps and cling to his Atlas shoulders. His

Oakleys—which I've never seen him without, always either on his eyes or pushed up on his head—are buried in his hair at the moment, the mirrored lenses glinting in the thick thatch of brown.

He glances sideways at me. "So. Where to?"

I stiffen my fingers and rake them through my hair to push it back from my eyes, and then tug the long, thick mass of coppery red over one shoulder. "Hmm. The plan was to head home and get some chores done, but now I'm car-less, and have work tomorrow." I blow out a breath. "You've probably got work to do, though, huh? I'd feel shitty taking up your whole day asking you to take me car shopping."

James rolls a thick shoulder. "Nice thing about being my own boss is that I can take the day off when I want to."

I groan quietly. "James, I can't take up that much of your time. Just drop me off at the used lot over near Target."

James shakes his head. "Nope."

"James."

"Nova." He gives me the James smile I'm more used to—a slight, subtle tilt of the lips, barely a grin. "We're ahead of schedule on all our jobs, it's Saturday, my girls are at a friend's house for the day, and the only thing on my agenda today was to help out at Imogen's. But Jesse and Franco have that locked down, and it ain't a rush anyway. So. You're stuck with me for today. Sorry, babe."

I chuckle. "Yeah, it's a real hardship, lemme tell you."

"What are you in the market for? Another SUV?"

I shrug. "You know, I've never even thought about it. I've owned that Explorer for so long, I have no idea what else I'd even like."

James scratches his beard. "I guess the first question is what is your budget?"

I give it some thought. "I have a bit of cash saved, but I was hoping to use most of it to do some remodels on my house." I shrug. "I guess I could go…maybe thirty or forty?"

James nods. "I've bought quite a few cars in my life, so my advice would be to find something you like that's gently used, no more than three or four years old, low mileage. Pay half or so cash minimum, or if you can really spare it, just buy it outright. Brand new isn't always a great deal as you take a pretty big hit in depreciation as soon as you drive it off the lot, whereas with a newer used car you get a decent newish vehicle with lower depreciation happening."

"Makes sense. I think I can handle thirty or forty in cash."

"You can get a pretty nice ride for forty grand cash," James says.

"If you say so. You know better than I do."

He pulls into a pre-owned lot, parks near the showroom, and we get out.

"Browse around, see what strikes your fancy."

I head for a cute little two-door Honda coupe, peek in the windows, and glance at the window sticker—well within my price range, that's for sure.

James thumps the roof with a big fist. "These go forever, but you live in Illinois, Nova. You want my opinion, you need something all-wheel, or a four-by-four."

I think about that. "The four-wheel drive on my Explorer did get me through some pretty gnarly storms," I concede.

"Exactly." James eyes the lot, and sees another SUV, a compact-crossover import. "Being a contractor, I need a pickup, but Renée owned one of these and loved it. I drove it a few times—it has the feel of a car, but it's great in the snow. I wouldn't do any real off-roading in it, but it'll get you through snowstorms and such."

I circle it, look it over, but end up shrugging. "I don't know. I feel kinda…meh about it."

James nods. "Well then, keep looking." He taps the price sticker: twenty grand. "You spend that much cash on a car, you should love it."

We spend almost half an hour looking over most

of the lot, but I don't really feel any kind of connection to anything.

As we get back into James's truck and drive away—much to the disappointment of the salesman who'd been stalking us—I glance at James. "Sorry, that was a waste of time."

"Not at all," he counters. "Now you know what you don't like. You've got it narrowed down."

I smile. "Huh. Never thought of it that way."

We go to a different dealer, this one is a used car lot connected to a Ford dealership. Another thirty-some minutes is spent perusing the various used models, and still nothing connects. I even look over some of the new cars, but still…no spark.

"I'm getting frustrated, James."

He nods. "It can be that way, especially if you haven't really thought about it. Usually, I know exactly what I'm looking for and it's just a matter of finding the right one at the right price."

"I mean, I know I don't want a sedan or whatever—you're right in that I want something bigger and more capable. I don't know."

James eyes me. "I have an idea, actually. Not sure how you'll feel about it, but it's an option."

I wave a hand. "Okay?"

"When I bought this beast a couple years ago, I was replacing my last truck. Which I still own. It's in my barn, actually."

I blink, thinking. "Is it like this one?"

He nods. "Similar." He glances at me. "Thus my hesitation at suggesting it. It's got the fancy wheels and tires, the lift kit, the light bar. Tires aren't as large, not as high of a lift, not as fancy of a light bar, but it's still pretty tricked out. The thing about that one is, the guys and I did some work under the hood, beefed up the horsepower and torque output, and put on an exhaust system that makes it rumble like a mother-fucker. Fairly low mileage, actually, considering the amount of driving I do for work."

I laugh, trying to envision myself in a truck like this. "I don't know, James."

He rolls his shoulder. "No pressure, just an option. I've been sorta reticent to sell it, because it's a great truck and I've got some sentiment about it. I'd love to see it go to someone I know who'll appreciate it, and us being friendly like, I could give it to you for a fraction of what I'd charge some random Joe."

"Don't do me any favors, James."

He frowns. "Why the hell not? Friends do friends favors. I ain't givin' it to you for free, babe. Just for a pretty hefty discount. I ain't lookin' to make money on it, I just don't want to see it go to just anyone."

There's something heavy in the way he talks about it, something in the sentimental value of the truck that has me suspect it has something to do with his wife. Which gives me hesitation.

But...

A good deal is a good deal. And I *have* always liked pickups. A bit macho, maybe, but if any chick can make a macho truck look cool, it's me.

"All right, let's go take a look. I might be interested."

He quirks an eyebrow at me. "Don't do me any favors, Nova."

I laugh at having my words thrown back at me. "I'm not. I'm genuinely interested."

He nods. "Cool. To the barn, then."

So, we head across town and into the rural stretches outside it, where James lives—only a few miles from me, as a matter of fact. He lives in the kind of neighborhood that's not quite the country, but not quite the suburbs either—he has neighbors on either side, but they're separated by an acre at least on each side. James's property is a fenced-in acre and a half of yard, with another five acres out back behind the fence, a pole barn at the back of the property. James clicks a button on a device clipped to his visor, and the large wrought iron gate swings open. He pulls through, closes the gate behind us, and then follows the driveway; it cuts past the house and garage to the fence line, and I see that a section of the eight-foot-high, wood-slat privacy fence is actually a large gate, so he can access the property beyond the gate. He stops a few feet away from the fence, shoves the truck into park and jumps out, leaving his door open. He swings the gate open away from the truck, and hops back in, driving down a track through the grass leading toward the barn.

The track is nothing more than a pair of ruts in the grass, and we bounce and jostle over pits and divots and bumps—it's so bumpy I instinctively cross my arms over my chest so I don't knock myself out with my own cleavage.

I don't miss the way James's eyes cut to me now and then as we bounce down the track.

I'm not sure what possesses me, sheer curiosity, perhaps—but, foolishly, I drop my arms and let the girls flop around and carefully but subtly watch his reaction.

Good thing we're driving slowly through a grassy field, because he glances to the side, and forgets to look away from the show. His eyes widen, and he coughs as if to cover an involuntary reaction.

He finally drags his eyes back to the road, discovers he'd driven off the track, and abruptly corrects. Another few feet, and his eyes cut over to mine, and I arch an eyebrow.

"Something wrong, James?"

"I…ah…no." He wipes his face with a palm. "Sorry."

I smirk. "Sorry? For what?"

He wriggles in the seat uncomfortably. "Um. Nothing." He tugs his Oakleys down over his face. "Never mind."

I laugh outright, now, and cross my arms over my breasts again. "I'm just messing with you, James."

He frowns. "Hysterical."

I laugh again. "I mean…it kind of was."

He twists his head to glare at me through his sunglasses. "Trolling me, huh?"

I shrug. "A little."

He shakes his head and lapses into silence as we pull to a stop on the wide concrete pad in front of his barn. It's an enormous pole barn, with green metal walls, a white roof, and huge white sliding doors. There's a basketball hoop on the wall above the doors, the red square faded to nearly nothing, the net fraying at the ends.

He parks at an angle, shuts off the engine, and hops down out of the cab. I slide out as well and follow him to the doors of the pole barn. He yanks one door aside and then the other, shedding daylight into the interior. Heading inside, he flicks on a trio of switches, and a double row of fluorescent tubes flickers on in three different areas.

The inside is a well-organized hodgepodge of masculinity; nearest the door along the right-hand wall is a weightlifter's paradise. There's a three-section Rogue power rack bolted to the concrete floor, with four Olympic bars in a rifle-style holder on the wall to one side and an elaborate storage rack holding thousands of dollars' worth of color-coded bumper plates in varying sizes on the other, along with a rack of dumbbells and kettlebells. There is a pair of thick ropes attached to an upright of the rack, several pull-up stations, a hex trap bar, a sled on a strip of artificial turf...god, he has *everything*, even a rowing machine and an air bike. On the left side nearest the door is a long, sleek bass boat, and beside it a smaller tin outboard boat. Farther down the left wall is a workbench built into the wall, scattered with tools of all kinds, and beyond that a set of tool racks. Opposite the mechanic area is a tarp-covered motorcycle, and the truck in question.

And holy shit, the truck is...a *lot*.

Ruby red, a full-size four-door cab, thick, knobby tires, a lift kit, big black wheels, a thick chrome bull bar covering the chrome grill, an LED light rack across the roof, and a soft black tonneau cover over the bed instead of the back rack and toolbox I'd have expected.

James walks over to the truck, running his fingers

along the side. "It doesn't actually have a very big lift, or crazy big tires, because I drive a lot of miles and tow a lot of trailers. Not sure how much you know about this stuff—"

"Nothing at all," I fill in.

He nods. "Well, you lift it too much and you'll need a fuckin' ladder to get into the box, and a special hitch to tow anything, and then you're straining your front-end suspension and end up going through parts faster. What I did was put the knobbiest, thickest-wall tires on fancy rims, and then lifted it a couple inches just for wheel well clearance. So it looks cool, but it's still useable as a work truck."

I eye the door. "I think I'll still need a damn ladder to get into the thing."

He grins at me, resting a foot on the chrome step under the driver's side door. "Nah. You'll have no trouble."

I arch an eyebrow. "It's an already big truck lifted several inches higher."

He nods, kicks the step. "These are custom steps, babe." He hesitates, and when he continues, his voice is low, quiet, and subdued. "I built this with Renée in mind. You wouldn't think it considering Renée was barely five-six. Tiny thing with short little legs. My truck before this one had stock tube steps, and she hated getting into and out of it. So when I pimped out this one, I put custom steps on it that were low enough for her to get into and out of easily." He opens the door, shows me the handle on the inside—it looks like it's carbon fiber, built into the rim just inside the door. "Give it a try."

I put a foot up onto the step, lean up and grab the handle, and climb in—it's actually very natural, just a little tug and a step, and I'm swinging into the camel-tan leather bucket seat. It's soft leather, deep, enveloping, comfortable yet supportive. Sitting in the driver's seat, I take the wheel in both hands, adjust the rearview mirror, and take stock of the interior. Upgraded audio receiver head and speakers, carbon fiber shifter knob, all sorts of little upgrades here and there that makes this feel more luxurious than I'd expect a truck to feel.

James circles to the passenger side and climbs in. He uses a small key on his keychain to unlock the glove box—inside are both of the actual keys for the truck, and he hands one of the keys to me. "Start'er up, let's take her for a spin."

I eye the rearview mirror. "Backing it out looks tricky."

James waves a hand. "There's plenty of space. Just crank the wheel and pull around."

I turn the engine over, and it catches immediately—the engine sounds like a bear snarling into a metal bucket, and the power of it sends a thrill through me. "Whoa."

James smirks. "This is the six-point-six-liter diesel, and we beefed it up. You could pull a house off its foundation with this bitch and drag it all the way to Canada."

I laugh as I carefully turn the truck around in the pole barn—James was obviously familiar with getting into and out of the pole barn, because there was plenty of space to turn around and pull out. I swing around James's truck and onto the two-track, through the gate, past the house, and onto the road. The tires hum loudly, but I can see the noise fading out of my awareness very quickly. Indeed, within a couple of minutes I barely notice it, especially with the radio playing country music.

James directs me on a fifteen-minute circuit around his neighborhood, and I do my best to put the truck through its paces—accelerating, stopping, turning. I even try parking; obviously I'm not going to be squeezing into any tight little spaces, but I don't park like that anyway. I tend to park in the back forty and walk across the lot to wherever I'm going, so that's not a problem.

We pull back into James's driveway, and I park in the driveway in front of the gate and switch off the engine. I sigh, unbuckling and twisting to lounge half sideways in the seat facing James in the passenger seat.

"So," I say.

James rubs his beard with a knuckle. "So. What do you think?"

I can't help a smile. "I like it."

James lets a small smile creep across his mouth. "You like it?"

I laugh. "It scared me at first, just the size of it, the utter and ridiculous masculinity of it, but…" I tug my hair backward. "It's just cool—it's fun. I actually enjoy driving it, and I really like being up this high. It feels…" I grin, laughing. "I feel like a boss."

James laughs. "That's why I do it. It looks cool and makes you feel like a boss."

I sigh. "Okay, be honest—would I look stupid?"

He frowns. "Stupid? Why would you look stupid?"

I shrug. "I dunno. It's this big, beefy, macho, hyper-masculine truck, and I'm a girl. Granted, I'm not some dainty girly-girl, but I'm still a chick."

James snorts. "Okay, number one, who gives a shit what anyone else thinks? Number two, no. You'd look like a boss-ass bitch. Just me, but a gorgeous woman driving a badass truck is pretty much the hottest thing on earth."

He turns away, rubbing his cheek with a

hand—he's blushing, I think, but it's hard to tell under the beard.

I try to stay composed and neutral. "Why, James Bod—was that a compliment?"

He frowns at me. "Don't act so shocked," he says, his voice gruff.

"I mean, I kind of am a tiny bit surprised."

"You're an attractive woman, Nova. I ain't blind." He adjusts his sunglasses, passes a hand through his hair—which only messes it up, leaving a section on the side sticking up.

My hand drifts of its own accord toward James's head—it seems to me we both watch my hand in slow motion as I reach out and gently smooth his hair back into place.

He stares at my hand as I drop it to the steering wheel again.

"Sorry," I say. "I don't know why I did that."

James clears his throat. "I—um." He fiddles with the glove box latch. "You wanna pull back near the barn? I'll grab the title and do a quick check to make sure it's good to go. If you're buying it, I mean. No pressure."

I think another moment or two, but I already know the answer. I like this truck. I feel cool in it, I know I'll never have trouble with bad weather, and I know it's been well cared for.

"How much do you want?" I ask.

He blows out a breath, tipping his head side to side. "For you? Twenty-five."

I frown at him. "James. You had to have put more than that in it just in custom upgrades."

He nods. "Sure. The truck is worth that much stock."

"Then what are you thinking, offering it to me for that price?"

He shrugs. "It ain't about the money. I got what I need, and enough to feel comfortable. It's just sitting there in my barn, and I gotta go out every once in a while to start it up and do maintenance on it. Truth be told, it kinda weighs on me. But I've got too much sentimental value in it to sell it to just anyone. So that's left me in a bit of a pickle—too attached to get rid of it, but it's taking up space and time, not to mention the emotional anchor of knowing it's there." He pauses, thinking. "Plus, the girls don't like seeing it, Nina especially. She remembers riding around with Renée and I in it. She used to ask for rides. She loved when I'd find a bumpy back road." He smiles faintly, sadly.

I frown again. "But won't seeing me in it be hard?"

He's quiet a while, thinking that one over. "Maybe at first? It's weird sitting in the passenger seat, weird seeing you drive it. Really weird, honestly." He makes a gruff sound in his throat. "Sorry. Bad manners to talk about that, though."

I shake my head. "No, it's not. We're friends, James. You can talk about it all you want."

"It ain't weird for you?"

I shrug. "I mean, the whole thing with us is already kind of weird, so that's not any weirder, you know?"

He nods. "Yeah, I get you."

"Why is it so weird seeing me drive it?"

He sighs. "I mean, because Renée drove it around a lot. At first she was scared of it, like you said. It being so big and powerful and all, but once I got her to try it, she drove it every chance she got. I got a big ol' kick out of seeing her tiny little ass climbing up into this thing, watching her hop down. But then she got pregnant and it became awkward to climb up into it, so we drove her CR-V everywhere. And then she… yeah. And I just couldn't drive it myself after she was gone, you know? She's just…in it. I still smell her in it, honestly. See her." He adjusts his sunglasses again, clears his throat. "Sorry."

"Do not apologize, James."

"I just…" He shrugs. "It's harder than I thought."

"Maybe it should just go back in your barn."

He shakes his head resolutely. "No. I want

someone to get some use out of it. I want it to be driven. I want it to be loved. Weird, maybe, but I'm a truck guy, and trucks oughta be loved." He pushes his Oakleys up onto his head and gives me a long look. "I want you to buy it, if you want it. I want *you* to have it. There's no one else I'd rather see this truck go to."

"Even if you have to see it a lot, and see me in it?"

He nods. "It'll be bittersweet, but yes."

"Then you have to let me pay you thirty."

He shakes his head. "Not taking a dime over twenty-five. And you need something fixed, you call me, not some damn shyster mechanic."

I stare hard at him—I know he's doing me a favor, but I think I'm also doing something for him, taking this truck from him. "Twenty-five?"

He nods. "Twenty-five."

"You know you're getting screwed on this deal, financially?"

He shrugs. "More to it for me than the money, told you that."

"How much of this is about you and me? Honestly."

James growls, but I can't interpret if that's out of annoyance or something I don't have a word for. "Why would you ask me that, Nova? I thought we agreed to leave it be."

"I need to know."

"Why?"

"I just...do."

James tugs his sunglasses back into place and stares out the window rather than meet my gaze. "Truthfully, it *is* about you, to some degree. But not like you're thinkin'."

"What do you think I'm thinking?" I ask.

He rolls a heavy shoulder, rolls the window down with a touch of the button, and rests his thick forearm on the window. "I think you think I'm selling it to you for cheap because there's...I dunno know how to put it—because there's an attraction between us. That I'm doing you a favor because you're a beautiful woman."

I sigh. "Yeah, okay—you've got that pegged pretty squarely," I say with a rueful chuckle.

He's quiet a moment. "I'm doing it for the reasons I said—I need to see it go to someone I know will appreciate it, and I know you will. I have sentiment towards it that's hard to let go of, and this way, it's still in my sphere, you know? Not like I'm keeping tabs on it, but... I dunno."

I nod. "I think I understand that part."

"And I mean...yeah, you're a beautiful woman, but that ain't why I'm giving it to you. I told you why. Not sure I see much point in going over it a third time."

I nod. "Okay."

He extends his hand. "So…twenty-five?"

"Deal."

We shake hands, and I quickly let go of his—not fast enough, though; I feel the sting and tingle and hum of energy rippling between us, lingering on my skin, sizzling up my palms like arcing electricity.

Ten minutes later, I've got the title, he's got a check for twenty-five grand, and I'm on the way to the nearest secretary of state to transfer the plate from my Explorer, and get my new truck registered.

Two hours later, I'm finally back home, new truck in the driveway and feeling pretty excited. Only now, I'm wondering if I opened a can of worms with James that I might end up regretting.

FIVE

MY PHONE RINGS AS I'M ON THE WAY HOME FROM
work a week later; it's been a busy week and I
haven't seen any of my friends, as I've worked back-
to-back doubles twice this week.

I answer. "Hello?"

"Nova. It's James."

I hesitate. "Uh. Hi, James. What's up?"

He's the one to hesitate now. "I...wanted to
check in and see how you're liking the truck."

"Oh. It's amazing. I love it. It kinda guzzles gas,
but I live pretty close to the hospital so it's not a huge
issue. That's really the only downside." I laugh. "I've
gotten a lot of compliments on it."

"I bet."

"And by compliments, I mean graphic sexual
propositions and wolf whistles."

"Don't you get those anyway?" he asks. "Woman
who looks like you do, I'd think you would."

I blush, but thankfully he can't see that. "I…well, yeah. But the truck has easily doubled it, and they've gotten even more grotesquely graphic."

He grumps a coarse laugh. "Not surprised. Like I said, a gorgeous woman in a badass truck is a killer combo."

"Unwanted male attention aside, I do love driving it. I've even started to like the experience of climbing into and out of it. It's like my own mobile command center or something. Boss bitch of the road!"

Another hesitation from James. "I also, um…I remember you saying you'd been saving for a remodel of your house."

"Yeah?"

"We're wrapping up the jobs we're contracted for at the moment. I've got some bids out and a few others lined up, but you being part of the inner circle or whatever, I thought I'd offer you a slot on the schedule." He sighs. "I'm fumbling this. What I'm saying is, if you wanted, I could swing by your place and you could tell me what you're looking for."

"Do I get an inner circle discount?"

"Nah. Full price, babe. Sorry." He laughs. "Kidding. Of course you do."

I give it a moment of thought; I was thinking of putting it off another year or two to save more for it so I wouldn't have to settle for less in terms of what

I want. But I spent a good ten or twenty grand less than I was assuming on a new car, so there's that to consider...

"Sure." I give him my address and we agree to meet at my house in fifteen minutes.

I'll be home in three minutes, but I need time to change out of scrubs and tidy up a bit before he gets here. The other downside of owning a lifted beast of a truck is that it doesn't fit in my garage, as it's a tiny old detached thing with a super low roof—my Explorer barely fit inside, and the truck is too tall by a couple of inches. It's got a remote start, though, so warming it up in the winter will be easy.

I park in the driveway, climb down, and head inside to change. It's a warm summer day, so I change into cotton shorts and a T-shirt, leaving my feet bare. And yes, this time I'm wearing a bra, so I'm not indecent...to James's chagrin, probably, but we *did* agree to ignore the chemistry and just stay friends, as he so recently reminded me.

Which is a little hard to do, and harder when I'm suddenly seeing him more than I'm used to. Harder yet to do, because every now and then I get a flash of memory from that stupid pool party; he kissed me in his kitchen, and the kiss turned into me with my back to the fridge and his huge body up against mine. It ended almost before it started, though, and we were both somewhat dumbfounded—by the intensity of the kiss, and by the fact that both of us immediately felt…weird about it. Awkward. A little guilty, maybe. And fraught with a wicked chemical, sexual, highly combustible tension I don't think either of us knows how to deal with.

No less ferociously attracted to each other, yes, but…weird.

Yet still, sometimes, I think about that kiss. The soft firmness of his lips, the heat of his mouth. The power in his hands as they scraped into my hair…

DING-DONG.

Caught by the bell. I'm flushed and flustered, but I answer the door anyway. And I immediately wish I'd taken a second to cool down. Because DAMN.

James is dressed in caulk- and paint-spattered dark blue jeans and a black Motörhead T-shirt, the sleeves stretched to bursting around his biceps. As always, his black mirrored Oakleys hide his eyes, and he has an ancient, battered, paint-spattered Bears hat on, his thick, shaggy brown hair curling under to peek around his ears and neck. His beard is neatly trimmed and brushed, and I catch a hint of cedar from him. He has a leather-bound notebook in one hand, open to a blank page, and a pen tucked behind his ear.

"Hi," he says, in that deep, gravelly bass voice of

his, staring at me inscrutably through those shades of his.

"Hey," I say, and I'm thankful I don't sound as breathless as I feel at having him on my doorstep.

Silence.

James clears his throat. "So." He juts his chin in a single macho movement at the interior of my house. "What'cha got?"

I back up and step aside to make room for him to enter. "Um…a house?"

He chuckles. "Uh, yeah. Gathered that much." He stands in my foyer and looks around. "Nice place."

"Thank you." I shrug. "I didn't really do anything except decorate. I painted the kitchen, ripped out the nasty old carpet in the rooms, and that's…well, really about it."

The house is a single story, two-bedroom, two-bathroom ranch with a detached garage, sitting on an acre corner lot. I bought it mainly for the lot size, and because of the giant spreading oak in the backyard. The house itself is dated and chopped up with a too-small kitchen and a lot of wasted space in the living room, not to mention the too-small, detached garage. James ambles around, knocking on a wall here and there, whipping a measuring tape from his back pocket and measuring seemingly at random, from one wall to another, ceiling to floor, and across the rooms, jotting the numbers down on his pad. He stands in the kitchen for a while, just looking around, then goes into the bedrooms but only pokes his head in briefly. He spends longer in the bathrooms, and then examines the wall between the master bedroom and the bathroom on the other side.

He goes out the back door and stares at the back of the house, goes around to one side and then the other, takes a few more measurements, and then clomps back into the kitchen. He leans his butt against a counter and focuses on me.

"So I have some ideas," James says, "but I want to hear what you're looking for first."

I shrug a shoulder. "Well, I dunno. More kitchen, less living room, basically. And if it can be a little more open, that'd be great."

James nods. "Kind of in line with what I'm thinking." He taps the page. "I'm not great at drafting on the fly, so I'll just sorta describe what I'm envisioning for your little cottage."

I arch an eyebrow at him. "Little cottage? This place is three thousand square feet. Not exactly tiny."

He snorted. "Just teasin' you, babe. You have a nice place, Nova. Good bones."

I frown. "I hear that a lot. Seems like a buzzword phrase to me. 'Good bones.' What does that even mean, anyway?"

He shrugs. "Just means the place is solidly built, with good potential." He sweeps the tip of the pen around at the kitchen. "Like you said, you need more kitchen space as a primary concern. For a house this size, this kitchen is a damn postage stamp, and the living room is cavernous yet most of that space is unusable, just open dead air." He moves to the wall between the living room and kitchen. "This wall *is* load-bearing, but put a big ol' beam across, and you're golden. The boys and I have done that plenty—we just did one at Imogen's house, actually, and this house isn't that old, so I don't see any surprises in the ceiling."

"You could really take out the whole load-bearing wall?"

He nods. "Those home remodel shows make it look a hell of a lot easier than it is, to be honest, but we can do it. And you're getting this at cost, basically, and labor is the most expensive part of putting in a beam."

I try to envision the room without the wall, but can't. "I don't even know what that would feel like in here."

He laughs. "It takes some practice." He indicates one exterior wall, currently separated by the wall between the kitchen and living room. "I'd extend your cabinets and counter space this way, which would mean we could bust out some space here." He gestures at the spot where currently there's a tiny sink and window. "Get rid of some counter and cabinet, and I can give you a nice big double farmhouse sink and a much larger window."

I feel a frisson of excitement at what he's describing. "That sounds amazing."

He grins. "Oh, I'm just getting started." He turns and indicates the load-bearing wall. "The wall we'd take out currently contains your stovetop and such, and it works well here, if you think about this as an open-concept room. So we rip the wall out and put in an island—lots of under-counter storage, a built-in cutting board with a garbage can beneath it, an induction range, a prep sink, an overhang facing the living room with some bar stools."

The frisson becomes a shiver. "You can do all that? Without costing, like, a quarter million dollars?"

He cackles. "Yeah, I can do that. And no, it won't cost even a fraction of that."

I want to squeal and clap my hands in joy, but I don't. "That sounds incredible. I've been dreaming of pretty much exactly that since I moved in, but I've always assumed it would cost an arm and both legs."

"Not to toot my own horn, babe, but the boys and I are pretty damn awesome." He indicates the wall on the other side of which is my second bathroom. "This part is where I'm getting a little…daring."

"Ideas are easy," I say.

He nods. "So, the bedroom and bathroom setup is weird. There's no clearly defined master, and obviously no master suite."

"Nope."

"And for a house this size to have two full bathrooms is kinda silly. Especially since this one on the other side is kinda oddly big, but again a lot of unused space, just open air that you can't do anything with. And when you're talking a three-thousand-square-foot ranch, dead space is the enemy. So my idea is to take this bathroom down to two-thirds of its current size, make it a three-quarter bathroom, just a toilet, vanity, and shower."

I frown in confusion. "And do what with the space you're taking from it?"

He smirks. "Pantry." He swipes his pen up and down in a couple of spots, side to side in others. "Walk-in pantry."

I blink. "A walk-in pantry? I didn't even know I wanted that!"

He laughs. "That's why they pay me the big bucks, babe." He angles away from the counter and heads for the hallway. "Next up, a master suite."

I grin. "No. Really?"

He nods, shrugs. "Easy enough. The other

bathroom shares a wall with your bedroom, so all you gotta do is move doorways around. Close off the door from the hall, and open up the wall between. I was thinking a nice rounded archway, just for a cool visual effect. That, or one of those barn doors on an exposed powder-coated black steel rail."

I'm vibrating with barely suppressed excitement. "A rounded archway?" This time, I do sound breathless.

He laughs. "Guess it's an archway, then." He goes back to the living room, where there's a small doorway leading out to three narrow steps down into the backyard. "You've got a great backyard out here, but only this one sad little doorway to get out to it." He grins, drawing an X in the air across the wall and doorway. "Boom, gone. All of it. The whole wall, from one side to the other, living room to kitchen. I found these awesome glass walls on this distributor website, and I've been drooling over the idea of putting 'em in somewhere—and your place is just begging for them. Basically, you've got glass from side to side, and certain panels swing open. It's pretty cool. Kinda thing you see in those multimillion-dollar mansions in LA or wherever, just on a smaller scale." He glances at me and then at the backyard, a speculative expression on his face. "You know, you have a huge lot, here. You could do an addition off the back, add a couple bedrooms and another bathroom or two, and attach the garage while enlarging it—taller door, for one thing, so you can get the truck in there."

I shake my head. "I think I'll have to stick with the original plan, kitchen and master suite. Maybe do the addition someday, but for now, that's just more than I'm thinking I'm ready for or need." I frown at him. "I've only got so much saved for this, you know."

"What's your budget?"

I roll a shoulder. "I...well, about seventy thousand, but I'd like to keep a bit as a nest egg, so under that if possible."

He nods. "Easy. You're getting us for materials cost, so you'll spend...well, a shitload less. And for that, you're getting a shitload more than you could otherwise afford on that budget."

I sigh. "I was planning on just getting the kitchen for that, and was thinking I'd have to settle for less than what I'd really like." I eye him with another sigh. "What you're describing should be...a hundred thousand, easily."

He nods, waves a hand. "Probably closing in on two, if you factor in the high-end materials I'm gonna use."

"James...I just want a little more open space. I wasn't asking for a whole remodel."

"I don't do shit by halves, babe."

"Is this like selling me the car?" I ask.

He nods. "Yeah, sort of."

I sigh, somewhat bitterly. "I hate having people do favors for me."

"I'm not—"

"You are, though." I knock knuckles against the countertop. "Growing up rich, favors were sort of... *de rigueur*."

"Say what?"

"Accepted practice. Everyone did everyone favors. If my father wanted to exert influence over a legal proceeding to make sure it benefited him, he'd do a favor for the son of the judge, get him an otherwise impossible to obtain internship the son was in no way qualified for, and in return my father got the ruling he wanted. My father wanted me to go Harvard—we had the money, and I had the grades, but I got denied at first because of an equality in admissions thing. Father dearest did a favor for the dean's niece, and I got into Harvard. Even getting the internship I did, working for the senator, all that—it was all at least in part done for me as a favor to Father, so he would scratch their backs."

"And ever since, you hate it when people do favors for you," James finished. "Because you want to earn things on your own merit."

"Exactly."

James crosses the kitchen and stands in front of me—we're not touching, but he's *way* inside my personal space; I'm forced to look up at him, and for the first time since he got here, he slides his Oakleys off his face and fits them onto the brim of his hat. His eyes are deep and brown, dark and unreadable and fierce.

His massive hands, big as a grizzly's paws, clasp around my arms. "Nova. Listen. I ain't the type to just go around handing out eighty percent discounts on my services. I'm a professional. This is how I make my living. I don't do shit for free. A buddy or acquaintance asks me to come over and help him build a deck, I say no, I'll do the deck, but you're hiring me. You do free shit one fucking time, and everyone expects free shit all the fucking time. So I don't do favors. I'm not doing you a *favor*."

"Then what is it, James? Because the answer you gave about the truck didn't quite scan for me. I needed the wheels and I wanted to save the money for this"—I wave at my kitchen—"and honestly, that truck just gave me a hard-on. But as much as I love your ideas for my house, I can't accept the answer you gave about the truck. Feels a little too much like a favor, and I'm not going down that road. Not when you're talking this amount of time, money, and work."

He doesn't blink. Just stares, jaw tensing. Hands clasped around my arms. "Dammit, Nova."

"It's a simple question, James," I whisper.

"No, it's not."

"Why not?" I'm pushing it. Pushing him.

This is dangerous ground. We've made it this far by basically ignoring each other and behaving like nothing more than casual acquaintances. By pretending nothing happened, by tacit agreement, we don't tread where things risk getting personal or deep. This...

This is taking it past that.

Way, way past that.

James abruptly releases me and paces away. "You don't want me to do the job for cost, fine. I ain't gonna force it on you."

"It's not that, James. It's that I want to know *why*—truly and honestly, *why* you're doing it for cost in the first place. Why you sold me your truck for half its value."

He's facing away from me. Fists clenched at his sides, head hanging. He's sucking in deep breaths, mighty shoulders lifting and heaving, broad back expanding.

"Last we discussed this, Nova, we agreed we wouldn't go there."

"Go where?"

"You know."

I huff. "You giving me steep discounts on the truck and the remodel is kind of you going there, no?"

He whirls on me. "I fucking *like* you, Nova, okay? I'm trying to pretend I don't, like you're just one of the crew, like Audra, Imogen, and Laurel. But you're not. I feel differently about you than I do about them, and not just because they're all shacked up with my best friends."

"James."

"What? You asked for the truth—that's the truth."

I did—I asked for exactly this. And now that I have the truth...I don't know what to do with it.

"James, I..."

He stares down at me, liquid chocolate eyes fierce and wild and dangerous. "You what, Nova?"

I swallow. "I don't know."

"You said you needed the truth, Nova. Now you have it." He closes in; my heart hammers in my chest, thumps in my throat. My pulse is pounding a mile a minute, my palms are clammy. My mouth is dry, my lips are cracking—I lick my lips, and watch James's eyes follow my tongue, and linger on my lips.

"James—"

Closer, closer. All I see are his lips. His shoulders. His beard. Feel his hands on my cheeks. "You keep saying my name like that, Nova. You can't stand there and demand my feelings and then clam up on me."

His hands are so rough, so huge, so hard...yet so gentle; his palms cover my entire face, from jawline to cheekbones, lips to ears, his fingertips slide into my hair around my temple, his thumbs brush my lips.

"I don't want to accept your generosity—your *charity*—"

"It's not—"

"Because I fucking *like* you too, James," I whisper, over his protestation, as if he never spoke.

His mouth slams over mine, and the moment his lips touch mine, I'm on fire. Alive as I've never been alive. I lift up on my tiptoes and press my mouth to his, because I can't *not* kiss him back, because I need this kiss like I need to breathe. I feel my arms rise, circle his neck, and his hair is soft and silky and thick in my fingers. He rumbles in his chest, and I whimper softly, because his mouth is making me delirious, making me forget myself, my name, my intention to stay clear of him.

That was hopeless from the start, I think, and the moment he entered my home I knew I made a mistake letting him in. Because now he's *in*—in my house, in my space, in my head, in my heart. In my veins.

And now, with his tongue gently searching, he's

inside *me*.

He presses against me, pulling me harder against the cliff face of his chest, and I feel him breathing against me, feel my breasts swelling against his chest. I open my mouth to his, and take his tongue into my mouth and offer him mine, and I taste him, feel the colliding tang of tangled tongues and meshed lips, and I carefully pull his ball cap and sunglasses off his head, set them aside on the nearby counter, and bury my hands in his hair, which is flattened against his scalp from being under a hat. I'm lost in the kiss, pressing harder and deeper, breathing him, feeling him.

And then we're moving—he's pressing me backward across the kitchen in a stumble, and I slam up against a countertop, the edge biting into my butt. I squeak in surprise, and he laughs into my mouth; I'm about to retort when his hands breeze downward from my face, carve over my hips, and curl up under my buttocks. God, his hands, his touch—I gasp, press closer into his embrace, and then I'm up in the air, held up by his strong hands, lifted up, his powerful fingers digging into the flesh of my ass, and then I'm slamming down to sit on the counter; I have no choice but to spread my legs wide and accept his narrow, angular hips between the V of my thighs, and now James is closer than ever, all of him pressed against all of me.

I feel *him*—his heart hammering as wildly in his

chest as mine is; I feel his lungs pumping as he breathes into my kiss; I feel his erection throbbing against me, and only two thin layers of cotton separate my core from his erection.

I'm pulsating. Aching.

He leans into me and his mouth devours mine and his breath is my breath and his chest and shoulders block out my kitchen and the entire universe. His arms close me in, envelop me, surround me, shelter me. His beard scratches and tickles and smells like fresh cedar and primal male. His hands, after setting me on the counter, scrape up to the small of my back and delve under the hem of my T-shirt, and now— god, now those mammoth hands are on my bare skin, hot and rough across my spine and so big he can almost wrap his hands around my entire waist...and I'm not exactly dainty.

I lift up, straighten my spine, lift my chest, tilt my face up, bury myself in him, in the kiss which goes on and on and tugs me in, drugs me with its dizzying potency.

As I lift up and lengthen my spine, his hands rise as well, his fingertips dancing along my spine, his thumbs grazing my sides, daring closer and yet closer to the underwire of my bra. I gulp at his breath, tangle my lips around his, searching and hunting for his tongue. I eat his moan. Swallow his grunt as I rake my fingers down his shoulders and under his shirt to scratch up the broad hard expanse of muscular back.

I feel wild. Out of control. I feel ravenous, like a snarling beast that hasn't eaten for days, weeks, months—*years*; and which now has a delicious morsel in its jaws.

James is my morsel, and I am a fury of sexual need.

My palms angle around his sides, under his armpits, and I cup his chest, feel the thick mat of hair and the hardness of his stomach and then the rolling mountains of his shoulders, tensing as he shifts. The kiss—god, the kiss; it breaks, a momentary lapse where lips desperately part from lips, and his shirt vanishes and so does mine.

Where does his shirt go? Where is mine?

Am I wearing a bra? I don't know. Was I? I'm not now. His hands are wild on my skin, caressing in swift circles over my back and shoulders, and I arch my spine even as I pull away to put space between our torsos to make room for his hands.

I gasp, and the sharp inhalation breaks the kiss again. Our eyes meet. We're both topless. I'm sitting on the counter, and he's wedged between my thighs. His zipper strains to contain his erection. My breasts are bare, swaying with my breath, hanging heavily between us, my nipples puckered and hard, gooseflesh rippling across my skin. His eyes fix on mine for an instant, and then slide down. I catch my lower lip in my teeth and suck in a breath, because no man has seen me naked for…so long.

His eyes widen, and his jaw falls open. "Jesus, Nova."

I wriggle. "What?"

"You. You're…you're fucking…" He shakes his head, and sucks in a breath as if to do so is difficult.

"What, James?" I need to know what he thinks I am.

"Incredible."

My breath catches. "It's just because I've got big—"

He gathers my hands in his, presses my palms over my chest, hiding me from his view, and his eyes latch onto mine. "No, Nova." His hands feather into my loose red hair, a thumb grazing my cheek. "You're so fucking beautiful it makes my head spin. You—who you are. Your face, your hair, your…just you, Nova."

I drop my hands to rest them on his waist. "So it has nothing to do with these?" I ask, shaking my chest to make my breasts jiggle.

He can't help but look, and I can't help but notice the way his hips flex forward, as if trying in vain to alleviate the mounting pressure behind his zipper.

He doesn't answer. Just stares, takes in the sight

of me topless, my fair skin pinking as I blush under his frank, hungry eyes, my nipples hardening to diamond points, aching, begging.

Begging for what he is teasing me with—his touch, his hands grazing down out of my hair, over my shoulders, to my thighs, resting on my legs over my shorts, halfway between the bare skin near my knee and the crease of my hips. I hook my fingers in the waist of his jeans, the denim tight against his skin. He glances at me, and then back at my breasts.

I want him to touch me. I need his hands on me—shit, I need his mouth on me. Everything.

My hair drapes into my eyes, and I see him through a curtain of red; his hands cover my breasts, and then I gasp, a loud expression of relief and pleasure as his hot hard hands cup over my breasts, his palms rough yet gentle against my rock-hard, hypersensitive nipples. I tilt my head back and close my eyes and moan at the feel of his powerful hands caressing me, now lifting them and hefting their weight, letting them rest in his palms, thumbs grazing over my nipples, flicking them. God, his touch is like heaven. It's been so, so long since I've been touched like this.

James touches me like he's never touched a woman before—which I know isn't true, obviously, but the almost-clumsy need in the way he caresses and cups and lifts my breasts is so eager, so needy. I fucking love it.

His left hand drops to my thigh. He leans forward, and I have a split-second warning before his mouth slants across mine and his tongue slashes over my lips, licking them, probing between them and I part my lips for him and spear my tongue into his mouth and gasp as his right hand continues to eagerly, hungrily caress my breasts, right side and then the left in turn, paying equal attention. His left hand, though—ohhh, god. He rests it at first on my knee. My shorts are modest enough when I'm standing up, hanging just above mid-thigh. But when I sit down they hike up, leaving most of my thigh bare. And now—now he has my flesh under his hand, and he wants more. I'm fully aware of each centimeter of movement, his palm slid-ing upward, toward my hip. Then his fingertips are daring under the hem of my shorts, and I ache, ache, ache. My thighs are spread wide to accommodate him, to allow his huge body between them. My core is damp. His fingers slide upward. I kiss him, taste his tongue and lips, arch my back to press my breasts into his hand, and wait for his fingers to slide higher and higher yet up under my shorts.

I'm reacting on instinct. Pure, raw female need.

This man is all that I want, he's everything, and he's here, he's virile and powerful and intoxicating and impossible, and he's huge and handsome and I need him. I need this. I've wanted this since we kissed at his pool party.

I don't want to want him like this; I don't want to need him. But I do. Dammit, I do.

I'm helpless—my needs and desires, this wild, fraught sexual tension between us has me fully in its claws and I cannot escape, cannot throw off the need, the furious drive of hunger inside me to feel a man's touch, to return that touch with my own.

His hand envelops my thigh, or most of it. I'm not breathing; don't want to, don't need to because he's breathing for us both. Our lips break, the kiss is paused, and I swallow hard, blink and meet his gaze, lock eyes with him as he lets his hand wander higher, higher. Neither of us breathe, then. His forehead nudges mine; his right hand cups a breast, holding it, his thumb idly rubbing over my nipple in circles, making me lose my breath and inhale in sharp short gasps at the sizzling searing thrill.

Touch me.

God, please, touch me.

His big thick thumb reaches the apex where thigh meets hip, and pauses. My underwear covers my core, and the pad of his thumb grazes over the gusset, over my core, tracing the damp cotton, the outline of my nether lips. I want to inhale, to beg him to touch me, but all I can do is moan—and even that is more of a whispered whimper.

He pauses, his thumb resting on the cotton, over my core. I gasp again, an attempt to regain control over my breathing, an attempt to restrain myself.

It's in vain.

Like the whole charade of not being attracted to him was in vain.

"James…" I whisper.

"Nova." He pulls his head away. "I tried not to want you."

"I did too."

"Just like I'm fuckin' tryin' not to let this happen." He shakes his head. "I need to touch you, Nova. I need to feel you."

I writhe my hips forward. "I need it. I tried not to, too. I don't want you to touch me, but I can't help needing it. It's so fucking stupid, but I just…god, James. This whole thing is stupid."

He gazes at me, his eyes fiery and wild, primal brown. "So stupid. I should have more self-control than this."

"So should I."

"But I don't," he mutters.

"Neither do I."

And then, his eyes on mine, my breast cupped in his hand still, he brings his thumb along the tendon at the utter apex of my thigh, his fingernail scraping the outer edge of my sex. I gasp. He growls, sighs. I tighten my fingers in the waist of his jeans, slide my hands together to meet at the fly; I need him. I need to touch him as much as I need him to touch me. But his touch has seared away my ability to do more than one thing at a time, and right now, all I'm capable of doing is waiting for his touch.

Which he gives to me…now.

Ohhh god. Oh god, I can't breathe. I'm dizzy.

His thumb slides over my bare flesh, gliding over the outside of my pussy, and then down the seam. He groans, and I know he's as affected by this as I am—as affected by touching me as I am by being touched.

His thumb slicks upward, and then, dragging through my lips, through the wetness of my desire. I don't breathe and neither does he, as his thumb slides through my core and upward, to the center. To *my* center. Where I ache most. Where his touch sizzles, sears, thrills.

I whimper.

God, his thumb feels so big, so hard, pressed against my clit, and I whimper again, a breathless sound of desperate need. He's so gentle—*so* utterly gentle. His touch is featherlight. Rasping in slow, meandering, teasing circles.

More, more.

I bite down on my lip and try to remember to

breathe, but his touch is too much, and my lungs won't work, don't work.

I can't help it. I need—I'm so needy; I need his touch, and I need to touch.

I rip open his fly. Yank the zipper apart.

Cotton bulges through the opening, and my fingers, acting with a hungry mind of their own, curl into the elastic of his underwear. Pause for a split-second, and then I can't wait another heartbeat. I pull the elastic away and tug down, and he grunts in surprise as I push his jeans and underwear down past his butt, baring him. I look, and I gulp.

The answer is, yes, he's as massively endowed as my dirty middle-of-the-night-fantasies suggested. As huge as filthy-minded Audra has suggested more than once.

He—is—*enormous*.

Thick as my wrist and more inches long than I care to guess, a fat, shiny, bulbous pink head, purple veins and so much tan flesh. A thatch of curly black hair around the base trimmed but not shaved.

I glance at James's eyes, see his need, but see also conflict.

His thumb continues its slow circuit around my clitoris.

My gut flips, my core throbs, my pulse pounds. I am afire with need—excruciating arousal slams through me, cranked higher and higher with each circle of the pad of his thumb.

And now, ohhhh god, now I have his cock in my hand. A huge, thick, soft, warm, iron-hard cock. A beautiful, perfect cock.

God, I *love* the way he feels, filling my hands.

I stroke him. Slowly. A sweet, achingly slow, greedy, needy caress of his length with both of my hands.

He gasps, a surprisingly quiet sound, and then he growls, a quintessentially James sound, a primal, bear-like rumble. His thumb moves, and my hips move with it. His right hand leaves my breast, travels downward to the waist of my thin cotton shorts, gathers fabric, and he yanks them down, roughly. Both hands, then, roughly, demandingly yanking my shorts down. I cling to his neck with one arm—refusing to completely relinquish my grasp of his cock—and I use his shoulders to lift my ass off the counter so he can yank my shorts down; I tug one foot free and wrap my leg around his buttocks, and he slips the bunched wad of shorts and panties off my other foot and now I'm utterly naked, totally naked, sitting on the cold laminate counter, and he's touching me, a long thick middle finger dipping inside me, sliding easily through my wet lips and into my squeezing channel. His other hand is busily smearing in slow circles around my clit, and with a finger inside me and two fingers on my spasming clit.

I have him in my hands, both fists wrapped around him, sliding up his length and squeezing around the plump tip and twisting down, and I watch my hands, stare at the beautiful sight of a perfect male cock in my hands—for the first time in so long; and I want it and need it so much, feel such deep, cutting, ripping, fiery need, a desperation I haven't felt in so, so long. Not since...

No.

NO.

I will not, cannot, shall *not* think of Craig, not now.

I focus on James, putting thoughts of anything else—any*one* else out of my mind. I look at James, at his conflicted, hungry, aroused eyes.

I realize his conflict—he's struggling with thoughts of someone else, too, and fighting to remain in the moment with me.

I gulp and writhe as he speeds his touch, and I change my own touch—one hand caressing in slow short strokes around his head, the other driving up and down the base in longer, faster glides.

His hips drive forward into my touch, and my own grind hard into the curling sliding movement of his finger and quick, slickly circling thumb. I stroke, he circles.

He grunts, I whimper.

His eyes lock on mine, and mine are on his, and then our gazes break and we watch our hands, and his lips slash across mine for a kiss, but we're too breathless, too caught up in this together to spare thought for even a kiss.

Another deep whimper from my lips, a taut line stretching from my core to my lungs is pulled to such tightness that I cannot breathe, can only grind and writhe and gasp as his touch incites wilder and hotter fire.

Another tense groan from James, his hips pushing his cock through my fists. I feel him—I feel how tense he is, every line of his body, every muscle taut.

I no longer groan or whimper—My legs wrap around his waist and my forehead rests against his chest, my hands between our bodies stroking him faster and faster, his hands tangled between mine to circle my clit.

I writhe. I'm helpless. I'm lost. I'm toppling wildly over the edge, and as I shudder to the shivering cusp of cracking, crashing, crackling, I cling to his beautiful thick hard cock and I plunder his length fast and fast and faster.

"Oh fuck, James—" I groan, my voice hoarse, my breath locked in my throat, clenched behind my gritted teeth. "I'm coming, James. Please, please—oh god, please, James."

I arch my back, leaning away from him, head thrown backward, eyes closed—a delicious wet hot tugging sensation rockets through me, and my eyes rip open to see James bent over me, mouth latched onto my nipple, and I'm stretched apart by his fingers, two of them slicking thick into my spasming, tightening, squeezing channel, his thumb rubbing madly around my clit, and his mouth slides to my other nipple and back, again and again, suckling my nipples to stretched points. His mouth is so wet, so hot, and his tongue lashes and his lips pinch and he sucks, suckles, licks, and his teeth saw not quite gently but not painfully around my erect flesh.

I come with a scream and a whimper, legs locked around his bare waist, my hands wrapped around his throbbing cock. I come so hard I weep, tears trickling down my cheeks, sob after sob ripping from me as I come and come and come and come, hoarsely sobbing.

And then James's hands leave my core and latch onto my breast and the back of my neck, and his hips thrust spasmodically, uncontrollably. He grunts, and then the grunt turns into a long, drawn-out groan. He arches forward over me, shoulders hunched and drawn in, head hanging. His eyes are closed. His breath comes in short sharp gasps, and he groans again as his hips begin undulating, grinding his cock through my hands. He's close.

I want it.

I want his pleasure. His release.

"Fuck, fuck, fuck—" The first words he's spoken in several minutes.

I plunge my fists down around him, slick them back up. He's dry—I release him with one hand and spit into my palm, smear my saliva around the head of his cock, and then slide my other fist around it, spreading the lubrication around him, and his groan now is hoarse and low and broken.

He thrusts helplessly.

I pull him closer to me, breathe in his ear, whisper his name, whisper encouragement to him, accepting his orgasm and relishing the vulnerability in this moment: "James, yes—come for me, James. Let me feel you come, James—yes, yes, yes." I'm whispering this in his ear, so softly and quietly I can barely hear myself over his nonstop grunts as he reaches climax.

I stroke him quickly, one fist above the other, and he's so huge that with both fists plunged down around his base, there's still at least a couple of inches of his beautiful organ sprouting out the top of my upper fist. I watch, rapt, as he tenses, goes utterly taut, jaw clenched around a curse:

"Fuck—f-f-fuuuuuck—"

He comes.

Beautifully, raggedly, James orgasms. His seed spurts in a thick white stripe out of him and over my belly in a hot thick pool, and I stroke and grind and twist and plunge, and he groans again, comes more, adding to the pool of cum on my belly.

He's heaving breathlessly, and he thrusts helplessly into my fists, spurting another, smaller squirt onto me. So…much…cum.

God, it's beautiful. He's beautiful. I've not felt this way—needed, wanted, desired—in so, *so* long. I've forgotten how it feels.

I'm still slowly stroking his length, and he jerks, judders, and a bead of cum dribbles down one side, and he groans long and loud.

"Ohhhh fuck. Fuck." He growls in his chest. "Holy shit, Renée."

SIX

I FREEZE.

He freezes.

His eyes fly open and meet mine. "Nova—Nova." His eyes are tortured, sorrowful, conflicted, pained. "Nova, fuck—I—I'm…" He backs away, stumbling as his jeans tangle around his knees. He jerks them up. "Goddammit—Nova, I'm sorry."

I can't speak.

It hurts. God, it hurts.

Knowing how easily such things can happen, especially to those like James and me—well, that doesn't help. It still hurts to hear another woman's name fall from his lips.

I have his cum cooling in a sticky pool on my belly.

I feel tears welling, and I blink them away, but I'm too late, and not strong enough to suck them back in. Not now, not weak from orgasm, not weak from having just felt so…so *wanted*.

I know, intellectually, that until the ultimate moment of release, he was fully present with me and aware he was with me.

I *know* this.

But he said *her* name.

"Nova—"

I swallow hard, shake my head. "It's fine, James."

He leans past me to grab the roll of paper towel off the holder, rips a handful of sheets free, and cleans me up in a few quick, economical wipes, folding the wad and wiping until I'm clean.

He throws the paper towel away and reaches for me, pulls me off the counter and sets me on my feet. His hands are so strong—*he's* so strong. I shiver at his touch.

I crouch and snag my clothing. "I…um. I'm gonna go get…get dressed."

I turn away and head for my bedroom, barely keeping it together. I make it to my bed, toss my clothing back onto the floor and collapse onto my bed, letting out the sobs.

How anyone his size, weighing as much as he does in solid muscle, can move so silently, I don't even know. I don't hear a thing, so I'm startled when I feel my bed dip, and then a blanket covers me.

I don't look.

I don't want him to see me crying, which is stupid, but there it is.

"Nova, I'm sorry." His voice is so quiet, deep and gruff and sad. "I don't know what else to say."

I roll to my side and bring the blanket up to my chin, peering at James through tear-blurred eyes. "Why are you still here?"

"You want me to leave?"

I shrug. "I don't know. No. Yes. I don't know."

"I'm here because I had to...say I'm sorry. You have to know I knew—the whole time, I knew I was with you. I wanted to be here with *you*." He rubs the back of his neck—he's still shirtless, his heavy muscles flexing and shifting as he moves. "I just...in that moment, I got...I want to say confused, but that's not right. I don't know how to put it."

I flop onto my back, heedless for a moment of the fact that the blanket doesn't come with me, and my breasts poke out—I follow his gaze, and tug the blanket up. "James, I get it."

"You do?"

I nod. "As much as I can, yes."

"I want to explain, but after what we just shared together, I don't want to talk about—" He stops abruptly, shrugging.

I press the blanket against my sternum and shimmy to a sitting position, and I wipe my eyes with my free hand. "Say her name, James."

"Nova, I—"

If I know anything at all about James, it's that the raw, brutal truth is always better than a pleasant fiction. "You said *her* name instead of mine as I made you come, James. You came *on* me, and you said your dead wife's name."

He flinches. "I know, Nova. And I'm sorry."

I ignore his words. "So, if you want to explain, then explain. And don't shy away from saying her name, James. It can't hurt me any more than it already has."

"I didn't mean to hurt you," he says.

I offer a sort-of smile. Not quite forgiveness, or acceptance, but...understanding, perhaps. "I know. The problem is, we don't have to *mean* or *intend* something for it hurt. It still hurts. You said her name instead of mine—it was an accident, and I understand. But it still hurts."

He sighs, long and slow. "Nova, I..." He wipes his face with a palm. His jeans are still undone, pulled up but unzipped; the gray cotton of his underwear is dotted with a spot where he leaked cum after pulling them up—or perhaps that was pre-cum from being aroused before I took him out. "There was only her. Ever."

I've heard bits and pieces and repeated parts of

stories, but that's not the same as hearing it from him. I stay quiet and keep my eyes on his. I wait.

"I met her in elementary school, same year as I met Jesse, her brother. I liked her from the moment I saw her—she was wearing a denim overall skirt, red tights, little black shoes, and her hair was in two blond braids."

I laugh. "You remember what she was wearing the first time you met her, what, thirty-five years ago?"

He shrugs. "Like I said, there was only ever her. We were friends until middle school. We antagonized each other in middle school and acted like we suddenly hated each other."

"As one does in middle school," I say.

He nods. "And then, the summer before ninth grade, we hung out together a lot, and then we kissed for the first time..." He stares at the ceiling, swallowing hard. "And that was it. After that first kiss, it was just the two of us, James and Renée. We were so inseparable we didn't just get...what's the term for combining a couples' names?"

"Shipping? Like Brangelina?"

"Right, that. We didn't just get shipped or whatever, our group of friends called us JR, as in James and Renée, like we were a single entity. If they wanted to know where one of us was, they'd ask, 'Where's JR?'"

I laugh at that. "Wow. That's relationship goals right there."

He shrugs, nods. "Yeah, I guess so." A long pause. "So, when I say it was only ever her, I mean that in every way. She was my first kiss, my first everything—and not just my first…my *only*." His eyes meet mine. "It has only *ever* been her."

"I get it, James."

He shakes his head. "I don't know if you do." He swallows hard again. "That time we kissed in my kitchen—that was the first time I'd ever, *ever* kissed a woman who wasn't Renée."

"Oh," I breathe. "Ohhh."

"Yeah."

"So…" I blink hard, trying to wrap my head around what he's saying. "So us, just now?"

"You are the only woman who has ever touched me, aside from her. And that was the first I've been touched by anyone since she…since Renée died." His eyes mist, and he blinks hard, turns his head to one side, away from me.

Somehow, his pain in this moment eclipses my own. I touch his cheek, turn his face to mine. "Don't hide it, James."

He grumps, gruff, blinks, shakes his head. "I'm just being stupid."

I rub a thumb across his cheek, under his eye.

"Quit acting macho. You're allowed to feel the way you feel, James, and you're no less a big, tough, strong, alpha male for shedding a few tears."

He stares at me. "After what we just did, and after what just happened, I expected you to kick me out, not let me whine about my stupid sob story."

I shake my head. "*Now* you're being stupid, James." I scoff, my own throat thick. "My story isn't quite like yours, but I *do* understand, to a degree."

He tilts his head to one side. "What do you mean?"

I'd told my story to Laurel and then to Imogen, and thus somehow just assumed James heard about it.

A long silence extends between us, as James waits for my answer.

"I lost someone I loved, too," I say. "Craig. We weren't childhood friends, or high school sweethearts like you and Renée, but...we were together for several years, and I truly, deeply loved him. I thought we'd get married. I was waiting for him to propose and was half planning our wedding while I waited. I thought it would be coming any day, you know?" I sniffle. "Then he started to get aloof and weird and secretive, and I assumed he was cheating, because that's been my experience when men act that way."

"He wasn't?"

"No," I say. "He had cancer. Terminal, inoperable cancer."

"Shit."

I nod. "Yeah."

"So, instead of a ring and wedding, you got a funeral."

I nod. I hesitate, and then just let instinct guide me. I slide off the bed, initially taking the blanket with me, and then I half laugh, half scoff. "Why am I hiding from you? You've already seen me naked." I toss the blanket back onto the bed and cross my bedroom naked, trying to feel confident and only partially succeeding.

On my dresser is a small wooden box, hand carved from cedar, with delicate scrollwork—a gift from Craig, made by him. I slide the top off—inside is a pair of diamond teardrop earrings set in platinum, a carat each, the only expensive thing my parents gave me that I've kept. Also in there is a delicate pearl necklace that belonged to Craig's great-grandmother, another gift from him, on our five-year anniversary; and a single ring, half a carat, plain gold band, solitaire setting. *The* ring. I take it from the box and hold it in my palm, go back to the bed and sit down, cover my lap with the blanket but remain topless.

I show James the ring. "He, um. He intended

to propose. He had the ring, and was planning to propose, and then he found out he was sick, and he couldn't. I think he thought he could push me away so I wouldn't have to deal with his death if I dumped him."

"You didn't."

"Fuck no." I sigh, deeply. "No. I stayed with him."

"To the end?"

I nod. "To the very end. I sat with him and held his head in my lap as he took his last breath."

"Jesus, Nova."

I laugh. "Funny, that's exactly what Laurel said when I told her the story." I shrug. "There's more to it, a lot that went on before Craig, and after, but…I guess I only tell you so you know I know what it's like to lose someone you love."

"I'm sorry you went through that."

"Me too." I meet his eyes. "Before, when you and I…whatever you want to call what we did." I pause again, swallow hard. "When I first, um…took you out of your pants." Another pause. "I, um. Craig wasn't my first, and wasn't my last. But he was…the one. The one that mattered, the one who really truly, deeply *meant* something to me. And I thought of him. When I first saw you, touched you, I thought of him. How I haven't…" I blink, swallow, and can't look at James. "I thought about how I hadn't…*needed*…anyone the way I wanted and needed you in that moment, not since Craig. And I...I hated thinking about him when I was with you, touching you, being touched by you, but I couldn't not. So...I get it. You accidentally saying Renée's name—I get it."

He takes the ring from me and spins it in the sunlight streaming through my open blinds. "I still have our rings...our wedding bands, her engagement ring." He hands the ring back. "I actually wore my band for three years before Jesse made me take it off."

"I wore that ring on my index finger for a while, and then I forced myself to take it off." I traipse over to the box, replace the ring and then sit back down on the bed, covering my chest and lap with the blanket this time. "It's not worth much, but I can't get rid of it."

"I know." He rolls a shoulder. "Why keep the rings? It's painful to see them, but it'd be like giving away the last reminder of her I have. Jesse and the guys helped me clean out her clothes and such a few months after she passed, and I've gradually given away the rest of her stuff, and replaced most of the pictures of us with pictures of the girls and me. Each of my girls has a picture of herself with Renée, and I have one of her and I in my top dresser drawer, upside down, under my socks. But everything else is gone. Except the rings."

Another long silence between us.

James shifts. Looks at me. "Do you regret it?"

I meet his eyes. "Regret what? Being with Craig? Staying with him to the end? Or what you and I just did?"

He scoffs, tilts his head back on his neck. "I meant what we just did. But...the rest too, I suppose. Since we're talking about it."

"No, I don't regret what you and I just did, James." I pin the blanket under my arms, against my sides. "I don't regret it at all. I...it was the best I've felt in...a very, very, *very* long time."

"Me too."

"Do you regret it?" I ask him.

He doesn't answer right away. "I...no. I don't regret it. But I'm still...I don't know how to put it. Fucked up about it. I feel...guilty, I guess. Like I betrayed her. But I know she's... gone. And before she died, she made me promise not to stay alone forever. So I...I don't think she would be mad, or whatever. That's a stupid way to put it, but I'm not very good with words. She wanted me to find someone. I was with her when she died. I held her hand. We were separated by the blue tarp thing they put up for a C-section, and she was bleeding out and she knew it, and no one could stop it and...she squeezed my hand as hard as she could and looked at me, and begged me to not stay alone forever. She knew me, I guess. Knew I'd...well, do what I've done: close up. And she loved me so much she wanted me to find some kind of happiness after she was gone. Even in death she was thinking about me." A tense, thick, sharp silence. "But I still feel guilty. Looking at you. Wanting you. Kissing you. Touching you. Wanting you as bad as I fucking want you? It feels like a betrayal of her. Of what we had for twenty fucking years. Of how I felt about her, how I loved her. And—and you touching me...that felt...so—god, I've had the worst...best...I don't know—the craziest, dirtiest dreams since we met, since we kissed, and you touching me...it was..." He shakes his head and trails off.

"It was what, James?"

He shakes his head, his mouth moving but no words coming out. He tries again, with a sharp breath. "It felt amazing. I wish I had better words to use, but I don't. Amazing isn't strong enough. It was incredible. But the guilt...*fuck*, the guilt." He looks at me, then, after long moments of staring anywhere but at my eyes.

"You dreamed about me?" I ask, a small smirk on my lips. I can't help but be a little pleased by the fact that he's dreamed about me.

He groans, head tilted backward again, hand

rubbing over his lips. "Yes."

"What kind of dreams?" I keep looking at him, watching him. "You said crazy, dirty dreams."

He nods. "Yeah."

"Tell me."

He shakes his head. "I felt shitty about that too."

"James, you have to know—"

"I do know. She's gone and I'm allowed to move on. I know." He shakes his head. "When I say I felt shitty about it, I didn't mean like that. I meant…in terms of you. I…" Another shake of his head, another trailed off sentence.

"What, James?" I ask. "Tell me."

"You're fishing."

"Yep."

He looks at me, brown eyes steady and wide and deep. "I had fantasies about you, Nova. Dirty stuff. You can probably guess what I dreamed about. You. What we just did. Other stuff."

"I've dreamed about you, too. Had thoughts." I pause, try to smile but the tension is too taut and thick, and I can't. "Wanted you, and tried to pretend I didn't. Woke up with dreams about you—about us—lingering, and feeling guilty about it, because we agreed we wouldn't…" I gesture toward the kitchen. "Do exactly that."

"So neither of us regret it," James says, "but…

now what?"

I shake my head and shrug. "I have no idea."

"That makes two of us." A phone rings in the distance, and it breaks the moment. James growls. "That's mine."

"You should answer it. It's probably important."

"It's always important."

"All the more reason to answer it."

"You trying to get rid of me?" he asks, and I think he's hiding a real question behind a joke.

"No," I say. "I'm not. But I'm really mixed up and confused right now, and I need to figure things out."

James nods. Slides off the bed, and I'm surprised yet again at how lithe and quiet he can be, for such a huge, muscular man. He exits my room and I hear him call back whoever had called him. While he's gone, I grab my knee-length plush robe from the back of my bedroom door and put it on, tie it. When James comes back, he's fully dressed, hat back on, Oakleys on the brim, shirt tucked behind the buckle of his black leather belt.

His eyes rake over me in my robe, and then fix on my eyes. "I have to go. A client's foundation is cracking."

"Not good."

"Nope. They're gonna want me to fix it, but you

really need a foundation repair specialist for that."
He shuffles his feet. "I didn't build the house, by the
way. When I put in a foundation, it don't crack."

I smile. "I know."

"Nova, I…" He trails off, shaking his head. "I
don't know what the hell to say, to be honest."

"I don't either. We kind of messed up our agreement, didn't we?"

He laughs. "Yeah. No more pretending we're
not attracted to each other, huh?"

"That was a pipe dream, I think."

He nods. "Yeah, it was." Another long silence.
"So, um. The remodel."

"James—"

"It's not a favor," he cuts in. "Yes, I like you. Yes,
I'm fucking crazy attracted to you. I just…I want to
do this for you. I'm not sure I can give you a reason
that makes any sense. It's not because you're hot, or
because of what we just did… It's…everything. It's
you. I want to remodel your house because I like
you, because of all the reasons I said I wasn't doing
it, and because I just…I'm a builder, and it's what I
do, and I'm a man attracted to a woman and we do
crazy shit like high-dollar remodels for cost when we
like a woman. I don't know what else to say."

"The obstinate, stubborn, independent part
of me is screaming at me to say no." I laugh. "But

I guess being selfish is winning. Because the vision you described for my house? James, I *want* that."

He stands in front of me—we're in the center of my bedroom, and he's towering over me, six inches taller and staring down at me with those intense, wild brown eyes. "There is one other reason I want to do the remodel."

"Why's that?"

"So I can see more of you."

I laugh. "Funny. That's the other reason I'm saying yes, and I'm glad you voiced it first." I sober, then. "Are we...we're not going to try and pretend this didn't happen, are we?"

"I don't think I can."

"Neither can I."

"But...just being totally honest—"

"You're not sure you can emotionally handle a repeat," I guess. "Or anything more."

He sighs, nods, and rubs his beard with one hand. "Yeah."

"But you still want to see me again?"

He nods. "Yeah."

"So things are going to continue to be awkward, weird, and complicated."

"I don't know how to make it different."

"Me either." I put my hands on his shoulders. Lift up on my toes. Kiss his cheekbone, just above his beard line. "Then it'll just be awkward, weird, and complicated."

He accepts my kiss on his cheek, and then twists his face and suddenly we're kissing again, and I'm on fire and tasting his tongue and whimpering—

"Dammit, dammit, dammit." He pulls away abruptly. "Complicated. So fucking complicated."

I touch my lips with two fingers. "Very complicated."

"I have to go." He growls this from across the room.

"Yeah, you do."

Without another word, without a backward glance, he leaves. Out of my room, out of my house, out of my driveway. I stay in my room, sit on my bed, and try to figure out if I want to laugh or cry or do both.

That just happened.

I put my hands over my mouth and let myself have a girly moment—I scream, kick my feet, and laugh hysterically. Because that's better than crying.

I need a shower: I'm still sticky...he missed a few spots when he was cleaning me up.

Never in any of my wildest, dirtiest wet dreams of James, ever, did I picture us doing what we just did. Even as a teenager, even in my promiscuous period, I never did anything that hot. That messy. It wasn't sex, so what was it? Dirty. Hot. Impetuous. Like we just...didn't have any chance of resisting the need to just *touch* each other.

God...

I need a shower, and then I need to talk to Audra.

SEVEN

Aᴜᴅʀᴀ sʜᴏᴡs ᴜᴘ ᴛᴡᴇɴᴛʏ ᴍɪɴᴜᴛᴇs ᴀғᴛᴇʀ Jᴀᴍᴇs leaves, parking her slick little white Mercedes convertible in the driveway behind my truck, letting herself into my house. She's dressed in shimmery, sparkly purple skintight workout shorts that only just barely cover her actual buttocks and give her mad camel toe. The shorts are paired with a violently yellow sports bra that looks painfully tight but still doesn't do much to contain her naturally massive mammaries. Her shoes are an eye-watering barrage of bright colors, and her hair is twisted back in a scalp-tightening French braid. She's coated in a sheen of sweat, and if I weren't a completely and utterly avowed straight woman, I'd have a hard-on for her, to be honest.

I'm still in my bathrobe, or rather, in my bathrobe again because I took a shower. My hair is damp and brushed straight back, sticking to my neck. Audra rummages in my cabinets until she finds a glass, fills it with ice and water, and drains it, refills it, and then arches an eyebrow at me.

"So. The doctor is in, my dear," she says. "Talk to me."

I shake my head and sigh. "I don't even know where to start."

She smirks. "It's the middle of the day and you just took a shower. Plus, you called *me* instead of Imogen or Laurel." She takes a sip of her ice water. "You fucked James."

"We didn't fuck," I say.

She narrows her eyebrows at me. "You did *something*, and you can't convince me otherwise."

I flip my hair away from my neck. "I'm not saying we didn't do anything, I'm saying we didn't have *sex*."

She frowns. "Intriguing. Go on."

"We…messed around."

"And? Why am I here? You wouldn't call me to come over and talk if you didn't have some sort of…I don't know—conflict."

I fill and turn on my electric kettle to make tea. "I guess I should give you the backstory. So, the pool party where I first met you guys—"

"I thought for sure you and James were gonna be a thing, like, as of that day."

"Under different circumstances, we probably

would have been. But we both have…issues."

"James lost his wife in childbirth, so I get his hang up, but you're little miss *'I don't talk about my past'*, so I have no idea what your issue is."

I laugh. "Funny thing is, I had a major panic attack about a week ago and showed up at Laurel's house at three a.m., sobbing. And I told her my whole story. And the process of telling her my story I realized I have to quit planning Imogen and Jesse's wedding, because of the aforementioned hang-up, which led me to having to tell her the story. Then I sort of told James some of the story when he was here quoting me on a remodel and we, um…yeah."

"So basically everyone knows but me?"

I laugh. "Yep. You're the last to know." I shake my head. "No. Laurel and Imogen are the only ones who know the whole story."

I give her a highlights version, and when I'm done, she's staring at me with interest.

"So that's why you're such a bitch all the time," she says, with a grin that tells me she's kidding.

"Yeah, exactly," I say, with another laugh. "I'm a bitch because life dealt me some shitty hands."

"So you and James have that in common, then—having lost a partner." She frowns. "I'd think that would bond you a little."

"You'd think. But in reality, it just makes both

of us reticent to trust anyone, and we feel guilty for doing anything with anyone. For enjoying anything, because it feels like betraying our dead lover."

Audra winces. "Oh."

I nod. "Yeah, oh."

"So, is that what happened? You guys messed around and now you have survivor's guilt or something?"

"Wish it was that simple or easy," I say.

Audra waves a hand. "So? What the hell happened? Don't keep a bitch waiting."

"Back to the backstory, first," I say. "The pool party. We clicked, you know? Like, instant chemistry. Attraction, sexual tension from the first glance, the whole shebang."

"But."

"We kissed," I say, staring out the window. "And by kissed, I mean, he slammed me up against the refrigerator and kissed me absolutely stupid. Like, I've never been kissed that way by anyone, ever, not even by my dead boyfriend." I pause, then. "And actually, that was my exact thought, verbatim—not even Craig ever kissed me this way. And I froze."

"Oh," Audra says, understanding dawning. "Oh boy."

"And it turns out James had a similar thought. Except in his case, it wasn't just a boyfriend, it was his high school sweetheart, the only woman he ever kissed, touched, dated, anything—not to mention the mother of his children and his wife of twenty years."

"Yikes."

"Yeah, so kissing me, and feeling like it was *that* good, as good or better than kissing his wife? Grounds for feeling a little guilty, I'd say."

"Must have been a hell of a kiss," Audra notes.

I snort. "You have no idea." I sigh dreamily. "Never in my life has a single kiss affected me that way—no touching anywhere except his hands on my face and mine on his shoulders. I seriously got wet from the kiss. If he'd touched me literally anywhere, I'd probably have spontaneously orgasmed."

"Jesus," Audra says, eyes widening.

"Yeah." The kettle comes to a boil and turns off, and I pour myself a mug of green tea; I wiggle an empty mug at Audra as an offer, and she shrugs and nods, so I pour her some too. "So, after the kiss, and our individually motivated freak-outs, we agreed that maybe it was best for both of us if we just…ignored the thing between us and acted like nothing had ever happened."

Audra nods. "Which is why things were so weird between you two for the last year." She laughs. "It totally worked, too, I bet," she says, her voice dripping sarcasm.

I sigh again. "I mean, yeah. It worked...until it didn't."

"Usually how that goes, in my experience."

"Because you have SO much experience pretending you don't feel sexually attracted to someone."

She fake-glares at me. "For your information, I TOTALLY held out on sleeping with Franco for, like, DAYS, at least."

"Wow," I say, deadpan. "Such restraint."

"Right? I know." She goes serious, then. "So you and James pretended you didn't have the hots for each other for over a year, and then...?"

"And then..." I shake my head. "If I'm going to actually tell you this, I need to sit down."

I take my tea into the living room and curl up in my favorite spot: my gray suede recliner I'd found for twenty bucks at a resale shop. I blow across the top of my tea, and then take a sip.

"So, I had a panic attack. Planning the wedding for Imogen and Jesse brought up all these feelings I'd kept buried for years—I designed centerpieces and stuff that was pretty much exactly what I'd planned for my own wedding to Craig...the wedding that never happened, because he got cancer and died without ever even proposing."

"Ouch."

"Yeah. I thought I could do it, when I first agreed,

you know? Like, it was years ago, I'm as over it as I can be, yada yada yada." I sigh, and then laugh. "NOPE. Not over it. The further I got into the planning, the more I started thinking about Craig. About the wedding I'd had planned. I mean, I had a whole binder of stuff. Dress ideas, centerpiece ideas, bouquet ideas, venue locations, everything. And I guess I was sort of subconsciously using all that for their wedding, and it just brought it all back up. I was dreaming about Craig. About the wedding that never happened—I saw myself with him at the altar, and then he wasted away before my eyes in time-lapse. Like he did in real life, only in a matter of seconds instead of months. I'd wake up sobbing. And the deeper into planning I got, the worse it became."

Audra winces in sympathy. "Shit, honey. No one blames you for quitting."

"Oh no, Imogen totally got it when I told her. And apparently Franco and Jesse had had a wager on *when* I would quit planning the wedding. Not *if... when.*"

"Wow. I've got news for Franco. I'll have to put a moratorium on spontaneous blowjobs for a week for that."

I wave a hand dismissively. "Don't do that." I frowned quizzically at her. "Wait, though. How many spontaneous blowjobs do you give the man?"

She wiggles her eyebrows. "A *lot*. Let's just say we don't necessarily have sex every single day, but he definitely gets a nice O every single day. Sometimes twice in one day, if I'm feeling particularly frisky."

My mind boggles. "How does that even work? Like, you suck him off in the morning and then fuck him at night?"

She nibbles on her lower lip. "He comes home for lunch most days. I've started scheduling free time around noon so I can go home for lunch, and he meets me in the kitchen. He makes us sandwiches, I suck his cock, he fingers me, we go our separate ways, and then we fuck while dinner is cooking. And sometimes again before we go to sleep."

I just blink at her. "Holy shit, Audra."

She shrugs. "I love the man, I love his cock, and he can make me come faster than anyone who's ever laid hand, finger, tongue, or dick on me or in me. It's mutually assured pleasure pretty much nonstop." Another wiggle of her eyebrows. "Plus, this way, I know he can't possibly want or need more than I'm giving him, which means I'm assured of his fidelity."

I frown. "I'm not sure giving him that much sex just to make sure he doesn't cheat is a good thing, Audra."

She laughs. "Ahhhh, I'm just kidding. He loves me, and I love him. He'd never cheat on me, nor I on him—we both have serious history with unfaithful exes, so that's a huge hot-button issue for us. I give him that much sex because I want it that much—I want *him* that much." She glances at me. "You've never wanted anyone enough to fuck them twice a day more than just occasionally?"

I blush. "I mean, if I was to have access to James every time I had a sexual urge, he wouldn't be able to walk."

Audra snickers. "So you know exactly how it's possible."

"Theoretically, yes. In practice, not so much."

"So…sounds as if your backstory is complete. But what actually *happened*?"

"I stayed at Laurel and Ryder's farmhouse last week. I didn't have any extra clothes with me, so I slept in a big old T-shirt of Laurel's."

Audra makes a face as if she's trying to contain laughter. "She's shorter than you and not as busty as you. How did you even fit in her shirt?"

I laugh. "I didn't. I mean, it technically covered the essential bits, but in actual practice it didn't really, um, conceal anything very well. Like, at all. I was pretty groggy when I woke up and wasn't even thinking when I went downstairs—I was just following my nose to coffee and food." I pause for effect. "And guess who was sitting at the table?"

"James."

"And Ryder. And Laurel's son."

"And there you are, in your ridiculously well-endowed glory, all but naked."

"Well, not all but naked, just...not dressed for being around people. James's eyes popped out of his skull, and I'm pretty certain he choked on his coffee." I huff a laugh. "Nate asked if the reason his mom's shirt didn't fit me was because my 'no-no's' we're so much bigger than hers."

Audra chokes, sputtering on her tea. "Oh my fucking god—he said that?"

I nod, cackling. "He did."

"He called them no-no's?"

"Ryder thought it was hysterical. He asked if I was having a '*tit*-uation'." I tilt my head, thinking back. "Actually, what happened was James was trying like the devil to not stare at me and failing badly, and didn't know what to do with himself, so he made excuses about having to go, and Ryder asked *him* if he was having a *tit*-uation."

Audra rolls her eyes. "Classic Ryder." She shakes her head. "So. James bolted."

"Later, Laurel pointed out that he left in a hurry, and was walking kinda funny."

Audra shrugs. "Well, if you were dressed like you describe, I can imagine him being pretty, ummm, affected."

"So I talked to Laurel a bit more, and then left. And then the next day, I knew I had to tell Imogen I was passing her wedding planning off on someone else, so I went over and talked to Imogen and explained everything. And then, barely two miles from home, my car died."

"Oh jeez."

"Yeah. I mean, I'd been expecting it for quite a while. It was over twenty years old and it had two hundred thousand miles on it. So I knew it was going to die."

"Still, having a car die on you is never convenient."

"Nope. To make matters worse, it died at a green light, in the middle of the intersection, so I had to put on my flashers—if you make a boob joke, I'll slap you—and get out and push."

"I think I know where this is going," Audra says.

"Yeah. All of the sudden, the car somehow got a lot easier to push. Whoever was helping me gets my Explorer to a parking lot out of the way. And guess who it was helping me?"

"James?"

"None other." I sigh. "So, he calls his friend who has a wrecking service, gets me five hundred dollars cash for my dead-ass car, and then offers to take me home."

"Whose home?" Audra asks, snickering lecherously.

I roll my eyes. "Nothing like that. So we're on the way home and I realize I now have no car, no way to get to work, and no way to even get to a lot to buy a new one."

Audra laughs. "Right, because James is *totally* the type to just say 'sorry, not my problem' and leave at you home without a ride."

"Exactly," I say. "So he drove me to a couple used car lots and even a new lot, but nothing really jumped out at me, so he mentioned he had a truck he wasn't using—he'd replaced it with his current one, but hadn't had the heart to get rid of it."

"That monster in the driveway is *yours*?" Audra asks. "I thought—I don't know what I thought."

I laugh as I swallow a mouthful of tea. "Yeah, it's mine. I went to James's house, and he showed me the truck. He and the boys had beefed it up under the hood, put on the lift kit and light bar and all that." I pause to drink more tea. "It had sort of turned into Renée's favorite thing to drive, whenever James wasn't using it for work. He had a lot of memories of her in it, and a lot of money invested in it aside from the sentiment, so he hadn't been able to bring himself to sell it to some random dude."

Audra's eyes widen. "He sold you Renée's truck?"

I nod. "And for, like, a fraction of what it's worth, considering all the aftermarket upgrades on it."

Audra scoffs. "That thing has to have nearly twenty grand in upgrades. Those wheels and tires are hella expensive, and I know lift kits aren't cheap, especially that high, plus the light bar, and whatever they did under the hood?"

I nod. "Exactly. He basically gave it to me."

Audra shakes her head. "It's weird, but I think you are the only woman who's woman enough to drive a macho mobile like that and still be all woman."

I laugh. "James thinks it's hot, apparently."

She rolls her eyes again. "Well, duh. I think you could roll in the mud and wear a paper bag over your head and James would think it's hot." She rolls a hand. "So, he sold you his truck, then what?"

I shrug. "I guess I'm not explaining this very well. The process of looking at the truck, him telling me about Renée loving it, how he didn't want to sell it to anyone but would sell it to me, and for a quarter of its value? It was intense. The whole chemistry we'd spent the past year trying to pretend didn't exist came flaring back to life." I sigh. "We flirted. I haven't flirted with anyone in *years,* and it's been even longer for him. But we just…couldn't help it. Every word, every look… was steeped in tension and chemistry."

"And?"

I shrug. "And nothing. That was it. Except for me calling him out for doing me a favor."

Audra frowns. "Of course he did you favor—he likes you, and your friends. Why wouldn't he?"

I sigh. "I hate favors. I explained this to him then, and again today. I grew up in a society where favors were social currency. I've basically lived my life in the polar opposite way to how I grew up, which means no favors. I don't do them, and I hate accepting them even more. Favors mean being in someone's debt, and I refuse to do that."

Audra nods. "I get it."

"But he insisted, and I needed the car, not to mention I really did fall in love with it. I love the boss feeling of driving it, of being up so high, having so much power at my disposal, the whole experience. So I took his favor." I pause. "I just…there's something about him. He makes it impossible to say no to him, to resist him."

Audra bites her lower lip. "Not saying a word on that score."

"Good," I snap playfully. "Don't."

"So when do I get to hear about what happened today?"

I finish my tea and shift positions, sitting cross-legged and making sure my robe covers my hoo-ha. Not that Audra would care if I accidentally flashed her, but still.

"So. Today, my phone rings. It's James, checking in to make sure I still like the truck and that there's no problems."

"How thoughtful of him."

"Right." I roll my eyes. "He also called to say he remembered me mentioning that part of the reason I was accepting his price on the truck was because I've been saving cash to remodel my house."

Audra's eyes narrow. "Really." She snorts. "An excuse to see you, more like."

I've sighed so many times I feel like a skipping CD. "Yeah. So, he came over. Looked around, took some measurements, and proceeded to describe remodel ideas that go a billion percent beyond my wildest dreams for this house. Open concept, glass along the entire back of the house, a new porch, master suite, everything I could dream of and more."

Audra's eyes widen. "That sounds amazing. And expensive."

I nod. "Exactly. And he wants to do it for cost."

She sputters in protest. "That's bananas!" She shakes her head. "I mean, Jesse has basically completely remodeled Imogen's house top to bottom for cost himself, but they're getting married and are having a baby."

I nod. "I know. Exactly." I hold my breath a

moment. "It got intense. I called him out again for doing favors for me out of some chivalrous, sexist bullshit or whatever, and he got mad because it was about me, about…everything between us. He didn't know himself, I don't think. Finally, he admitted he just liked me." I bite my lip. "And that was the catalyst."

"Oh boy." A grin slides across Audra's lips. "Now it gets good."

"He kissed me. Like…like he *had* to kiss me." I tip my head back and stare at the ceiling, remembering. "God, what a kiss. It made the one in his kitchen seem tame in comparison."

"No shit?"

I shake my head. "No shit." I bite my lip again and grin at her. "And the kiss just…never stopped. It turned to…a *lot* more. Touching. Clothes coming off. Next thing I know, I'm naked as the day I was born and sitting on my kitchen counter and James is making me feel like…well, better than I've ever felt in my entire life. I'm naked, he's naked, and things are hot and heavy and getting way, way out of control."

Audra sits forward. "Was it good?"

"Good?" I stare at her incredulously. "It was beyond words. Touching him, the way he touched me? It was…*everything*."

"Except actual sex?" Audra asks. "What did you actually do?"

"It was all just hands," I say. "But, god…it was…
it was heaven."

"Did you both…you know?"

I nod, biting my lip and blushing. "*So* hard."

"You did?"

I nod. "Explosively."

Her grin widens. "And he did?"

I nod again, my grin and my blush both going
furious. "Very, *very* explosively." I lick my lips, gesture
at my stomach. "Explosively…and all over me."

Audra's eyes widen. "No! The first time you guys
go past a kiss, you let him come *on* you?"

I can't restrain my cackle of embarrassed yet
aroused laughter. "I know, right? It was crazy. I still
can't believe it happened. But it just…nothing has
ever felt so right." I sigh, sobering. "And yet, not. I
still feel guilty, because even though I've had sex since
Craig died, it was…purely physical, and while it was
fun, it was rarely more than just fun, and thus, not…
intense. It felt good, but it was essentially forgettable.
The sex I had after Craig died—there was, honestly, a
lot, for about two years, and then I stopped completely
because I got tired of it, tired of the games, tired of
feeling…I don't know…like I was using men to try
to forget Craig, which was impossible. I thought of
Craig while I was messing around with James, and I
felt awful."

Audra winces. "That's understandable."

I bark a laugh. "Hold that thought, babe," I say. "In the moment that James finished—and yes, he finished all over me, and yes, it was hot and messy and awesome—he…he said *her* name."

Audra gasps, hand clapping over her mouth. "No! He did?"

I nod. "He said, 'holy shit, Renée.'" I sigh, long and sad. "He immediately realized his fuckup, and was as upset about it as you would imagine. And so was I—I mean, we'd just shared this hot, incredible moment, and he forgets he's with me? It fucking hurt."

Audra nods sympathetically. "Of course it did. How could it not?"

"I mean, I understood. Especially when he told me the kiss in his kitchen was the first time he'd kissed anyone else—not just since Renée died, but anyone except her *ever*."

"Holy *fuck*," Audra breathes. "Really?"

I nod. "Really. So him and me kissing was a huge deal for him. First kiss after she died, and first kiss with anyone not his wife, who he knew and was with literally his entire life, since third grade."

"God*damn*."

"Yeah. So us messing around, making each other come? That was…beyond a huge deal. And in the heat of the moment, yeah, I absolutely get how he would accidentally say her name. How he would be... in a very weird, agonizing place afterward."

"Doesn't make it any easier for you."

"No."

"So...now what?" Audra asks.

I laugh. "Exactly! Now what? That's why you're here." I roll a hand. "I have no idea. I feel like I got a taste of something truly and incredibly epic, and a huge part of me wants more, but I'm...afraid, I guess. On one hand, I'm afraid of moving on from Craig in a way I never really have, and scared of what trying to make things happen with James might do to him. I don't know if he can get over Renée. Can he be with me and give me emotionally what I need?"

Audra makes a face that's somewhere between sympathy and a wince. "James is kind of a mystery to me, honestly. He's forty-whatever years old and he's only ever been with *one* woman, until today? I don't know what to do with that. He honestly may never get over that, Nova."

I laugh bitterly. "Wow. Awesome. Very helpful and supportive."

"I'm sorry, I'm just being honest." She shrugs. "What about you, though?"

I tilt my head. "What about me?"

"Do you think you can overcome your past? If

James was suddenly like hell yeah, babe, let's be a thing right now…do you think you'd be able to jump in with both feet?"

I groan. "I want to say yes."

"But you can't."

I roll a shoulder and stare out the window. "I think I could get there. It would take time and work, but I just don't know if I can…I don't know."

"You know you can't stay alone forever," Audra fills in.

I nod. "I can't do casual sex anymore—been there, done that, got the T-shirt, and donated the T-shirt to resale." I toy with the teabag in my mug. "I also can't do relationships where we both know it's not serious, but it's not casual either. I tried that too, and it just doesn't work. It ends up being casual, and either I feel gross about myself, or stay closed off. Usually both. But the longer I'm alone, the more closed off and cranky I get. At this point, honestly, you may as well just give me half a dozen cats and call me a crazy cat lady."

Audra tucks her feet under her thighs. "I guess it's a matter of what you think you have to lose by not chasing James. Or you can wait and see if he makes a move? He did make up an excuse to see you, after all."

I wipe my face with both hands. "But if he calls me, how do I know he's making a move out of emotion, and not just thinking with his dick?"

"Would it be a problem if he *was* thinking with his dick?"

"Um, yeah? Because if all I wanted was dick, I could walk down the street and snap my fingers and I'd have all the dick I could handle."

"But it wouldn't be *his* dick," Audra argues. "And it's his dick you want."

I drop my eyes. "And it's not *just* his dick."

"But sometimes, the fastest way to a man's heart is through his penis."

I laugh. "True, but what if I don't want to get James's heart via his penis?"

Audra laughs, and it's not a mean laugh, but it's not kind either. "Then you shouldn't have jerked him off onto your stomach."

I groan. "You're not being very helpful, Audra."

"If a man has cleaned his cum off your belly, he's gonna be thinking about you in sexual terms. And once he's thinking about you in sexual terms, it's a simple step from that to at least some kind of closeness in the afterglow. And the afterglow, my dear friend, is the best time to grab a man's heart."

"That sounds manipulative."

"It is," she agrees. "It's totally manipulative. The problem is, in general, men often have trouble getting in touch with their emotions. After really great sex, though? They're more open. You're naked together, you just shared this really great experience, and it's easy to sort of just feel…close. And you can tease that closeness out of him, try to keep it growing beyond sex. He starts to see you all the time like he does during and after sex, and suddenly he realizes he has these feelings for you…"

I can't help but laugh. "Is that how you snagged Franco?"

She snickers. "Nah, that was a case of good old-fashioned can't help falling in love, and I eventually just quit fighting it and embraced the mushiness."

I frowned at her. "Yet you're recommending that tactic to me…why?"

"I'm not necessarily recommending it. Just saying, it's an option." She taps her chin. "Now that I think about it, I don't know if it would work on James anyway. He seems pretty emotionally locked down. It might take more than afterglow snuggles to get him to open up."

My laugh was definitely bitter, now. "Wow. You are…*not* helpful today."

She blows a frustrated raspberry. "I'm sorry, Nova. James is kind of opaque, to me. James is just… James. He's a great guy—I have no doubt he'd give you the shirt off his back. If you could get him to open up, I think you guys could be amazing together.

But losing Renée, when, like you said, he'd known her since third grade and had never been with anyone else in any capacity, ever? That's a pretty big obstacle. Not absolutely insurmountable, but...definitely a biggie. And to be totally honest, Nova, you deserve to be loved. Everyone does, obviously, but my point is that if James isn't willing to open up at all, I'm not sure what you're gonna get from him besides a lot of noncommitment."

"He flat out said he likes me, though."

"I'm not saying it's hopeless."

"What *are* you saying?"

"You have to decide how much you're willing to risk."

"I don't even know."

"And neither does he, I'm willing to bet."

I rake my hand through my hair. "I'm glad we talked, because it feels good to talk about what happened, but I'm not sure you really helped me figure out what I'm supposed to do."

She laughs. "Well, sometimes you just need to vent, and eventually you'll either know what to do, or the decision will be made for you."

"Awesome. So I just sit on my thumb until something does or doesn't happen, at some vague point in the future?"

"Well...how strong are your feelings for James?"

I think about the kisses we've shared, and the way he made me feel…up until he said the wrong name, at least. I look down and shrug. "Pretty damned strong."

"Strong enough to be willing to risk getting hurt again? And possibly hurt worse than him accidentally saying his dead wife's name at the moment you make him orgasm?"

I swallow hard—that *had* hurt, and it did still sting. Could I handle that happening again? Could I handle something even more painful happening?

"I guess I'll have to think about that one," I said.

Audra smirked at me. "The question is, will you be thinking with your brain, your heart, or your vagina?"

"I hate that you're right about there being a pretty drastic distinction," I said.

"We're women, Nova—if it was easy for us to have head, heart, and body all in agreement all the time, we wouldn't be so damn complicated."

I laugh. "Now *that's* the truth."

EIGHT

ANOTHER COUPLE OF DAYS PASSED WITH NO SIGN OF James, which was just as well. Because I couldn't stop thinking about him. I couldn't stop thinking about the way he'd looked in my kitchen, shirt off, and heavy muscles rippling and shifting. How he'd looked with his jeans shoved down around his thighs. How huge he'd been—and not just his cock, but *him*. Every part of the man was enormous—his shoulders, his chest, his arms—even his hips, as narrow and trim as they were. His thighs were like…well, at the risk of sounding like a bodice-ripper, they'd been like tree trunks. And yes, his cock was…god, it was glorious.

So thick, so long. Pink, beautiful, soft and warm and iron hard as it slid and stuttered through my hands.

I find myself daydreaming about him at work, leaning against the desk in the neurology department, visions of James thrusting into my fists dancing in my brain.

Of course, every time my imagination got to the point where he was about to come, I heard him say her name, and my fantasy soured.

It got to the point of distraction where my boss asked me if I was okay, and if I needed a day off. Which was the last thing I needed—work was the only thing keeping me from breaking down and calling him just to see where he was about everything, and I really didn't want to be the one to make the first move.

Finally, after two consecutive double shifts, I have three days off in a row, which I'm equal parts excited about and dreading. Years of waking up at five a.m. every day have made it impossible for me to sleep in, even if I wanted to, so, since I'm awake by six on my first day off, I figure I might as well hit the gym for a nice hard workout.

Only, when I get there, my gym is, inexplicably, closed. I go to a small, locally owned place—the owner is the only employee, and he lives above it, so he's always open. Even if he's not there, he leaves it open for his select clients, like me. But the gym is closed, locked, and the lights are off, which means something has happened. But without any way of contacting the owner, Richard, I don't have any way of knowing if and when he'll open again. Which leaves me without a gym.

I sit in my truck, trying to think of solutions.

I call Audra, and she doesn't answer, but calls me back within a minute. "What's up, Nova?" she asks, out of breath. "I'm in the middle of something though, so make it quick, babe."

"My gym is closed for some reason, and I need a workout."

She tsks. "Unfortunately, we're closed for a private CrossFit event, so I can't really slide you in like I normally would." She muffles into the phone and says something, and then addresses me again. "You know, Franco said he, Jesse, and Ryder were all going to James's place this morning. Apparently he has a pretty sweet setup. You might try him."

I laugh. "Are you trolling me right now?"

"I wish."

"I'm not asking for a training session, just access to a power rack and some free weights."

"I know, babe, and you know I'd never deny you if I had a choice, but this one is out of my hands. Sorry."

I groan. "Fine. Be that way."

"Nova, this is a qualifier event for the international CrossFit Games. I can't just—"

"I'm kidding," I interrupt her. "Mostly. Thanks anyway."

"Any other day, I'd get you in and lift with you, it's just today has been scheduled for over a year."

"It's cool. Richard is probably there, actually. He usually leaves the gym open even when he's not there, though."

"Try James. If all the guys are there, it may be awkward, but at least it'll be safe, you know?"

"Nothing is safe. I've been daydreaming about him."

"Oooh, that's no good. Bad sign."

"I know. My boss wanted to send me home."

"You're that spacey?"

I laugh. "Guess so."

"You've got it bad, girlfriend." A voice on the other end shouts her name. "Hey, listen, I'm up at the wall, so I gotta go."

"Okay, bye."

We end the call and I sit in the parking lot, staring at my phone, my thumb hovering over the contact entry with James's name on it.

Do I dare? This seems like inviting disaster.

Or, possibly, something else.

Or maybe nothing. Maybe we'll just work out together and nothing weird will happen.

Ha. Right.

I call James, my stomach flipping in my chest. It rings three times, and then he answers, and he's slightly out of breath too. "Hey, Nova. What's up?"

I don't even know what to say. My throat is closed,

and my stomach is not just doing flips, but twists and all sorts of acrobatics that make it hard to breathe. God, this is dumb.

"I, um. I normally workout at this little gym my friend owns, but it's closed and I have the day off and I haven't had time to lift since last week, and—"

"We just started lifting. Come on over."

"You're sure? I don't want to mess up your rotations or anything."

"As long as you don't mind working out with a bunch of ugly, sweaty, loud, foul-mouthed gorillas."

I laugh. "I wouldn't call you ugly, James. Far from it."

"I was talking about Ryder, but thanks."

"I'm not ugly," I hear Ryder say. "I'm just...very lived-in."

"If you were to look in a mirror, your reflection would run away screaming," I hear Jesse say.

"Fuck you," Ryder says good-naturedly. "At least my hair doesn't look like a seagull made a nest on a homeless bag lady's head."

"Which one of us has a bald spot?" Jesse shoots back.

I can't help laughing. "You guys are *mean* to each other, aren't you?"

James chuckles. "The meaner we are, the more it's meant with love. It's a guy thing."

I flip my ponytail with my free hand. "You're sure I won't be in the way?"

"Not at all." James's voice is quiet, familiar, and gruff.

"I'll see you guys soon, then."

I hang up and head to James's house. The gate is open, as is the back gate leading to the pole barn, and I pull through. All four men have their big, diesel, macho-mobile trucks parked in a line in front of the barn, and I park next to them, laughing at the fact that my truck fits right in.

The doors to the barn are wide open, and a Megadeath song blares. James is in one slot of the rack, squatting three sets of forty-five-pound plates with ease; Jesse spots Ryder as he benches in the second slot, straining to finish a rep with two forty-fives and a thirty-five; Franco is out front of the last slot, doing cleans with a single forty-five on each side, every rep smooth, fluid, and practiced.

I hop down from my truck, and focus on acting like I'm not intimidated by the amount of weight the guys are pushing. Even more importantly, I focus on acting like I'm not self-conscious about what I'm wearing: short, tight, black running shorts and a red sports bra under a baggy muscle shirt. The shorts cover my butt, so it's not like I'm wearing anything revealing, but still. I don't dress to impress at the gym, so the shorts are a little old, a little faded, fraying and ripping at the hems, and I know for a fact they ride up pretty high when I squat. The bra and muscle shirt are also both old—the bra is my favorite workout bra, with great support and super comfortable, strong enough to keep the girls well-contained even during sprints or cleans but without being so constrictive that they hurt. But, it's also faded and fraying, with loose threads and permanent boob sweat stains. The shirt is a Harvard Powerlifting Club shirt, with sleeves I cut off myself with a pair of kitchen scissors.

Even my shoes are old and ratty—well-worn, well-loved, never untied New Balance cross trainers I've had since college.

Face to face with a man who I can only describe as my crush, I feel…underdressed.

Which is stupid, because the men are all shirt-less, wearing even rattier shorts and shoes than mine. Objectively, I fit in pretty well. It's just that, if I'd known I'd be lifting with James today, I'd have worn a more flattering outfit.

Which is stupid.

I suck in a breath, let it out slowly, and enter the barn. "Hey, guys," I say.

Ryder, Jesse, and Franco all stare at me, and then at the truck, and then back at me. Jesse's eyes narrow, and he helps Ryder rack the bar before turning on

James, who in turn racks his bar.

"You gave her the truck?" Jesse growls. He sounds…pissed.

James shrugs. "Yeah."

"You said you sold it," Jesse says.

"I did sell it," James growls. "What's the deal?"

Jesse trades places with Ryder, sliding on the bench under the bar, stretching his arms as he scoots and wiggles into position. "That was Renée's truck."

"Actually, it was *my* truck. She ended up driving it, but it was my truck. You didn't say shit when I sold her CR-V."

"Because…" Jesse snarls wordlessly, gripping the bar hard, adjusting his position slightly, and then sucking in a deep breath—he grunts in exertion as he unracks the bar and knocks out five slow, smooth reps before racking it again, Ryder guiding the bar into place without actually helping too much. "Because she was my sister, goddammit. I don't know. It's just different, I guess."

I stand in the barn, unsure of how to handle this. "I—I'm sorry—I didn't realize it would be an issue for you, Jesse."

He shakes his head as he slips off the bench and takes his place as spotter for Ryder; Franco is still methodically knocking out cleans, doing at least twenty reps, studiously not addressing the current drama.

"Nah," Jesse grumbles. "It's not about you. I'm sorry, Nova. I'm being a dick."

"Would you rather I sell it to some random dude on Craigslist?" James asks. "At least this way, it's *around*."

Jesse doesn't answer until Ryder is done with his reps, and then they both step away from the rack. "No, you're right. I guess it was just weird seeing Nova get out of what I think of as Renée's truck. You said you sold it and I didn't think much about it—it was odd walking in and the truck not being here, but it didn't register. And then I see it rolling up, and for a second, I...I half expected to see her climbing down out of it."

James nods, head hanging. "I know, Jess."

"It was just weird for a second."

James looks at him, their eyes meeting, exchanging a long, deep, significant stare that only lifelong friends could interpret. "I *know*, Jess."

Jesse looks at me again. "I *am* sorry, Nova. I'm not usually like that. I'm glad you're driving Ruby. I really am."

I glance at James. "You didn't tell me she had a name."

"Slipped my mind," James mumbles.

"*Bullshit*," Ryder coughs into his fist.

James glares. "Something to say, Ry?"

Ryder shakes his head, a shit-eating grin on his

face. "Nope." He coughs again, this time a normal cough, rather than a cough meant to disguise snark. "Just got some dust in my throat."

I grab a 24kg kettlebell off the rack and set to work warming up with a set of two-hand swings. I feel the men watching me, but more to assess my form. I can't help showing off, then: I do a few one-hand snatches with the 24, which is a feat I've been working on for quite a while. It's a lot of weight to snatch, and I know it's impressive. I do five each arm, and then set the kettlebell down, out of breath now, and probably more warmed up than I need to be.

James laughs. "Don't even think about it, Franco," he rumbles.

I glance at Franco, who I realize is eying the 24kg kettlebell speculatively. "What?"

James answers. "He's jealous. He can do double snatches with the sixteens, but those twenty-fours have been giving him shit. He's not quite ready to level up yet, and he feels inadequate now that a woman has done what he can't do."

"Fuck you, James," Franco snaps. "I do *not* feel inadequate."

I laugh. "I did a total of ten reps, one arm at a time, and that's all I can do," I admit. "I was kind of showing off a little."

Franco holds out his fist for me to tap, which I

do. "Well, consider me impressed," he says. "But if you're gonna work out here with us, you're gonna take some shit. I hope you know that."

"And if I'm gonna take shit, you know I'm gonna give it as good as I get," I shoot back.

James juts his chin at the power rack. "What lift you wanna start with?"

I head for the station where he was squatting. "I like to squat first, if you're done."

He nods. "I'm good. Go for it." He taps the end-most 45lb plate. "How much to start?"

I grin. "As much as I'd love to pretend I can compete in your league, I'd just end up killing myself," I say. "I'll start with one plate. My one RM is just shy of two plates, which is my goal."

James nods without replying otherwise, and takes off two plates on one side while I remove the two on my side. I slide the clamp back on and settle under the bar, aligning the center knurl low on my neck, and then slowly push up with my legs to accept the weight. Once balanced, I step back from the rack, glancing down to make sure I'm aligned with the spotter arms, and then slowly but fluidly squat down until my butt is past parallel with my hips—a full squat. I tighten my core and exhale loudly through my teeth as I press back up. I'm hyperfocused on retaining perfect form through each repetition, stopping at eight reps. After eight, I rack the bar and step away, rolling my shoulders.

"You have impressive form," James says. "Nice and deep, and your back is straight all the way through."

Ryder snickers. "Yep. Niiiiice and deep."

James and I give Ryder identical glares.

"Shut up, Ryder," I say. "Let's see you do better."

That shuts Ryder up real fast, and James laughs. "He's not answering because he knows he cheats on his squats."

"I do not!" Ryder protests.

"At a proportionate weight, you don't squat anywhere near as deep as she does."

I laugh. "That was my warm-up set," I say. "I'll start cheating on my form once the weight is nearer the upper end of my working range."

"You don't have to make him feel better," James says. "He needs the inspiration. He knows he cheats his form."

"I don't fucking cheat!" Ryder insists.

Jesse laughs. "So put another pair of plates on there and let's see."

I watch as Ryder and Jesse slide two more forty-fives on each side of the bar, clamp it, and then Ryder settles under the bar, lets out a short, sharp exhale, and stands up under the weight. Slowly and under extreme control, Ryder squats down, and he does go deep…but after three reps, he's struggling to get back up. He finishes five full reps, going deep each time, and then racks the bar roughly, with a loud clang.

"Boom, motherfucker." Ryder jabs a pointer finger in my direction. "Five clean, no-cheat squats at three-fifteen."

I laugh. "Hey, I never challenged you, that was all James." I point at the bar. "Not a fair comparison anyway, because there's no way three-fifteen is a warm-up set weight for you. I was doing a warm-up set, and you were doing a working set."

Jesse laughs. "You know your shit, Nova."

"I've been into powerlifting for a long time," I say, and then knock out my second set.

James and Franco pair up for benching, while Jesse takes over doing cleans and Ryder squats next to me.

Things are quiet for a while, except for the occasional comment or joke here and there. I go through five sets of squats, ending up at 205 by the last set. I could've gone higher for a few reps, but I decided against risking failing a rep my first time working out with James and the guys. I transition to a set of cleans next—I notice a dry erase board on the wall by the rack of weights with today's workout written out on it—5x5 squats, one set of 25 cleans, 3x10 bench, and an overhead press/pull-up drip set. Challenging as hell, and I enjoy it. The guys make it easy to rotate in with them, and I never feel judged or rushed. I end up leaving the set of bench presses for last, because I need a spotter for that lift and everyone else is busy; I showed up after their first set, so they're all done by the time I'm ready to do those.

I position myself under the bar, 175 on the bar. Not my highest, but good for 5x5 at the end of a tough workout. Gripping the bar, I decide to play a little game of roulette:

"Can I get a spot?" I call out, intentionally not addressing anyone in particular.

I hear heavy footsteps tread over to me, and when a pair of hairy-knuckled, bear paw-sized hands touches two fingers under each side of the bar—guiding rather than helping, as a good spotter should—I know it's James without having to look beyond the hands. I'm not sure if I won or lost that game of roulette—or whether I wanted James to spot me or not.

I get through the first set without issue, but by the end of the set I know I've bitten off potentially more than I can chew trying to bench 175 for five sets of five at the end of the workout. I'm shaking as I rack the weight, panting hard.

James doesn't say anything, but I feel his eyes on me.

I rest about a minute or a minute and a half, and then go to work on the second set. Again, I make it through the set, but barely. And this time, I know James is adding at least a tiny bit of pressure under the bar.

I glance up at James as I rest between sets two and three. "No helping," I say, wiping sweat off my forehead.

His eyes crinkle with a small smirk—a look I'd almost call sassy. "One-seventy-five may have been a bit ambitious," he says. "No shame in dropping down a notch or two."

I narrow my eyes at him, stick out my tongue, and put my irritation at his needling into my lift. Which, I realize, was his goal all along—motivation via insult.

"You are such a guy," I snap as I pause at the top of the press.

He follows the downward motion of the bar, and I notice for the first time how close he gets, bending over me, making sure he has the leverage to lift in case I end up failing a rep. I can feel his breath, I can smell him—his sweat, his beard oil, a faintly cloying hint of BO that should gross me out but doesn't.

"Glad you noticed," he mutters.

Set four is hard. The fifth and final rep requires a lot of strain, a lot of shaking. I finish the last rep and rack the bar, breathing hard.

James's eyes are on me; I've sweated through my sports bra and my shirt. I rest, and then adjust my grip on the bar.

I hesitate, meeting James's gaze. "Eyes on the bar, tiger," I say.

He arches an eyebrow. "That's a big ask, babe."

"There's nothing to even see," I mutter, pushing the bar off the rack and preparing to lower it. "I'm wearing the tightest sports bra I own and a tank top."

"Memory and imagination, Nova," James says, following the bar as I start the first rep of my last set.

I push through reps two, three, and four, but I'm struggling, straining and shaking as I barely finish the fourth rep. I pause with the bar at the top of the movement, gasping and contemplating whether I can gut out a fifth or not.

James glances at me. "Going for five?"

I nod, and grit my teeth. I slowly lower the bar, and when it touches my chest, I push hard, snarling through clenched teeth, pushing my feet hard against the ground and arching my back off the bench for added leverage. I feel James putting a tiny bit of assistance on the bar, but I'm honestly not sure I'd be able to get the rep without it, so, as much as I hate being helped, I accept it. The bar is barely moving, but it *is* moving upward. Inch by inch, straining with every fiber, I get the bar up, and James takes it and racks it for me.

The other three guys are all watching me, impressed.

"That was a hell of a set," Franco says.

An awkward silence, then, as I sit on the bench and try to recover my breath.

One by one, the guys check their phones and shuffle their feet.

I realize these are lame signals to one another to leave James and I alone in…

Three…

Two…

One…

"So, I, uh…" Ryder checks his phone again, even though he just did. "I have a potential client looking for a bid, so I have to go."

"Same," Franco says. "I have a custom armoire to finish. Needs a bit more sanding and a couple coats of stain."

Jesse looks at Ryder and Franco, and then at James, and then at me; his grin is mischievous and shit-eating. "Not me. I ain't got shit to do. You wanna shoot some hoops, J?"

James rolls his eyes. "Funny, Jess. Very funny."

"For real. I ain't got anything going on." His grin says he's enjoying fucking with James.

"Yes, you do," Franco says, kicking Jesse's foot. "You're helping me with the armoire, remember?"

Jesse isn't letting it go. He glances at me, winking. "Ohhhh, I see what's going on. You guys want to be alone so you can pretend to not like each other some more."

James hurls a clamp at Jesse. "You are such a jackass."

I smirk at James. "I mean, it *was* kinda funny."

James frowns at me. "Do NOT encourage his dumb ass, Nova."

I snicker, and James rolls his eyes, trying to hold the frown, but he can't. Eventually he starts laughing, and waves at Jesse. "Get out of here, moron."

Jesse tosses the clamp back to James and heads for his truck. "If I'm a moron, what does that make *you*?"

There's a chorus of diesel engines coughing, snarling, and grumbling to thunderous life, followed by thick-knobbed tires crunching in gravel, and then James and I are alone. James has a canister of antibacterial wipes, and he's wiping down the benches; I take a couple and wipe down the bars and plates and rerack everything in its own place.

"You don't have to help," James says.

I just shrug. "Thanks for letting me crash your workout."

"We're here Monday, Tuesday, Thursday, and Friday mornings at six," he says. "You're always welcome."

I look at him, gauging his sincerity—in my experience, people sometimes offer things but often half hope you'll decline. I kind of do want to accept; I've been working out alone for years, and I miss the camaraderie of having friends to razz me into finishing the rep, friends to shoot the shit with between sets.

But I don't know that being around James that much is a great idea. Honestly, I'm being pulled in opposite directions right now: half of me wants to throw myself at him, and the other half wants to bolt for the door.

The weights are racked, the barbells are slotted back in their holder, the benches are wiped down and pushed in; James shuts off the lights and heads outside, and I follow. He rests his forearms on the hood of his truck, and his eyes fix on me.

His gaze is speculative, filled with thoughts and feelings I don't know how to read. "Gonna make a protein shake. You want some?"

I do. I want to be in his kitchen with him. I want to talk to him. Be near him.

I want a repeat of what happened in my kitchen.

I want more than that.

But I'm scared. Of him—of my feelings. Of his

feelings. Of him not returning my feelings. Of him being unwilling to indulge in his feelings out of guilt or loyalty to Renée. I can't compete with a ghost, and I will not try.

I stare at him steadily, and decide to try. He's making a step toward me, letting me crash his workout, and now inviting me, alone, into his kitchen.

"Sure," I say.

"You off today?" he asks, opening his truck door.

I nod, climbing up into my own truck. "Yep. Next three days. Longest stretch I've had off in months, actually."

"Got plans?" he asks, hesitating before turning his engine on.

I shake my head. "Not really. Organize some closets, maybe. Catch up on reading, and maybe catch up on a few shows. I've got some episodes of *Schitt's Creek* I've been saving for a stretch of time off."

"Sounds exciting," he says with a laugh. "Meet you at the house."

I head out first, and he follows, hopping out after he's pulled through the fence to close and lock the gate behind himself. I park at the end of the driveway, the nose of the truck facing the street. When I go in through the side door into James's kitchen, I find him chopping the heads off fresh strawberries.

I watch. "You said you were making a protein shake?"

He nudges a giant canister of whey protein. "I am."

"I thought you meant, like, in a shaker bottle."

He taps his blender, which is filled, so far, with chunks of banana, handfuls of spinach, blueberries, and apple slices; he's finished with the strawberries and tosses them into the blender. "I like to blend. Makes the shake more fun. If I'm on the go, sure, I'll just toss some protein in a bottle with water and shake it up. But if I have time, I like to fancy it up a little."

He adds almond milk, half a dozen scoops of berry-flavored whey, some ice cubes, and then fastens the top on to the blender and starts it up. A few seconds of noisy clatter as the ice breaks up, and then the mixture begins to smooth out. Once it's done, he pours the shake into two large plastic tumblers and hands me one; we tap our tumblers together, and drink a few sips in silence.

I wait for James.

He's looking at me like he has something on his mind but, so far, hasn't said anything.

Half my shake is gone, and the silence is beyond awkward and into downright agonizing.

Finally, staring into his tumbler, he sighs. "Nova, I…" He takes another long drink, more for something to do while coming up with what to say than anything, I think. "About the other day, at your house…"

I wait in silence, keeping my eyes on his.

"I just…" Another heavy sigh. "I've relived that moment a million times, and it hurts more every single time."

"Which particular moment, James?" I ask, even though I know.

He looks at me, pained. "You know, Nova." I don't answer that, and James swirls the dregs of his shake. "I know I've already apologized and explained, I just…I can't get it out of my head."

"And I told you I understand as well as anyone can."

"Doesn't change it." He finishes the shake and rinses out the tumbler. "You were crying when I went into your room."

I nod. "Yes, I was." I shrug; I go for blunt honesty, not to hurt him but because it's just my way. "I don't cry easily, James."

He winces. "You don't seem like the type." He hesitates. "It really hurt you."

I nod. Go for more brutal truth. "After Craig passed away, I…I guess you could say I sort of went through a period of time where I did everything I could to pretend to myself that I was fine. I grieved, sort of—cried a lot, lay in bed for days until friends dragged me out of bed and forced me to shower and eat, that whole scene. But then I snapped—not like a stick breaking, but like a rubber band. I didn't crumble, I didn't turn to drugs or drinking." I swallow hard. "Until then, I'd been very…conservative, sexually. Few partners, and only ever with someone I was emotionally involved with."

I pause. Think. Gather words. I'm not sure why I'm telling him this. I'm not ashamed of it, but I'm not proud of it, either. My feelings about it are, to be honest, very complicated.

"Craig was my last romantic partner. The last person I was involved with emotionally." I hesitate again. "I stayed alone for a long time. Six months? Close to a year, maybe, while I recalibrated, trying to figure out what I wanted out of life after losing Craig. I moved away, went back to school. I knew no one, had no friends, no family around—I was just utterly alone. And so, so lonely."

James nods. "That's rough. I always had Jesse, Franco, and Ryder. I don't know what I'd have done without them."

I sigh. "I got sick of being alone and lonely. I needed…companionship. So I tried going on a date." I laugh bitterly. "That didn't go well."

"No?"

"Panic attack. Straight up panic attack. Couldn't

breathe, heart palpitating, the whole nine yards."

"Ouch."

I nod. "I tried a couple more times, but I couldn't make it through a date without panicking. And then one day I got invited to a party by a classmate." I roll a shoulder. "I got a little tipsy, and out of sheer desperation to feel anything besides pain and loneliness, I let the guy who'd invited me take me to his apartment. I was…not quite sober, but only buzzed enough that I could get past my hang-up. Sort of. He started feeling me up, and I stopped him, told him I couldn't stay the night, hoping he'd catch my drift. He just laughed and was like, I wasn't planning on asking you to. So that was that. And for the first time in my life, I had a one-night stand."

James keeps his expression neutral. "I see."

I drop my eyes. "That was the start of what I guess I'd call an experimental phase. I coped with my fucked-up feelings through sex. Casual, short-term, no-strings sex." A pause, and let it all hang out. "A lot of it. But none of it was…" I drift off, hunting for a word.

"Real?" James suggests.

I nod. "Yeah."

"Did it work?"

"No." I scoff, and then frown, tilting my head and rethinking that. "I mean, yes, to a degree. For about two years, I tried to cover the heartache and loneliness with sex, and for a while it was fun. I did enjoy myself, I'm not gonna lie about that. Unless something touched on my hard limits, I went with it." I blush, because it's hard to talk about this with James. "But after a while, it became…harder and harder to pretend I didn't feel weird about it. I think by nature I'm just a monogamous person—a one-man kind of gal. Things just caught up to me, I guess. I really don't know how to put it. I didn't feel guilty, and I don't now. I don't regret it, and I'm not embarrassed by it. I learned a lot about myself, and about what I liked and wanted, and what I didn't."

James nods. "Good. You shouldn't be ashamed or feel guilty."

"I guess with you having only ever been with one woman—"

James cuts me off. "That was a choice I made for myself. I found the woman I loved early on in life, and I was damned lucky to have her in my life for thirty years, married to her for twenty of them. But just because I chose her and only her doesn't mean I pass judgment on others for making different decisions."

"I appreciate that," I say. I finish my shake and rinse out the tumbler, leave it in the sink with James's. "So, anyway, once I realized my little experimental, casual sex phase was over, I realized I'd only put off the real work of dealing with things."

James chuckles. "Boy, do I identify with *that*. Grieving is one thing, but really healing and moving on? That's a lot fucking harder."

"No kidding." I pause, meeting his eyes. "After that, I...closed up shop, you might say."

James blinks. "Totally?"

I nod. "Totally and completely."

"For how long?"

"A long, *long* time," I say.

"How long?" James repeats.

I frown. "Three years. Or, almost." I sigh. "I went about...two years right after the experimental phase, and then I met a guy when I first got the job in the hospital here, a nurse in the palliative care ward. I liked him, and I thought I could...I don't know. I thought I could work past things."

James rests his forearms on the island between us, leaning closer to me. "Not so much, I take it."

I shake my head. "Nope. We went on a few dates, and I only just barely fought off panic attacks on each one. I had to get tipsy to get to the point where I could even kiss him, much less anything else." I groan. "We got to the point where things were...it was either full speed ahead, or a full stop."

James winces. "Let me guess. Full stop?"

I nod. "I kept thinking of Craig. I didn't want

to, but I couldn't help it. I tried and tried to get past it, and the guy was honestly super sweet and understanding about it, but eventually I ended things with him because it wasn't fair to him. We'd get close, and then I'd freeze and not be able to go any further, because Craig kept popping back up in my head. And after I broke up with Vince, I just...I didn't see a point in trying anymore. So I didn't, and I haven't."

James sighs. "Until me."

"Until you."

"And you did get past it—with me. And then I said Renée's name instead of yours at the critical moment."

I nod. "Yeah." I drop my head again. "And I'm not gonna lie, it fucking hurt, James. A lot. I felt like I was finally making progress...like maybe, with you, things would be different. I was able to shut down the Craig-comparison-guilt loop and focus on you." I look up at him, and I hate the pain and guilt I see in him. "And then...yeah. You said her name. And please, *please*, believe me when I say I understand, and that I don't hold it against you."

James is silent awhile, and I let the silence stand.

After nearly two full minutes of dead silence, James straightens, walks away to stand at the door looking out over the backyard.

"You and Renée couldn't be more different,

honestly. You're tall, super strong, athletic, with long hair…and you're, um…" I can hear the blush in his hesitation, the hunt for a word or phrase. "You're well-endowed."

I sniff a half-hearted laugh, unsure how else to respond to that.

"Renée was…none of that. She was short, five-five. Hated working out. Had one of those ridiculous metabolisms where she could eat whatever she wanted and never exercise and she was just always relatively fit. Short hair, pixie short, like Audra's, only the same color as Jesse's. She had blond highlights for a while…" He shakes his head. "Anyway. She was short and skinny, a fact which she bitched about constantly." He laughs. "One time, she spent literally three full weeks eating junk food and burgers and milkshakes and just crap. She said she was trying to, and I quote, eat her way to bigger tits."

I cackle. "Oh my god, no! Really?"

He nods, laughing. "For real. Eventually she started feeling sick and gave up, and then actually spent, like, four full months working out somewhat regularly because she did gain weight from it, but it all went to her belly and thighs, and not her butt or boobs. That really pissed her off."

"I bet," I say and can't help another laugh. "It doesn't work like that."

"So she discovered." He sighs. "She was wildly outgoing. Like, Audra and Ryder rolled into one—a tiny, foul-mouthed pixie with a wicked sense of humor and no filter. She and Audra would have either hated each other or be best friends, I think. She had a T-shirt made for herself, once. It said 'Itty Bitty Titty Committee' across the top, with arrows pointing to each of her boobs, labeled 'chair' and 'co-chair.'" He shook his head, laughing. "She did crap like that all the time, made fun of herself."

I just listen, let him talk. I'm not sure where he's going with this, but I sense he needs to get it off his chest.

"She made fun of me like it was her sole job in life. Growing up I was teased a lot. Bullied. I've always been big, but in elementary and middle school, before I really hit my growth spurt and discovered sports, I was just this tall, gangly, overweight, shy kid who never spoke. And Renée was my protector. She'd attack, verbally and physically, anyone who tried to pick on me, but then she'd turn around and make fun of me. But she always did it with love, and when we started dating and took things physical, she started using psychology on me." He pauses a moment. "Pavlovian, you might say. She would tease me, make fun of me, and honestly it would get pretty brutal at times, but then she would...um, instigate things. Until

I started equating her teasing me with things getting hot physically. Crazy, and something only she would think to do. It was intentional, too. She was sick of me being withdrawn and lacking confidence, so she went on the offensive. Psychologied me out my insecurities from being bullied, encouraged me to try sports, and eventually I...well, I guess you'd say I found myself. Took over the role of her protector, because she had her own hang-ups. She used humor to cover her insecurities over being so tiny."

"Sounds familiar. I make fun of myself in similar ways about being so tall. Not so much anymore, but I used to. I got teased a lot for looking like a boy. I was always tall, but puberty hit late: I was fourteen before I started filling out. So then I was a boy with huge boobs. My mom messed up a haircut the summer that I got my boobs, and I had to get it all chopped off, so I had, literally, a buzz cut, *and* these giant new boobs that I didn't know what to do with. So, to cover my insecurities, to cut people off before they could hurt me, I started making fun of myself."

James nods. "It was the opposite for Renée. She hit puberty and filled out a little—went from being a literal stick to having some softer edges, some curves, but in all honesty, she was never anything but a short skinny chick. No boobs, like at all, and no butt." He's silent a long time. "God, she was *beautiful*, though.

She kept her hair short, and it just suited her. She had these high, sharp cheekbones and a mouth that looked like a million bucks, but that mouth could flay the paint off a barn if something annoyed her."

I think I'm starting to sniff out where he's going with this, but I continue to let him play it out at his own pace.

"I was so attracted to her, so in love with her. I'd have killed for her, died for her. I'd have walked through fucking fire for her."

His love, his pain—it's so raw, so real, so palpable. I ache for him. I'm not jealous, either. I just hate his pain. I want to soothe it, to comfort him, but I don't dare. He needs to say this.

"I was absolutely gone for her. I never even *saw* other women when I was with her. I mean, sure, I'm a red-blooded heterosexual male, and this world is full of beautiful women, so I noticed them. But they were just...*people*. I don't know how else to put it. No desire, no attraction. She fulfilled me in every way there could possibly be."

"She sounds amazing."

"She was," he agrees. "And then she died. And I wanted to die with her. I probably would have, were it not for Nina and Ella, and my boys. Those five people saved my life. I don't think I'd have killed myself, but I think I would have just...died. But I had to keep going for my girls, so I did. I put my nose to the grindstone and set about rebuilding my life. Alone, with the girls. Being a single father. Running a business. Those things have taken up every single spare minute of my time." He lets out a slow breath. "I never wanted to see anyone else. There were women around, obviously. We're at Billy Bar a lot, and there're always chicks around, and some of them have thrown themselves at me pretty hard. But I just…" He shrugs. "I haven't been able to summon the will to care. It's like…I don't know how to put it. Like when she died, I *did* die, and I had to learn to live again without her. And for the most part, I have. I eat, I get dressed, I work, I spend time with my girls, and I have fun with the guys. But that part of me, the part that feels… well, anything…for women? It's still dead."

"James, I—"

He keeps going, and I lapse back into silence. "Then Imogen invited you to the pool party, and… for the first time since Renée died, I noticed you. As a woman, not just as a person." He glances at me over his shoulder, briefly, and then turns back to the window. "I *saw* you. And once I did, I couldn't…I don't know. I couldn't unsee you. And believe me, I tried. Not that I didn't want to see *you*, I just didn't want to see *anyone*. I believed that part of me was dead and I was better off that way. Despite the promise I made to her right before she died, I just never had a desire or an intention to even try to reawaken that part of me. Renée was it for me, and she was gone, so why bother?"

Another long pause.

"It's the only promise I ever made to her that I haven't kept." He laughs bitterly. "And there's a weird, ironic sort of guilt about that, too. But missing her, hating life without her...is still so strong." He turns now and gazes steadily at me, with a deep pain in his expression, mixed with...something else. I don't know what. "But I *saw* you. I saw *you*—as a woman. I was attracted to you, as a woman. And Nova, that's brought on more guilt than I even know how to express, much less deal with. Because you're *so* different from her. You're everything she was not—and I don't mean that as a comparison, like she was lacking anything or vice versa. Just that you're polar opposites in pretty much every way. But I guess most of all, it's the physical aspect that messes with me the most. Emotionally, I don't think we've pushed into territory that prompts this level of guilt, but physically? My attraction to you is just...a fucking problem." He shakes his head. "Shit, man. I don't know how to even say it."

I shrug. "Say it how it is. Don't mince words. You and I both appreciate hearing the blunt, raw truth, even if it's brutal."

He nods. "Yeah, okay. So…" A moment of thought. "I'm just trying to put it into words. For myself, if not for you. I guess it's that I'm so crazy physically attracted to you, and that you're so differently built." Another pause. "She was so self-conscious about being flat-chested. She wasn't generally jealous, but if a girl with big tits was around, she'd sometimes ask me if I wished she looked like that, or did I want her to get implants."

"Ahhh. Now we come to the crux of it." I keep my eyes on his. "You feel guilty being attracted to me, in part because I have the body Renée was always worried you'd leave her for."

He nods, tearing his gaze from mine, emotions boiling in him. "Yeah," he whispers. "Exactly. It's taken some soul-searching to realize that, too." He groans, rubs his face with both hands. "I never felt that way. I never wanted to change her. If she'd wanted implants, I'd have supported her, if it was something she felt was important to her, but she only ever talked about that when something messed with her own insecurity. Like I said, I was totally in love with her, and even if there was a girl around with big tits or whatever else, even if they were literally hanging out in the open— which did happen once, on vacation—I only had eyes for her. And normally, she was confident in that, in my love for her. But sometimes, those insecurities would flare up."

"So you feel guilty for even being attracted to me in the first place."

He nods. "Yeah. Like I'm betraying her, betraying my attraction to her by being so attracted to you, being built the way you are—like you said, the embodiment of what she felt self-conscious about *not* being." He frowns. "I'm not sure that made any sense."

"It made perfect sense to me." I let out a breath. "So where does that leave us? Because I can't change the way I look. I've worked hard to be confident, to love myself for being six feet tall, for being a dedicated powerlifter—having big guns and thick thighs and broad shoulders."

"I'm just explaining why I'm fucked up," James says. "I'm glad you love yourself for who you are—you're a gorgeous, amazing woman. You should be proud of yourself."

"James…" I sigh, hunting for words. "Honestly, I don't know what to say." I throw up a hand. "I'm attracted to you, James. That's no secret at this point. I like you. What happened in my kitchen the other day—it was one of the best experiences of my life… until…you know. Not just since Craig, but…ever. Objectively, comparatively, it just was that good. I felt that good with you. And yeah, I feel guilt over that. It was like, Craig is gone, he's dead, and here I am having a sexual experience that's better than pretty much everything Craig and I ever shared. I loved the man—we had chemistry. We had good sex, sometimes even great sex. And you and I didn't even *have* sex, not really, yet it was still just *that* good."

He swallows hard. "Same here." He tilts his head back, growls—as if forcibly pushing down emotions he doesn't want to fully let out. "That fucks me up, too. That's a different guilt, piled onto everything else."

"There's a huge part of me that really, really wants to explore this with you, James. Physically, sexually, I want to know more, feel more, see what could happen if we kept going, if we indulged and really gave into everything. Emotionally, I feel a connection to you, too, and—and yeah, I want to explore that, too."

I hold his gaze, and don't try to hide the wild, turbulent emotion in my eyes. "But I'm scared. I'm scared of getting hurt, I'm scared of being rejected, and I'm scared I'll get attached and then lose you." I pause, swallow hard. "Most of all, I'm scared that every minute I spend with you, I'll be competing with a ghost, James. And I just can't do that. I *can't*. No one can."

"I know," he whispers—and his whisper is fragile. It's heartbreaking to hear such a thing from so strong and powerful a man. And the vulnerability I see in him…it's…intoxicating and terrifying and so brave. "It's not fair to you. I know that."

"So where do I go from here, James?"

He shakes his head. "I don't fucking know. That thing you said—competing with a ghost. That's right on target. I *feel* her, Nova. In this house, in my head, in my heart.

"Then I look at you, and I give in to wanting you, to being attracted to you, and it's…god, it's wild. For a few seconds, for a few minutes, I feel like—I don't know—like a kid with his first crush, the first time you feel that rush of need for someone, you know? That's how it was with me and Renée—the summer before ninth grade we went to a public pool together and even though I'd seen her in a bikini any number of times before, I was suddenly hit by a different kind of attraction to her, need for her. It was like being hit by a Mack truck.

"And it's like that with you, every time I'm around you. But then my brain or my heart or whatever brings up Renée—and my immediate thought is to quash those feelings. But then I feel guilty for trying not to think about her, and that starts a spiral. I don't want to forget her, but I'm fighting her ghost too, and I don't know how to hold on to her memory without it holding me back from living my life."

His eyes bore into mine, brown and intense. "And I *do* want to explore things too. But I can't, and won't, make you compete with a ghost. And I don't know what to do."

"I wish I could answer that for you, James."

He shakes his head, hands scraping through his hair. "I can't answer it for myself."

"That leaves us at an impasse, I guess." I sigh. "I want what I can't have, and you can't have what you want."

James growls again. "I'm sorry, Nova. This is why I tried to avoid letting things even get started with you. I didn't and don't want to hurt you. I never meant to, and I'm sorry that I did." His eyes search mine. "I don't regret what we did, Nova. Not a second of it—the only thing I regret is that moment when I said her name instead of yours. I said it then and I'll say it again—I knew the whole time who I was with and what was happening. I was *not* trying to...I don't know, put you in her place or whatever. I got lost in the moment and my mouth spouted off something from my subconscious, or something. I don't know how to explain it. I've never said any name in moments like that except hers, and I guess it was..." He shakes his head. "I'm fucking this up. I don't know what else to say."

"Not instinct, but more...long-ingrained habit,"

I say.

He nods slowly. "Yeah. Exactly."

"You don't have to explain anymore, and you don't have to apologize." I smile at him sadly. "I just don't know where to go from here."

"Me either."

I sigh bitterly. "The first time I've been able to have both an emotional and physical connection with a man, and it's impossible." I laugh, even more bitterly. "It figures."

"Nova, I—"

I shake my head. "I should go."

"Nova."

"We're just going in circles, James. I'm not going to push you. But I'm not willing to get into something purely physical, even though I know both of us could probably use the relief."

"I think about you enough that I need the relief," he murmurs.

"Same here," I admit. "But with you, I need the emotions, too. I can't do casual anymore, James. I gave that up a long time ago."

"I've never done it and I'm sure as hell not going to start now," he says. "But I also don't know that I can just…pretend this doesn't exist between you and me. And the thought of not being around you, not being your friend, not seeing you?" He shakes his head. "I can't do that either."

I choke. "Neither can I." I turn away before he sees the tears fall, and I blink them away. "So what do we do, James?" I whisper the question.

He's silent. "I don't fucking know."

"Me either." I move for the side door. "I—I have to go."

I'm out the door and heading for my truck. I get the door open, and climb in. Then he's there, hauling me back out, manhandling me as if I weigh nothing. Pinning me up against the frame of my truck. Kissing the ever-loving shit out of me.

Kissing me breathless in that way he has—making me feel dizzy, making me feel wild and primal and needed in a way I've never felt before.

And then he backs up, and I can see him shaking with the intensity of it—as I am. "Don't give up on me just yet, Nova. I'll figure this out."

"How?" I whisper.

He shakes his head. "I don't know." He backs up a step, as if he's a powder keg and I'm an open flame. "Just…give me some time."

"I think I can do that," I whisper.

NINE

TWO DAYS, THREE DAYS...A WEEK. TWO WEEKS—NO James. Not a word. The word from the rest of the crew is that he is working insane hours, working out like a fiend, keeping to himself outside of work... and taking mysterious, unexplained, hour-long lunch breaks twice a week.

I'm at home after work one Friday evening, and there's a knock at my door—my heart flips in my chest, and I answer the door with shaky hands and trembling knees. But it's Jesse and Franco, dirty and dusty, wearing tool belts, covered in drywall dust and mud, both wearing their hats backward and Oakleys upside down on the brims.

I frown in confusion. "Um, hi guys. What's up? Come on in."

They both hesitate, glancing down at their nearly identical filthy tan Timberland boots. "We're dirty, so we'll hang out on the porch," Jesse says.

I shrug. "I can sweep. It's not a big deal."

They enter, but remain near the door. Jesse fiddles with the hammer in his tool belt, and Franco has a leather business folder like James's in his hands.

"We're here to show you the drawings for the remodel," Franco says, lifting the folder. "And, if you're cool with them, we can actually get started demoing."

I blink. "Oh. Um. I guess I didn't know that was still happening."

Franco shrugs. "James is super slow at getting drawings done. He's crazy meticulous, which is why it takes so long. Usually for big jobs, he outsources it, but if it's a job he has a personal connection to, he does it himself." He juts his chin at my kitchen table. "Take a seat and I'll run through it with you."

"I can't read that shit for shit," Jesse says with a rueful chuckle. "Which is why he's explaining it. I'm just the muscle."

Franco rolls his eyes. "You know, you're nowhere near as stupid as you make out. I mean, you *are* stupid, but not *that* stupid."

"Shut up, twink."

"Guys. Focus." I lead the way to the table, and while they take a seat, I bring a six-pack of beer out of my fridge and pass one to each of them, and then open my own. "So. James explained his vision. Is that a drawing of what he said, or something different?"

Franco shrugs. "Dunno, I don't know what he told you." He opens the folder and withdraws a carefully folded piece of thin, gridded tracing paper; on the paper is a top-down blueprint of my current floor plan. "He got the blueprints for your house as a starting place, so this is your place now."

I nod, tracing the outline of the kitchen with my fingertip. "Yeah, I see."

Franco withdraws a second piece of tracing paper and overlays it on top of the piece with the original layout. This second layer shows what James is proposing.

"So, the idea is to remove walls here, here, and here," Franco says, touching the lines indicating walls—between the kitchen and living room, between my bedroom and the bathroom next door, and the entire back wall of the house between the living room and kitchen. "Open up the kitchen, switch things around so your stovetop is in this island, which we'd build from scratch to suit. New countertop—marble, slate, concrete, butcher block, you and Jess can make that call. If you want a butcher-block counter, though, I can hook you up with something super cool. I've got some giant pieces of black walnut that would look pretty great."

I frown at Jesse. "Why would you make that call? I'm just curious. I thought James was the lead, or whatever."

Jesse and Franco exchange glances. "James is the builder, so he leads the general stuff. Lines up sub-contractors as necessary, assures quality and standards, makes sure things are code, all that. But when it comes to the aesthetics of interior design, Jesse has the best eye of any of us." He chuckles. "Funny enough, he really does have the best taste in terms of interior design."

"Plus, James is working through some shit right now, so he's pawned the start of this project off on us," Jesse says.

Franco nails him in the shoulder with a fist. "You weren't supposed to say that, you tool."

Jesse shrugs. "What? It's true. And it's not like she's not gonna figure it out. She's a smart chick, bro."

I sigh. "I figured as much when you two showed up." I hesitate, but then figure I may as well just trust these guys with the truth. "I also know he's working through things. We talked after the workout a few weeks ago, and he said he needed time to work on things." I eye them. "Do you happen to know what exactly he's 'working' on?" I ask, using air quotes around the emphasized word.

Franco and Jesse both shrug.

"Nah, not really," Franco says.

Jesse says, "I've known him longest, and I'm only guessing, but I'd say he's finally trying to come to grips with losing Renée. He grieved as well as anyone can, but he never dealt with it in terms of, like, moving on. He's gone for an hour, hour and a half every other day for lunch and won't talk about where he's going, or what he's doing, which makes me think he's seeing someone." Jesse pauses, then stumbles over his words. "Seeing someone, like a therapist, I mean. Not another woman. I mean, the therapist could be a woman, but not seeing her like that...I mean—"

I laugh. "I know what you meant, Jess."

Franco rolls his eyes with a sigh. "You're a blabbermouth, you know that?"

"Was it supposed to be a secret?" Jesse asks. "Besides, I'm just guessing. He could be...I dunno, doing something else during his long weird lunch breaks he won't talk about."

I tap the blueprints. "Let's focus, guys. Conjecture about what James is doing is futile. He'll explain what he's doing if and when we need to know. For now, let's stick to talking about my house."

"Sounds great to me," Franco says. "So. Kitchen gets rearranged a little. Stove in the island, larger window over the sink, which also gets replaced. New countertops. Push this wall here backward, taking room from the bathroom, which becomes—not quite a powder room, but not a full bathroom. Toilet, vanity, and a small shower in the corner. The extra space from the bathroom becomes a built-in refrigerator and freezer unit. Something by Subzero, probably. Nice and big, with beautiful cabinet exteriors to match the new cabinets everywhere else."

I think about that last part. "When he was here, he talked about it being a walk-in pantry."

Jess nods, answering for Franco. "Yeah, he said that. But then he realized in taking out the wall you lose not just the stove, which is gonna be a cool induction unit, but also the fridge, and it has to go somewhere. It makes more sense to use the space for a built-in freezer-fridge combo—and by combo, I mean a full-size fridge and full-size freezer side by side. Super lux, super upscale. Big splurge, but it'll take the kitchen from an eight to a ten. It'll be cool and it'll be worth the expense just in terms of resale value alone."

"And new cabinets everywhere?" I ask.

Jesse nods, excited. "Oh yeah. If you do a nice dark butcher block like Franco was talking about, I'd like to see some cool white cabinets—either open-face, or glass fronted. Dark floors to match the counters, so you have dark floors and counters, white cabinets, white ceiling, and we're putting in a huge thick dark beam—probably a piece of the black walnut Franco has, so it'll all tie together. It'll look amazing."

I visualize it, and my stomach flips. "Like

something out of HGTV."

Jesse brings his fingertips together and then explodes them outward. "Kaboom, baby. This place is gonna be *lit*."

I laugh. "Lit? What are you, fifteen?"

Jesse just laughs and shrugs. "I'm cool enough to get away with slang."

"Sure you are," Franco says drily. "Keep telling yourself that, big guy."

Franco taps the bedroom and bathroom wall. "This wall won't be removed entirely, just opened up for a doorway—James mentioned you liked the idea of an open archway."

I tilt my head. "I don't know. He also mentioned one those barn doors on an exposed rail. I like that, too. I live alone, but I still like to close the door while I take a shower, so I think I'd feel a little weird having my bedroom be totally open to the bathroom. I don't know." I glance at Jesse. "What do you think?"

He rolls a heavy shoulder, adjusting his hat and sunglasses on his head. "I guess I'd have to wait to make that call. Get the wall opened up, update the bathroom." He hums. "Both ideas are cool, it'll just depend on how you want the final product to look and feel."

"Do you guys want to take a look at the rooms now? Maybe that will give you a better idea."

"Sure, good idea." Jesse hops up and ambles to my bedroom, looks around, then pokes his head into the bathroom and looks in there, and then returns to sit at the table again. "So, just from an initial impression, I'd say an archway makes more sense. You're not working with a ton of space in either room. Most of your square footage is in the living room and kitchen, which is actually ideal, but it just means your bedroom and bathroom are smaller. A sliding barn door may make the bedroom feel smaller, whereas an open archway will add to the feel of space. Right now you have a shower-tub combo, a huge—and, frankly, hideous—vanity, and a linen cabinet. None of that is using the space efficiently. I'd take the bathroom down to the studs, put in a small, marble-tiled shower stall, a soaker tub, a small, delicate, elegant vanity—a pedestal, maybe, with a glass or hammered copper bowl and a fancy faucet. Rip out that stupid cabinet and make a shelf for towels out of bare pipe and squares of black walnut to tie in with the kitchen. Efficient use of space, and it looks cool. You'll feel you have more space in the bathroom, but you'll have a marble shower with a rainfall head *and* a soaking tub. You have the space in there, you just have to use it right."

I blink. "Wow. I love that idea." I glance at Jesse speculatively. "You know, when you start talking design, you turn into a whole different person."

Franco laughs. "He actually sounds smart, doesn't he?"

Jesse flips Franco off, totally unfazed by Franco's constant insults to his intelligence. "I may be a dumbass, but I'm not a total moron." He then gives Franco double middle fingers. "Unlike you. You're a dumbass, a moron, *and* a fuckface."

"Ooh, you really dug deep for that one, didn't you, little buddy?" Franco says. "Careful coming up with those witty retorts, Jess—wouldn't want you to strain your one brain cell."

"At least I have a brain cell. You've outsourced your thinking to your butthole."

I cackle. "Hey, Tweedledee and Tweedledum— do you two ever stop?"

"Nope!" they both say in unison.

I shake my head. "So immature."

Jesse snickers. "Hey, I've overheard you and the girls talking. You're not much better."

I laugh. "I can't argue with that." I lean over the blueprints again. "So. What else?"

Franco traces the outer wall facing the backyard. "This whole wall becomes a glass wall—apparently James has a specific product in mind. A deck, some paint here and there, and I think that covers it."

I think a while. "And cost?" I ask eventually.

Franco pulls out a third piece of paper, this one

a computer printout with a line-by-line estimate. "You're paying for materials, plus about ten percent of the cost of labor. If you want to go lower, we can pick less expensive materials—James has figured pretty high-end stuff in here. So if you want to spend less, we can help you pick slightly less expensive but still quality materials."

The number on the sheet would mean pretty much every dime of my savings, plus I would probably figure some extra for unexpected costs, which always crop up, in my experience. But for what James is proposing...it's theft. Actual theft.

I sigh, conflicted. "How much would this cost, at normal rates?"

"If you were just some random client?" Franco says, leaning back and thinking. "I dunno. Jess?"

Jesse tilts his head to one side, thinking, calculating. "Oh, let's see...the kitchen alone would be fifty, at least. Maybe twenty or so for the bathroom. The wall and deck? Another ten, easily. That's conservative. If you could do this for under a hundred, you'd be winning. Fifty for the kitchen is probably way under. You could easily blow a hundred grand on this kitchen without going nuts."

I wince and sigh. "I don't know if I can accept this. You guys are going to put in, what, weeks of work? Months?"

Jesse shrugs. "Nah, not months. We'd bring in a crew for the grunt stuff. We have some guys who are expert deck builders—that's all they do, and they give us good prices. I'd say a month, two at most, barring unforeseen complications, but this place isn't that old, so I don't see too much of that."

Franco leans forward on his elbows, flipping a pencil around his thumb with his middle finger. "Nova, listen. All of us are doing really well. Business has never been better. We have more jobs lined up than you can imagine, and we've increased our profit margin by quite a lot over the last year or two. We're not hurting, okay? So, you can take this bid and get an amazing remodel. It'll take your resale value and nearly double it, I'd say. This neighborhood is getting better by the year, which means your comps will go up in value, making your personal home value go up. My point is, you'll see a big return on this, even if you paid full price."

Jesse rolls his eyes. "You're so dry and boring, Franky boy." He gazes at me earnestly. "What Franco is trying to say is that we're doing this for you be-cause we want to. You're our girl, Nova. Part of the gang. Audra moved in with Franco and Laurel moved in with Ryder so their places were already done, but Ryder, Franco, and James all helped me redo Imogen's house, and we'll all help James redo yours."

"But we're not—"

"Nova, listen," Jesse cuts in. "He's working on it. We all know that's what he's doing. He's been a miserable fucking bastard for years, to be honest, and since he met you, I've seen hints of the old James. Just hints, but more than I've seen in him since my sister died. So, we're all rooting for you two to figure your shit out—and no one more than me."

"Even though your sister was his wife?" I ask.

Jesse winces, sighs heavily, and nods. "I hated them together at first. Classic older brother, right? I actually decked him when I found they'd slept together. But she loved the fuck out that big dumb jock, and she made him better." He smiles faintly, eyes misting. "And god knows James was stupid for my sister. He'd have fought Satan himself barehanded and bare naked for that woman, and he kept her grounded. She was a wild woman, flighty and kooky, and…" He shrugs, lifts his hands palms up, and shakes his head, lets his hands thump heavily onto the table. "But she's gone. And she wanted him to find love again."

Franco nods. "I knew her well enough to know she'd have wanted him to get his head out of his ass and find some kind of happiness again."

Jesse blinks hard. "I—she…um. A few days before she—before she died, Renée called me." Jesse hesitates. "No one actually knows this. But, um. She called me at like four in the morning, sobbing. She'd had a nightmare—she dreamed she'd died in...in childbirth. She told me she knew it was silly, and just a hormonal pregnancy dream, but that it had felt... different. More real, or something. She was more scared and upset than I'd ever heard her, ever. She made me promise that—if by some freak or fluke or whatever, something did happen to her, that I'd make sure James didn't bury himself. That's how she put it. Bury himself. And it's what he's done. I haven't had any success trying to help him dig out, but god fucking knows I've tried. He's a stubborn bastard, though, and he's refused to...to—" Jesse shrugs awkwardly, visibly choked up and emotional. "He just won't get his head out of his ass."

Another pause, his eyes on me. "Until you came along. He's fighting it, but I see some of the old Jamie in him, when you're around. And I—I like it. I like seeing that. And I keep finding myself hoping that I can do something, anything, to help you and him figure shit out, because that would mean I'd have done something to keep that promise to my sister—the last promise I ever made her. And the only one I've been unable to keep."

I'm choking. "Jess, it's not—"

He taps the blueprints. "So, what I'm saying is, I'd build you an entire house with my bare hands, from scratch, if it meant giving you and James time and space to figure it out. If it meant…" He shrugs, trailing off. "I dunno."

I cover his hands with mine. "He has to be ready for it, Jess," I say, my voice low and quiet.

He nods. "I know. It's just that I'm a fixer, and his broken-ass heart is the one thing I can't fix."

"No one can," I say. "I can't fix his broken heart. He has to be willing to be with me with a whole heart. There'd be pieces missing, and seams and cracks, but he has to offer it as a whole. I'm worth more than just accepting the fucked-up mess of him, just to have a part. I want more than that—I deserve more. If he can get there, I'll be here waiting. I've got nothing but time, Jess. I'm not going anywhere, and I told him that. I'm willing to wait—because I think he's worth waiting for." I smile at Jesse. "If he can get his head out of his ass and work on rebuilding his broken-ass heart, he'll be worth waiting for."

Franco slaps the table. "All right. Mushy time is over. I'm all for everything you guys said, and I want my friends—both you and James—to be happy, however that happens, however it looks. In the meantime, I need to know if you're giving us the green light to get to work in here. We can start right now—I've got a roll-off dumpster on hold and it can be here inside of thirty minutes. We can start in the kitchen, get the biggest and messiest part of the demo over with first."

I blink, surprised. "Wait, like, *now*, now?"

"I didn't wear my work clothes for the fashion statement," Franco says.

I look around at my house. I think about the bank account I've been scrimping and saving and pouring every extra dollar into for years. Then I close my eyes and try to picture my house as James, Jesse, and Franco are describing—open, airy, white cabinets and dark counters, a soaking tub, a marble shower, a master suite, a giant built-in fridge and freezer?

"Let's do it," I say. "But I want to help with the demo."

Franco nods. "All right—done. Let me make the call to get the roll-off dumpster over here."

Jesse gestures at the kitchen with a broad sweep of his hand. "We gotta clear out in here, then. Dishes and stuff out of all the cabinets, mainly. The fridge can stay as is, we'll demo around it." He looks me over—assessing, rather than anything inappropriate or untoward. "You'll want to change, if you're gonna help with demo—that shit gets messy. Jeans and a tee you don't mind getting messy, and probably a ball cap so you don't get your hair dusty."

So I change into get-messy clothes and Jesse and I get to work boxing up my dishes and pots and pans, as well as the food from the cabinets and all the cleaning supplies under the sink. By the time we're done, Franco is back with three sledgehammers and three sets of safety goggles, and announces that the dumpster will be here within about ten or fifteen minutes, and that we might as well get started.

He and Jesse unplug my fridge and move it across the kitchen, plugging it back in and leaving it basically in the middle of my kitchen near the pile of boxes containing the contents of my kitchen. Once the fridge is out of the way, they haul my stove away.

"Wait—where is my range going?" I ask.

Jesse gestures at the appliance. "Well, are you in love with this one?"

I shrug. "Not really. I replaced the appliances when I first moved in, but I went for the bottom of midrange, in terms of price. So...the appliances aren't great."

Jesse traces a giant rectangle in the air. "The island is going to be the new hub of your kitchen. Induction cooktop up top, with side-by-side ovens beneath it, more storage space on both sides, and a bar overhang with stools facing the living room. It'll be pimp, trust me."

I laugh. "Well, if you say it's gonna be pimp, then by all means, let's do it." I gesture at the microwave and dishwasher. "So we're replacing all the appliances with high-end then? What do we do with the old ones?

They're only a few years old and in great condition."

Franco, speaking over his shoulder, says, "Sell them on eBay, if you want, or if you'd rather, I've got a connection that handles donating used appliances to families in need. Your choice."

I grin. "Donate them, by all means. If I'm getting this amazing remodel for so little, then I'm sure as hell gonna pay it forward a little."

Franco grins back. "Atta girl. I'll get ahold of my friend and arrange a pick up once we've picked out your new stuff."

Jesse hands me a sledgehammer and set of goggles; I don the goggles and grip the sledgehammer in both hands, leaving the heavy head resting on the floor at my feet.

Jesse gestures at the wall. "First swing is yours, babe."

I swing away, and the head of the hammer bites into the drywall with a shudder and a crunch, leaving a giant hole in the wall. I laugh, yanking the hammer out and glancing at Jesse, who just shrugs and gestures at the wall.

"Go nuts," he says. "Make a hole."

I glance at Franco, who is holding a pair of massive crowbars; he just grins. "Demo is the fun part," he says.

I heft the hammer, let the handle slap down into

my palm, and then wind up and swing hard—and this time, the hammer goes through the wall completely, sticking out on the other side. I wiggle, tug, and then give it a hard yank, and the hammer comes free, taking a giant chunk of drywall with it. I can see daylight through the hole I've made, and now Jesse moves up to the wall a few feet away and swings his hammer with far more accuracy and power than me—his bites all the way through on the first swing, and then his second swing brings almost an entire sheet of drywall down. Franco tosses one of the pry bars onto the floor and uses the other to start ripping the upper cabinets off the wall, making quick work of it—within five minutes, he has a huge chunk of cabinetry on the floor.

I hear a beeping outside, and then a deafening metallic screech, a hydraulic whirr, and a thump—the dumpster is being delivered. Without missing a beat, Jesse finishes making a hole in the wall big enough for him to step through, and then sets aside the hammer and starts carrying chunks of drywall outside.

The afternoon passes that way, and by six in the evening, there is no more wall separating my kitchen from my living room—we left pairs of studs far left, middle, and right for ceiling support, until they can get a brace up and the new beam in place. The three of us are leaning against my counter, covered in dirt and dust, sipping beers, admiring our handiwork.

"Good start," Jesse says.

Franco gestures at the wall where the built-in fridge is going to go. "That's next. Rip out the bathtub-shower, knock out the wall."

I wipe sweat off my forehead with the back of my wrist and then take a sip of beer. "Tomorrow?"

Franco nods. "Yep, along with the rest of the cabinets and counters in here, and the floor."

I hesitate. "Will it be just you two, then?"

Jesse shrugs a big shoulder. "Dunno. No telling with James, and Ryder is working on a big contract for a new event center. When we need electrical work, he'll pop by and knock that out real quick, but that won't be for a week or so yet."

I nod. "I see." I look around at my half-demolished kitchen and abruptly start laughing. At quizzical looks from both guys, I wave at the rubble and remains of studs where the wall was. "I just realized I have no idea how I'm going to make food."

Franco laughs. "I'd say have your favorite delivery on speed dial until this is over."

I groan. "Oh, hell no."

Franco eyes me. "No?"

I shake my head. "I eat in as much as I possibly can." I slap a hand against a buttock. "My metabolism is a stubborn piece of shit. Delivery food will go straight to my ass, so I like to make my own food. I prep meals a week at a time." I open my fridge and show them the stacks of Tupperware containers. "One for lunch and dinner for six days of the week. I don't eat breakfast, and I eat what I like on Sundays."

Franco nods, swallowing a sip of beer and pointing at the fridge with his can. "Impressive that you find the time to do that working the hours you do."

I shrug. "I usually get at least one day, if not two, off every week. I spend a couple hours cooking and prepping for the week. Little enough effort to expend, especially if it keeps my ass from ballooning into something with its own damn zip code."

"Speaking of an ass with its own zip code," Jesse says, "I should get home to Imogen. She's gonna be craving corn chips and peanut butter about now, I'm guessing."

"Jesse! Not nice!" I frown and laugh at the same time. "And I thought cravings only happened in the first trimester?"

"She told me she'd rather I tease her about it than pretend like nothing's changed. So I tease her. She knows I'm kidding, and it's on her request." Jesse shrugs and shakes his head. "And as far as the cravings go? Hell if I know. That's what the books she made me read said, but they also said some women experience cravings for specific things the entire pregnancy, and for Imogen, it's been corn chips and peanut butter." He laughs again. "Funny thing is, I tried it, spreading peanut butter on corn chips, and it's actually pretty fucking good. I'll probably keep doing it, honestly."

Franco makes a grossed-out face. "Corn chips and peanut butter? Are you kidding me?"

"Hey man, don't knock it till you try it." Jesse touches two fingers to his forehead and salutes. "Have a good night, kids. See you tomorrow, bright and early."

Franco hesitates a few minutes longer, lingering over his beer, and I realize he's got something on his mind. I kick his steel toe boot. "What, Franco? I can feel you working up to say something."

He rolls a shoulder. "It's…" He sighs. "Audra is the kind of girl who won't ever ask for anything, you know? Like, she'll rarely ask for help, even from Imogen who she's known for fucking ever."

I nod. "I get that about her. I'm the same way, so I sympathize." I wiggle my can at Franco, offering another, but he shakes his head. "Is there something going on?"

He hesitates again. "She'll probably kill me for this. But she's so damn stubborn and I just feel like she needs support but won't ask for it."

"She sick or something?"

He shakes his head. "No, nothing like that."

Another long hesitation. "Imogen being pregnant has Audra all twisted up."

"She wants a baby?"

He nods. "Yeah. She never thought she would, and neither did I. So when she floated the idea of trying, I was kinda shocked, but open to it."

"I guess I kind of had her pegged as someone who didn't want kids."

"Because she always has been that way. But us being together has sort of changed us both. Softened us, opened us up some, you know?" He tosses his empty can into a nearby open contractor-grade garbage bag.

"So where do I come into this? I feel like you wouldn't be talking to me about this unless there was some issue."

He nods. "She went off birth control and we've been trying for a while."

"Nothing doing?" I surmise.

"Right. And she recently went to her doctor to see what's up." He pauses, considers his words. "Fact is neither of us are exactly young anymore, you know? And her doctor basically said it wouldn't be impossible, but unlikely for her to conceive, and a pregnancy would be difficult and risky at her age, even if she did."

"I see. That's tough."

Franco nods. "She's struggling with it. She needs

to talk it out, and I know Imogen knows something's up, but I think it may be more than a one-woman show, you know?"

I smile at him. "Absolutely. I'll talk to her."

"Thanks."

TEN

A WEEK AND A HALF LATER, AUDRA, IMOGEN, LAUREL, and I are at Imogen's house. I talked to Imogen, and we decided this was a conversation for the whole crew, so we talked to Laurel, and decided to blindside Audra with a dinner party intervention.

We planned an Italian night, so Audra and Laurel are working on a lasagna, Imogen is making an antipasto salad, and I'm doing cheesy garlic bread. Out of deference to the fact that Imogen can't drink, being pregnant, we made it an alcohol-free dinner party, serving sparkling water instead of wine.

Which, considering the seriousness of the subject at hand, is probably a good thing.

We collaborate on a fabulous nineties music playlist to cook to, put *Friends* on in the background, and basically just have fun. Dinner is delicious, and drama free. Dessert is a tiramisu purchased from a local bakery—because we're committed to the theme, but not *that* committed; tiramisu is *hard*.

Finally, we're all sated, full of salad, lasagna, garlic bread, and tiramisu, and we're sitting around Imogen's living room sipping herbal tea and watching *Friends*. We're all having so much fun.

Imogen eyes me, and I eye her back, and she gives me a significant look and I return it.

Finally, Audra snorts. "You two are so fucking obvious, it's adorable." She gestures at the four of us. "What's this intervention about? Don't get me wrong, I've had more fun than I thought was possible without booze, but you two have something up your dorky little sleeves."

I laugh. "We're that obvious?"

She laughs. "You've been making weird eyes at each other all evening. If I didn't know you two were both slutting it up for sexy men, I'd think you were going lesbo together."

Imogen blinks. "There are so many offensive elements to that statement, I don't even know where to start listing them."

"I'm not slutting it up for anyone, thank you very much," I say.

Audra arches an eyebrow. "What, no repeat of the kitchen incident?"

I narrow my eyes at her; I only told her about that. "Nope."

Laurel leans forward on the sectional. "Kitchen incident? What incident?" She eyes Imogen. "Do you know of any incident?"

Imogen shakes her head. "Nope." Her eyes go to me. "Do tell, Nova."

I give Audra the finger. "Nice redirect, bitch."

She just cackles. "Can't corner me, slutty-buns."

"James and I had a little...moment of intimacy," I say. "In my kitchen, a couple weeks ago."

"You slept with him?" Laurel says, squealing.

"In your *kitchen*?"

I groan. "No, I did not *sleep* with him." I hesitate. "We just...fooled around."

"And?" Imogen presses.

I shrug. "And...he's not there, yet."

"Meaning?"

I focus on Phoebe, who's doing the "Smelly Cat" song. "Meaning...we talked again in his kitchen, a few days later, and he just needs time."

"Needs time for what?" Laurel asks.

"To figure out...life," I say. "To figure out single-hood and moving on."

"Oh." Laurel nods. "That makes sense." She stares at me, scrutinizing, searching. "And you?"

"And me, what?"

"Where are you in the whole thing?"

I shrug again. "I don't know. I like him. I really

enjoyed…what happened with us. I'd like more, but only if he's all in. And he just can't commit to that. At least, not the last time we talked, which was almost a month ago, now."

"A *month*?" Imogen says.

I nod. "He's been MIA and totally beyond communication, at least for me. I see plenty of Jesse and Franco though, and they say he's around and still going on those mysterious long lunches. Two or three days every week."

"Are you okay with that?" Imogen asks. "Him being incommunicado? And not being ready?"

I make a face and shrug a third time. "I mean, do I have a choice? It's not something you can force." I groan. "And why are we talking about *me*? This was supposed to be about Audra."

Audra looks around at everyone. "Why is this supposed to be about me? I'm fine. Everything is hunky-fucking-dory in Audra's life. Legit, I've never been happier."

I sigh. "I talked to Franco."

She goes…opaque. "Okay?"

"Let me just preface this with the fact that the only reason Franco even talked to me about this was because he loves you and he's worried you're not dealing with this very well."

"With what?"

Imogen moves from her seat in a deep leather recliner to curl up on the couch next to Audra. "Sweetie. I've known you more than half our lives. You don't have to put up a front. It's me—it's *us*."

Audra is still opaque and shut down. "I don't know what you're talking about."

I sigh. "Audra...I *talked* to *Franco*."

She tilts her head back and sighs, rubbing her face with both hands. "I'm gonna kill him."

"He knew that," I say. "But yet he still talked to me about it. Which means you know he has to have a serious concern if he's willing to risk pissing you off."

Audra blinks, her expression still carefully blank. "Just so we're all on the same page here—what exactly did Franco talk to you about?"

I glance at Imogen—being Audra's best friend, it's probably best for her to take point on this.

Imogen wraps an arm around Audra, who stiffens, goes rigid as a two-by-four. "I've known something was up with you for weeks, and I had a pretty good idea what it was about even before this. So don't think you were snowing me with your 'everything is fine' routine. Don't forget, I *know* you, bitch."

Audra snorts. "What the actual hell are you babbling about?"

"You being infertile," Imogen says.

Audra visibly flinches. "Fuck." She sniffles, and

her expression abruptly crumples. "Goddammit," she whispers. "Goddamn you, Franco."

"You can't blame him," I say. "He's worried about you."

"He shouldn't be," Audra snaps, but her voice is weak, quiet, and unconvincing. "I'm fine."

Imogen outright laughs, but it's a loving laugh of amusement at Audra's stubborn insistence on pretending she's fine. "Honey. Franco only came to us because when you get like this, it's damned near impossible to get past your walls. He loves you, but men just aren't equipped to handle shit like this. It takes a best friend to handle something like this."

"Three best friends," Laurel says.

Audra sniffles again. "I'm not infertile," she says eventually. "I'm just old."

Imogen tightens her grip on Audra's shoulders. "You're not *old*, Audra."

"I'm almost forty-two, hon. Kinda old. And definitely too old to be thinking about having a kid."

Imogen hesitates at this. "Audra...since I've known you, you've had one hard and fast rule for life, and that's that you'd never have kids."

"I know. I know."

"So, when did that change, and how, and why haven't we talked about it?"

Audra shrugs, dropping her eyes. "It was gradual.

I mean, I also swore I'd never fall in love, and here I am, in love with Franco and his stupid sexy body, and his stupid romantic heart." She sniffles. "I fell in love with his stupid ass, and got all soft and mushy about everything, and started thinking."

"Oooh, thinking—that's dangerous," Laurel quips.

"No kidding. So, yeah. I fell in love, and got all mushy and soft-headed," Audra says, sniffing a laugh. She reaches out and rubs Imogen's big, round, taut belly. "And then this happened."

Imogen rests her hand over Audra's on her belly. "Ahhhh. I see."

Audra nods. "So, it's your fault."

Imogen laughs. "Blame Jesse."

Audra flattens her palm against Imogen's belly, eyes going wide. "He's kicking!"

Imogen smiles. "We actually just got the gender ultrasound the other day." Her grin deepens, goes soft and bright and emotional. "It's a girl."

Everyone squeals and claps and hugs her, and then Audra lurches off the couch, shaking off all the affection.

"See? That shit right there is what makes me crazy." She shudders. "The mushy shit—you bitches squealing and sighing and acting like goofy-ass little girls." She stands at the picture window overlooking

Imogen's front porch.

"Quit acting like some macho alpha male," Imogen says, rising off the couch to stand next to Audra at the window. "This is us, babe, you can be real with us."

Audra's shoulders shake, and her head drops. "I don't *want* to want a baby. It's stupid. I'm almost for-ty-fucking-two. I'd be a senior citizen by the time the kid graduates high school."

"So?" Imogen leans against the window and faces Audra. "You're fit as hell. You'll be a spry old lady. And a hell of a cool mom."

Audra can't even respond. "I just…I want it with him. I lay awake in bed at night staring at Franco, watching him sleep, and I imagine a little baby with his face and my eyes. I can see him holding a little baby, rocking it…I see a little boy, for some reason. I don't know why. It's so fucking weird. It's almost like a compulsion, like some drive deep inside me— biological and hormonal rather than emotional, or based on some logical, rational decision. I fought it and fought it for months, but eventually Franco was like, what the fuck is wrong with you, because I kept acting weird, especially after sex. I was…we were su-per careful, you know? Like, I've been on birth con-trol since I was a teenager and I haven't ever missed a dose—and we only ever had sex bare once, at the condo in Florida after you left. Since then, it's never bare. But even though we always had protected sex, I would lay there thinking about what it would feel like to be with him bare again, and how it would feel to be pregnant, to have a baby...and I found myself not being scared of it."

Imogen laughs quietly. "Oh, it's scary all right. But exhilarating and exciting and amazing too."

"But my doctor says it would be super risky."

Imogen just rolls a shoulder. "Eh, I'm technically high risk, being over forty myself. It just means a few extra ultrasounds, and a few more doctor appointments throughout the pregnancy. We're both super healthy, and you even more so than me."

"I just...I don't know how to reconcile the part of me that's still, like, NO WAY, no babies, never ever, and the part of me that's like, GIVE ME BABY." Audra touches her belly—flat, with six-pack abs. "I almost feel it sometimes. Like it's already real. Even though I know it's not."

"You guys have been trying?" Imogen asks.

Audra nods. "I went off birth control a couple months ago. It took a while for my cycle to reassert itself into a normal rhythm—and after having super short, light periods if any at all for so long from the birth control, having a heavy flow fucking *sucks*, let me tell you." She laughs. "And yes, we've been...

trying. A lot."

Imogen laughs. "You guys fuck like sixteen-year-olds who just discovered sex as it is."

Audra's eyes widen. "You have *no* idea. It's even more, now. Like, once we both got on board and committed to actively trying to get pregnant, it's like our sex drives went into overdrive."

Imogen rears back, eyes wide. "*Your* sex drive is in overdrive? I…I can't even fathom what that means."

Audra laughs, shakes her head. "Morning sex almost every day. I put my feet up, and he brings me coffee. He comes home for lunch most days and we fuck again. And then, most nights, we fuck a third time before we go to bed." She laughs harder. "It's honestly kind of exhausting, even for me, but I just…I fucking *want* him. ALL. THE. TIME. I want his cum inside me. Sorry to be so graphic, but I just…it's a craving. I'm not even blowing him anymore. Like not at all, the poor guy. I think he misses the spontaneous BJs."

"He's getting sex three times a day," I say drily. "I think he'll survive."

"He's used to getting a BJ several times a week at least. Now it's down to literally zero. But I just don't want to waste it. I want it inside me." Audra shakes her head, as if she can't believe what she's saying. "I want his baby juice inside me, and I want it in a way

I can't explain. I barely understand it myself, but it's like this crazy biological imperative."

Imogen sighs. "Audra, god…" She twists and faces Audra again, touching her on the shoulder. "Let's just be real, here, huh?"

Audra frowns. "I *am* being real, Im."

"Calling it the work of some mysterious biological imperative is a copout and you know it, hon."

Audra tips her head backward and groans. "God*dammit*, Imogen. Can't you give me one little white lie?"

Imogen shakes her head. "No. Because you wouldn't give me one, and you know it."

Audra turns away and paces across the room, slumping to the couch, head hanging, face buried in her hands. "I'm fucking terrified," she whispers. "Of being a mother. Of being *my* mother. Of being a terrible mother." Her voice drops until we almost can't hear her. "And yet I'm even more afraid of not being able to get pregnant, and never knowing."

Laurel comes to sit on the couch, and suddenly all four of us are crowded together, the three of us huddled around Audra—who, for once, doesn't fight the affection as she weeps like I've never seen her weep.

"As the only one here who has already had a child, I can tell you this, Audra: that fear of being the worst part of your parents?" Laurel's voice is a quiet murmur. "That will drive you to be the best mom you could possibly be. You'll make your own mistakes, but you sure as hell won't make *their* mistakes. I can tell you that you'll never be ready. I can tell you that it'll be hard—Imogen will testify to the fact that being pregnant is hard, unless you end up being one of those annoying bitches who has an easy pregnancy. But it'll be worth it."

"I don't even know if I *can* get pregnant," Audra says. "And that's the scariest part."

Imogen laughs. "I was told I *couldn't* get pregnant," she says, and then palms her belly. "And look at me. And we weren't even trying. I thought I couldn't get pregnant so we never bothered with a condom, and obviously I wasn't on birth control. And the one morning I suddenly started throwing up, and I missed a period..." She shrugs. "So I took a test, and promptly freaked the fuck out."

Imogen wipes her eyes. "So you guys don't think it's stupid to try for a baby?"

I snort. "Why the hell would it be stupid? You're in love with the man, yes?"

"Yes."

"And you're committed to him for life, yes?" I ask. She nods. "Absolutely."

"So what possible reason is there to not have a

baby with him?"

She frowns. "Being old."

Laurel scoffs. "You're forty-one, Audra, not six-ty-one. Big difference. People have kids at our age all the time." She indicates Imogen. "Case in point."

Audra nods. "I guess you're right."

Imogen rests her head on Audra's shoulder. "I want to be a mommy *and* an auntie. I want us to be auntie-mommies together. So, you just have to work on becoming more fertile."

Audra frowns at Imogen. "And how does one do that?"

Imogen shrugs. "I mean, you're already doing most of it. Natural fertility doctors would say more sex, better diet, exercise." She grins. "You've got the sex part down. More of the sex should be positions that put you a bit more inverted so his spermies don't have to swim upward as much. Putting your legs up, like you're already doing. There are supplements you can take, which I can help you find. I'd say in your case actually reduce your exercise—less high-intensity, less high-impact. More food high in healthy fats. Reduce stress, maybe even take up yoga and meditation. The more you stress out about it, the harder you make it on yourself. The more you relax and just enjoy the process, the easier it'll be."

Audra laughs. "Well, I definitely enjoy the

process. No worries there."

Imogen lightly whacks Audra's shoulder. "I mean the *whole* process, dummy, not just the sex." She leans against Audra, arms around her waist. "Enjoy being in love. Relax into the feeling of wanting a baby with the man you love, and while you're laying there with a pillow under your thighs and Jesse's baby juice draining up inside you, think baby—think pregnant, think love, think openness, think acceptance. Don't fight it, honey. You're fighting the whole process. You have to relax and accept it and enjoy it."

"Easier said than done," Audra whispers.

Imogen nods, kisses Audra's cheek. "You're safe, Audra. You're loved. You're accepted. He's not going anywhere and neither are we."

Audra looks around at each of us in turn. "Promise?"

We all wrap her up in a big suffocating bear hug.

"You're stuck with us, bitch," I say, feeling oddly emotional about this myself. "Get used to it."

Audra meets my eyes through the scrum of hair and arms and shoulders. "You're not out of the woods, you know," she says to me. "Just because we're talking about me doesn't mean we're done talking about you."

I sigh. "That's fine, because there's nothing to talk about."

And no amounting of wishing or talking will change that. And at this point, I'm wondering if I was stupid to tell James I would wait. My heart hurts from waiting, and it's been barely a month. How long can I wait with an open heart?

How long before I shut myself off again? Because if I do that…there will be no curtain call—not after this.

ELEVEN

ANOTHER WEEK PASSES—MY KITCHEN IS NEARLY DONE. The island is finished, and the floor is in: dark wide planks. The cabinets are almost in, brand new white open-face cabinets custom built by Franco. The opening for the fridge is roughed in, and Jesse has been working on the bathroom while Franco does the cabinets. Ryder has come by a few times—once to reroute the electrical so I have light switches for the kitchen by the hallway and by the back door, and a couple more times to just generally help with the remodel.

But no sign of James.

Not a word.

In fact, the guys have clammed up about him, too, and I worry there's something they're not saying. I don't push it, though.

Late one evening, it's just Jesse putting the finishing touches on my new three-quarter bathroom—touch up paint around the switch plates and installing the new light fixture, caulking around the marble shower, changing the doorknob and installing the cabinet pulls.

"Jesse?" I say, leaning against the doorframe while he puts a powder-coated black iron cabinet pull on the cabinet and screws it in from inside.

He grunts a response, not looking at me.

"What's going on with James?"

Jesse finishes and leans back on his heels, head hanging. "He's been struggling these past few weeks."

"Struggling? How so?"

A shrug of Jesse's heavy shoulder. "Just with…everything. Memories, I guess. Letting go. I don't know and I'm not sure it's my place to say even if I did."

I nod, and sigh. "I won't ask again."

Jesse eyes me. "Nova…" He flips the screwdriver in the air, catches it with a slap against his palm, and then stands up, raking a palm through his loose, messy brown hair. "I'm not saying give up. I'm just saying he's trying to work through things he's been suppressing or not dealing with for years. It's a lot. I know he's trying, but he…he can't do this just for you."

I shake my head. "It has to be for him, and for his girls. If he goes through all this and he's in a better place, I'll be happy for him, even if he concludes he and I can't be anything." I ache inside just saying that.

Jesse pulls his hair back and then lets it go. "I don't think he'll come to that conclusion. I guess I'm just not sure how long it's going to take for him to feel like he's ready to offer you anything."

"And I don't know how long my heart can hold out, Jess."

"And he'd tell you to do what *you* need to do." Jesse slaps the sink. "I'm gonna go."

"Thanks, Jesse," I say.

He nods. "We'll be done with your kitchen soon, and then we'll start on your new door wall."

"What about the master suite idea? I guess I thought that would be next."

Jesse hesitates. "James said he planned on doing that himself."

"Oh." I blow out a breath. "I guess at this point I assumed he wasn't planning on actually doing any of this." I realize I sound ungrateful, possibly. "Not that it matters. I don't want to sound like I'm—"

Jesse laughs, holds up a hand. "Hey, I've been thinking the same thing myself."

"You guys are amazing. My kitchen is incredible."

Jesse grins. "Appliances get delivered Monday. Once those are in, you'll have a kitchen again."

I clap excitedly. "I'm actually giddy with excitement, Jess. Seriously. Thank you so much."

He exits the bathroom and I follow him into my mostly complete kitchen, which is just missing appliances and some floor trim, which Franco is working on now that the cabinets are in. "My pleasure." He grabs his toolbox off the floor and heads for the door, pausing halfway through it. "Don't give up just yet, Nova."

I smile weakly. "Trying, Jess. I'm trying."

Once he's gone in a rumble of diesel clatter, I stand in my kitchen and look around, in awe of how open my house feels now. I stare at the framed-in opening where the fridge is going to go—it still needs drywall, mud, and paint, and then the actual appliance, and I try to picture the completed space.

I spend a few more minutes trying to visualize the whole place being done, but it's hard, because I'm not really a visual person. And the mental exercise, to be honest, is more about distracting myself than anything.

Because it's all too easy to remember James in here, to picture him. To feel him.

Gahhh.

I get ready for bed and curl up under my blanket, watching *Dexter* on my iPad until I eventually fall asleep.

I wake up abruptly, and try to figure out what woke me. I'm groggy—I don't wake up easily, and when I do, it takes me a while to regain anything like coherency.

I lay in bed, blinking at the ceiling, waiting to see if whatever woke me up will happen again.

There it is—a fist pounding on the door...the back door.

I slide out of bed and tiptoe hesitantly out of my room, down the short hallway, and into the living room. Another knock—more of a pounding, honestly. Franco left his tools here, so I grab a hammer from the toolbox—the thing is something Thor would use, not just a normal hammer, but a two-foot-long thing with a huge, heavy head. I wield it in both hands as I approach the back door. I grip it one-handed, yank open the back door and kick the storm door outward, and then grab the hammer in both hands again, ready to clobber whoever the hell is at my back door at whatever the hell time it is.

James.

He's weaving on his feet—absolutely hammered. "Nova." His voice sounds oddly clear, however, even though he's visibly obliterated.

"James...um. Hi." I toss the hammer on the porch and reach for him as he sways, nearly falling off the little porch. "Whoa, there. Grab onto the door-frame, James. You're too big for me to catch if you go down."

He reaches for the doorframe, misses three times, and then gets it, and I hear the wood crackle under his grip. "Hi, Nova."

I rear back from the potent reek of alcohol on his breath. "Wow, um…hi."

He's shirtless, although I see the shirt hanging from his back pocket. His jeans are filthy at the knees and one hip, as if he'd fallen in the mud and struggled to get back to his feet; his hands are similarly muddy.

" 'M drunk, Nova."

I nod, wide-eyed. "Yeah, I noticed."

"No. No-no-nonono. I'm really, really, *really* drunk. Like super-duper McShwasted. Drunky drunk drunk."

"Yeah, I noticed."

"I started drinking at Billy Bar, but then I was too drunk to drive, so I started walking home. But then I missed."

"You…missed?"

He nods, a wobbly, circling sort of movement. "Uh-huh. I missed the house and ended up at a liquor store down the road."

"Um."

"I think my truck is still at the bar." He digs in his pocket with one hand—a long, laborious process— and comes up with keys. "See? I stopped driving. Not a driving drunker. Drunker driver. Drive drunker.

Whatthefuckever. Buddy in college killed a guy doing that and went to jail. Told his stupid ass not to drive. Tried to wrestle his keys away, but he was a boxer and he knocked me out. Lucky punch, but still. Tried to stop him and I couldn't. Should've. Never drive drunk. Never never never."

"You walked here?"

He nods. "Uh-huh. Walky walky walk." God, he's so silly it's almost cute, but there's a darkness to this, a heaviness masked behind the silliness.

"Why are you here, James?"

He blinks at me. "I missed you."

I only just barely suppress a pained sigh. "You need to come in and sit down."

He follows me in and stops just inside, looking around. "Looks fuckin' great. Just like I pictured it." He touches the island, comically missing it the first few times, but once his hand finds the countertop, his touch is professional, examining the workmanship of the island and the cabinets. "Franco did great on this. The cabinets too."

I nod. "He sure did. The guys have been working their asses off." I realize it sounds vaguely accusatory.

James looks at me—drunk as a skunk, but the awareness in his gaze is potent. "Don't, Nova."

"Don't what?"

"Act like I don't care."

"I didn't say that, and I wasn't suggesting that."

He abruptly misses a step and falters backward, stumbles, catches himself on the counter, and then slowly slumps down onto the floor. "Whoops. Guess I'm sitting down right here, huh?" He rests his head against the cabinet. "I care, Nova."

"I know." I have several cases of bottled water on the floor, and I take three, open one and hand it to him.

He drinks it all, crumples the plastic and twists the top on to seal it and opens another. "I drank a lot."

"I bet."

He shakes his head. "No. You don't even know. My tolerance is dumb. The guys on my football team called me The Beer God."

"How much did you drink, James?"

He holds up his hand, tries to count his fingers, only managing to touch three out of five. "One, two, three…ten. I drank ten."

"Ten bottles?"

He shrugs. "I dunno. Maybe. Lotta lotta lotta beer." He blinks at his hand. "I walked from there. I was gonna drive, but I couldn't find the keyhole, so I said fuckit, let's drink more. So I walked to the liquor store. I bought a whiskey."

"How much whiskey did you drink?"

He stares at his hand again, as if the answer is

written there. "A big guy. Really big guy. My ol' buddy Evan. Big, big, big guy. A glallon."

"A *gallon?*" I repeat.

He nods. "Uh-huh. I drank it all. Every last drop."

"Oh *shit*. I think we need to take you to the hospital, James."

He blows a raspberry. "Nahhhh. Not me. Not good ol Jamie. I stopped trying to get drunk, you know. I don't drink all that much mostly, because it takes too much to get me drunk. Too esspensive. Takes too many drinks to make me not feel nothing." He blinks at me. "You're so pretty, Nova."

I close my eyes briefly—it's painful to see him like this. "Where are the girls, James?"

He rolls his head on his neck, as if trying to figure out where it's supposed to go. "Disney World!"

"James. Where are Ella and Nina?"

"Tol' you. Disney World." He holds up his left hand, and my eyes widen: on his ring finger is his wedding band. "Every year I send Mom and Pop O'Neill with the girls to Disney World."

"Every year?"

He nods, staring at his ring finger. "Every year. This weekend, every year."

I'm starting to suspect what's going on. "This weekend, huh?"

He twists the ring on his finger. "This weekend."

He glances at me—or, at least, toward me. "Don't tell Jesse. He'll be pissy. He wanted to drink with me tonight, but I dodged him. I esssss-*caped* him. He wanted to be a babysitter, because he knows. He *knows*, Nova. I mean, of course he knows. But...he *knows*."

"What does he know, James?" I ask, grabbing a bucket that has dried drywall mud crusted at the bottom and set it next to James, just in case, and then I sit on the floor next to him.

He pokes the bucket with a huge forefinger. "You're silly. I won't puke. I never puke. I—I can hold my liquor. All the liquor. I licked the liquor, and then the liquor licked me. It licked me tonight, Nova. It got me."

"Yeah, it did." I rest my head against the cabinet and stare at him. "What does Jesse know, James?"

"He knows. It's this weekend. It's tonight."

"What is, James?"

He stares at the ceiling, now. "Six years ago. Exactly six years ago today." He looks around. "What time is it?"

I shrug. "No clue."

He rummages his pants pockets until he finds his phone, peers at it. "Four? Does that say four?" He shoves the phone toward me. "I'm too drunk to read it."

I glance at it. "Four twenty-three a.m."

He nods, drops the phone on the floor between us. "Six years, eight hours, and five minutes." He pauses. "Renée died six years ago at eight eighteen p.m."

I flinch. "I see."

His eyes go to me, lucid and sharp, despite his inebriation. "You see."

I nod. "I see."

He shakes his head. "No, you don't see. You don't see a goddamm fucking thing." He sounds…angry.

"What don't I see?"

He drinks more water. "Doc Rich said I have to let her go. I don't *want* to let her go. She was my fucking *wife*. My best friend. How do I let her go? Doc Rich—stupid Doc Rich. He said letting go of her doesn't mean forget her. Just let go. Stop holding on to her memory. But then what? Then what? He doesn't fucking know, the dumbfuck. Let her go, he says. But how? Doesn't fucking know that either." He twists his head to look at me. "It's your fucking fault."

I flinch. "What? What's my fault?"

"I was content being miserable, damn you. I was happily miserable. Lonely old fuck, and fine with it, that was me. And then you. Then you came along, with your fucking beautiful hair and your fucking beautiful face." His eyes fix on me, on said hair, said face…and then rake downward, and I remember I went to bed like usual: T-shirt and underwear, and nothing else. "You, and your fucking hair like fire, like the sunlight on brand new copper. Like the flame from a welding torch reflected off a piece of copper. Your eyes like…fuck, I don't know. Like the sky, like sapphires. You, and your…your fucking body. Those big perfect tits, and that big round tight perfect ass. Fucking…fucking abs, and fucking hips like a church bell. You're fucking perfect, goddammit, and you made me just miserable. You made me realize that I wasn't happily miserable or fucking—fucking *content*, or any of that bullshit. I was just lonely and I'd accepted it as my life. And then *you*. Goddamn you. You made me *want* you. You made me fucking *need* you."

I've never heard him talk like this—or this much, or with this much vulgarity. It's shocking, scary, and painful.

"James, I—" My throat is tight.

I know he's drunk, but he's not incoherent; he's talking the kind of truth that often only come out when the filters have been washed away like they are right now.

He cuts in as if I hadn't spoken. "She's *dead*, goddammit."

"I know, James," I whisper.

"I loved her so fucking much."

"I know that, too."

He swallows hard, and I see moonlight glinting off the tears I don't think he's aware he's shedding. "She made me promise I wouldn't be alone. *'Swear to me, James,'* she said. *'You're not built to be alone. Find someone.'*" Tears flow. He doesn't wipe them away. "Find someone. And I promised her." He tips his head backward. "I found someone, but now I don't know how to—how to do it."

"James—"

"I've been seeing a therapist. Dr. Richard. He makes me talk about things. Talk, talk, talk. How I felt inadequate, sometimes. Like I wasn't a good enough husband or father. How I loved Renée, but some-times—sometimes I *did* think about what she would look like with...*more*. You know? I wouldn't have ever wanted her to change. I loved her as she was—I fucking loved her. *Loved* her—loved the actual shit out of that woman. And I felt guilty about that—about sometimes thinking about what she would look like with bigger tits, more of an ass. And I'd be like, I'm such a fucking asshole. Because I didn't care. I really didn't. Not just didn't care—I loved the way she was built. I loved her tiny tits and boy hips and her bony little butt. And then *you* came along. And you're like, a wet dream come true, and all that guilt, plus so much more guilt on top. All the guilt. And Doc Rich says I have to forgive me—I have to forgive myself. I loved her, he said. I loved her, and I lost her and I'm here and she's not, and I'm allowed to love again. Loving again doesn't mean I never loved her. It doesn't mean I'm replacing her. Forgetting her. But it feels like it."

My throat is so tight. Hot and thick, filled with a lump I can't swallow. I don't know what I'd say even if I could talk right now.

He shakes his head, scrubs at his face with the back of his wrist. "Dammit. Crying like a little bitch. But I don't care." He looks at me with a tear-tracked face. "Do you care?"

"That you're crying?" I wipe at his face with my fingertips, so gently, so carefully. "No, James. I don't care."

He nods, captures my wrist and peers at my fingertips, glistening with his tears. "Weeks of therapy. Months. Three times a week, talking it all out. Hoping for some…some…" He shakes his head. "What's the word, for when you suddenly realize something life-changing?"

"Epiphany," I say.

He nods. "That. Ephi-f…epip—fuck. E*piph*any. There you go." He sighs. "I thought I'd have one of those. But I haven't."

"No?"

He shakes his head. Holds up his left hand again and stares at the ring on his finger. "That ring. She put it on my finger more than twenty years ago." He swallows hard. "She died on our anniversary."

I choke. "You're fucking kidding me."

He shakes his head sloppily. "Nope."

"Holy hell, James. No wonder this weekend is hard for you."

"She was gonna have our baby on our anniversary. I was excited about that. Thought of all the presents I'd buy every year, a birthday and our anniversary on the same day? So many presents. And then she died, and our little baby boy died with her, and our anniversary became the anniversary of the day she died and the day our baby died. Too much on one day. And usually I spend it alone with Jesse. We drink a little and talk about Renée and get sad and that's it. Today? I couldn't do that. There's more than sad inside me, and I've been keeping it bottled up, Doc Rich says. I've got to let it out, he says."

"He's right, you do."

"You're the punching bag," he murmurs. "I'm sorry."

"Don't be. I'm strong. I'm tough. I can take it."

"Shouldn't have to."

"Let it out, James."

He shakes his head again, and a weird look crosses his face. "Whoa. Maybe—oh god. I haven't puked from drinking since I was fourteen." He grabs the bucket, gags, and then pukes into it, again and again and again, and I rub his back until he's done. "Jesus."

"Feel better?" I ask.

He nods, wiping his mouth. "Yeah. A bit." He shakes his head. "God, that fucking sucks."

I hand him another bottle of water. "Drink. Rinse and spit and then drink."

He does so, and then sighs. "I'm still really drunk."

"Puking it up will help, but you're gonna be hammered for a long time."

"Benny." He mutters this, his eyes closed, head resting back against the cabinet. "Our boy. We were gonna name him Benny. After Benny Goodman. Renée was a big band freak. Loved that shit."

"It's not just about her, is it?" I say.

He shakes his head. "It's about him, too." He squeezes his eyes closed. "I held him. He was stillborn. So tiny." He holds out his cupped hands. "This big."

I crack. "God, James. I'm so, so sorry."

He's quiet a long, long time. "I think about you constantly," he says, eventually.

"I think about you, too," I whisper.

"I didn't know I was going to end up here." He's tilting sideways, sliding toward me.

"James?"

He slumps. His head hits my shoulder, and his weight drags him further downward. His face scrapes down my chest, smashes against my breast, and then he lands in my lap on my bare thighs.

"James?"

He groans. "Sleepy."

"Should I be worried about you?"

He grunts a negative. "I'm indestructible. Wish I wasn't. I'll wake up and remember everything."

"Let's get you up."

He grunts a negative, but then makes a valiant effort to get upright. I scramble to get my feet under me, crouching with my shoulders under him, and use all the power in my thighs and core to leverage him up to his feet.

"You're a fucking beast, Nova," he says.

"Well, I've been powerlifting since college," I say. "Gotta be good for something."

"It's fuckin' hot," he mumbles. "Everything about you is hot."

I laugh. "You're just drunk."

"Yeah. But that doesn't make you not drunk. I mean, hot. It doesn't make you not hot." He opens one eye and peers at me. "I mean it. You're so fucking beautiful."

I half carry him out of the kitchen—a single

glance at my couch tells me he'll never fit there. The only option is my bed—I have the extra bedroom, but I use it as storage. So that's where I take him—to my room, staggering under his weight. I get him onto my bed. Untie his muddy boots and haul them off. And holy shit, his socks stink—those go too, and both socks and boots get tossed out into the hallway. I undo his jeans and tug them off, trying to avoid getting dried mud on my bed. He's a deadweight, but he's mumbling under his breath, so I know he's not passed out yet. Once his jeans and boots are off, I take them out of my room and toss the boots outside and the socks and jeans into the washer with a load of my clothes that have been sitting there since last night. When I go back into my room, James is more fully on the bed, on his back, his left hand across his chest. He's still mumbling.

I get his legs under the blanket, and then realize he will probably need the bucket again. I dump the contents of the bucket—straight booze, it smells like—down the toilet, then go outside and rinse the bucket with the garden hose. I bring it back inside and set it on the floor next to him. Then I give him a couple of extra-strength Tylenol with more water which he swallows clumsily, half asleep.

I'm trying to be nurse-like about this—he's in nothing but a pair of tight black boxer-briefs, which do nothing to hide how massive he is, even limp. His chest is so big—his arms, his shoulders…he's just a powerhouse of virile, masculine strength, and I'm valiantly searching for a nurse's objectivity, but it eludes me. This is too personal, too real—taking care of a drunk James caught up in the grip of his tragedy.

I think for maybe ten seconds about sleeping on the couch. Then I climb into my bed, on the right side. My side. He's on the left. Still mumbling incoherently.

I watch him, wondering if I should try to get him on his back. He blinks his eyes open. His left hand lifts, hovers in the air over his face.

He touches his ring, the golden wedding band on his ring finger. Wiggles it. Twists it.

His head flops to one side, and he looks at me. Drunk, but lucid.

A heavy sigh. "Renée…"

Hot, sharp agony slices through me. "James, it's me. It's Nova."

He shakes his head. "No—I…I know." He twists his head to stare at his hand again. Then, in a slow, careful, deliberate movement, he removes the ring from his hand. "I'm saying goodbye."

"Goodbye?" I whisper.

He nods. "Goodbye." His hand flops out in a sudden motion, and then he sets the ring down, very, very carefully, on the bedside table. "I'm saying goodbye to Renée."

The hot sharp pain increases, then, rather than decreasing. "James…"

"The epiphany." He sucks in a deep breath, lets it out slowly. "I had the epiphany."

"You did? When?"

"Just now." He wipes at his cheeks again. "I can't keep holding on. It'll kill me. And I…I have to survive, for Nina and Ella."

"Yeah, you do."

"I'm not letting go for you, Nova." His voice is faint, fading, but lucid and coherent. "I'm letting go for me. For them."

The hot sharp pain in my chest, in my belly goes hotter and sharper. "I know, James."

"I want to live."

"Good, James. I'm glad."

He looks at me. "I didn't always."

"I know. I've been there." I lift my wrist: I've worn the plastic hospital bracelet for so long I've all but forgotten about it.

Until now.

I stare at it. Tears swim in my eyes as I reach up, hook a finger in the plastic where it's fastened together and tug, once, sharply. The plastic snaps, and I feel a tear on my cheek as I set the bracelet on the bedside table next to James's wedding ring.

"I want to…" His eyes fix on mine, sharper than ever—sharper even than when he's sober. "I want to do more than just live, Nova."

I try to breathe and fail. "James, I—I don't know what to say."

"It's not all better. It's not magic like that. I just…" He fades, momentarily passing out, and then jerking awake again. "I promised her. The girls…for them. I have to…for them. They need me to be more than just making it. Holding on to fading memories."

"You'll always remember her, James."

He nods, a mushy, sleepy movement. "I know."

"It can't be about me."

"It's not." He fades again, for longer. "But it is. It *is* about you. Not *for* you, not *because* of you. But you're part of it."

A long, long, long pause.

"Goodbye, Renée. I love you."

Another, longer pause.

"Nova?"

"Yeah?"

"Just…" A quiet breath.

Nothing—silence.

His breathing evening out, slowing, deepening.

It took me a lot longer to fall asleep.

TWELVE

No matter what time I go to bed, or how little sleep I get, I wake up around five in the morning. But tonight, I'd been woken up half an hour before I usually get up, so when I finally did get back to sleep, I fell into a deep, hard sleep.

I don't wake up again until many hours later. And when I do wake up, I'm disoriented, which is typical. But this morning it's a new type of disorientation.

Something is off. Different. But what?

I'm not ready to open my eyes yet. I try to go back to sleep, but I know it's futile.

I groan, stretch, and that's when awareness jolts through me like a lightning bolt to the skull. I'm not alone in my bed.

James.

We're not just platonically sharing a bed.

My head is on his bare chest. My hand is wrapped around his shoulder and neck. His arm is curled around me, sheltering me, enveloping me in a warm cocoon of strength and safety. His hand rests with casual possessiveness on my hip. His breath huffs hot on me.

I panic.

I'm totally frozen; I can't breathe. How did this happen? How am I *cuddling* with James right now? When I fell asleep, he was on his back on the edge of the bed, and I was on the other side, rolled to face away from him. Yet now, here I am, wrapped up in his arms.

And feeling more content and more safe and sheltered and just...*happy*...than I've ever felt in my life. Just waking up in his arms.

Tears prick my eyes and I have to force myself to breathe. Breathe in, breathe out. Calm. The panic recedes a little, and the pricking heat of pooling tears abates. I focus on the moment. This doesn't have to mean anything, right? It was an accident of habit— we've both had long-term relationships where the habitual norm when sleeping was to seek comfort in the arms of the other person. James especially—he spent twenty years with a woman, and those habits die hard. If he, even unconscious and passed out drunk, is in bed with a woman, his subconscious is going to take over, bring me into his arms.

And if I'm being honest with myself, a huge part of my unhappiness and loneliness is sleeping alone. I

HATE sleeping alone.

Breathe in, breathe out. Be in the moment. Don't panic.

This does feel really nice. He's so huge, so strong—and speaking as a six-foot-tall woman, and one with the physique of a powerlifter at that, feeling delicate and protected and sheltered has not typically been something I'm familiar with. The majority of men simply cannot, through no fault of their own, make me feel that way. James is simply so big and so strong that I feel...utterly feminine. It's nice, quite honestly.

His hand on my hip feels good. Warm, powerful. Rough calluses from a life of manual labor, but his touch is gentle. Just resting on my hip, cupped and lax.

He snores softly, a hoarse breath deep in his throat. Snorts. Shifts restlessly, makes a small, boyish sound as he seeks a more comfortable position. James rolls into me, and, without a conscious thought, I roll with him; just like that, we're spooning. He's behind me, now. A huge hot hard wall of man behind me, wrapped around me. His hand slides down my thigh, rests near my knee. Pauses, and slides back up to wrap around my belly, high, just under my breasts. His nose brushes my spine, and I feel his hips pressing against my butt.

So much of him—all James, all around me.

I'm not aroused, which is somewhat odd considering he's pressed against my butt and his hand is inches from my boobs—I'm just comfortable. I feel safe. I feel sheltered, and that gives me a sense of…god, what? A kind of bone-deep, gut-twisting, chest-cracking kind of joy that's too much, too big, too expansive to contain.

I feel sleepy again.

I peer at the alarm clock on my bedside table—9 a.m. Jesse and Franco told me they had a deck build they were doing today, so they probably won't be here at all today, which means I can go back to sleep without worrying about them walking in and seeing this.

Not that I'm ashamed, or feel like this needs to be a secret. It's just…

I don't know. James was wasted last night, and even though it seemed like he was letting go of things so we could be together, he may feel differently in the light of day, and sober.

So, for now, I'm just going to go back to sleep and enjoy, for as long as it lasts, the comfort of having James's arms around me.

If nothing else happens between us, at least I'll have had this—this feeling is something I'll treasure.

I fall back asleep with my hand over James's, trying desperately to keep at least a tiny shred of objectivity.

THIRTEEN

I WAKE UP AGAIN, AND I'M ALONE IN THE BED. JAMES probably got up and left. Maybe he regretted coming here—or he remembered everything he said and needs time to process it. Who knows? Either way, he's not here and I knew that was coming.

I have to pee.

I slip out of bed, groggy and still half asleep, my brain, body, and heart all working at different speeds and on different conundrums: my brain is trying to wake up, my body says I've been ignoring my bladder for hours, and my heart is trying to come to grips with James leaving.

When I'm half asleep, my brain doesn't really process what's going on around me. I don't notice things right away. I've been known to sleepwalk, and to have entire conversations that I don't remember.

So, when I get up out of bed and trudge to the nearest bathroom—the one that's going to become my *en suite* master bathroom—I'm half asleep and not paying attention to anything except relieving my screaming bladder. I shove down my underwear, sit, and pee for a very, very long time, sighing in relief. And my boobs itch, so I reach up and give them a good rub and scratch, lifting my shirt to get at them more easily.

I finish up, wash my hands...

And that's when I realize something is...not quite right.

I blink, and realize the bathroom is filled with steam.

Steam?

Uh-oh.

I twist in place, and there's James. My shower curtain is see-through, so he's on display.

Standing with wet hair plastered back against his scalp, covered in shampoo, beard straggly and dripping. Big chest swelling and receding as he sucks in slow breaths. Cock hanging against his thigh—and growing, it looks like, as he stares at me.

His big brown eyes are wide.

"Um." I blink at him. "Hi."

He just stares. "Hi."

"I, um. I tend to not notice obvious things when I'm out of it." I can't stop staring at him. "Like someone in my shower, for example."

He nods, like he's as unsure how to handle this scenario as I am. "I see." He pauses. "I woke up feeling like shit. So I made coffee and figured I'd jump in the shower. Thought I'd be done before you woke up. Sorry."

I shrug, my eyes raking over him—taking in all of James, naked and wet and in my shower. "It's okay."

"It's okay?" he asks.

I shrug again. I'm staring—as I watch his cock go from hanging mostly limp to standing rigid against his belly. "Yeah. It's okay."

"I'm sorry about last night," he says. "I was a fuckin' mess."

I shake my head. "Don't be sorry. I'm not." I meet his eyes. "Unless it was just the booze talking."

He doesn't answer for a moment, his eyes fixed on mine, intense and unreadable. And then, abruptly, it's like a curtain falls, and I can see a wealth of emotion in him:

Uncertainty. Fear. Embarrassment. Desire.

He shakes his head slowly. "No. It wasn't the booze talking." He lifts a shoulder in a half shrug. "I mean...the booze got me talking, but it wasn't *just* the booze."

"You remember it all?"

He nods. "I don't black out. I remember every word." His heavy shoulders lift with a deep breath, and then lower as he lets it out slowly through his teeth. "I meant every word."

Silence, except for the hiss of the shower.

I swallow hard. "James..." I close my eyes, take a shuddery breath. "I'm afraid to want too much too soon."

"I know." His eyes flick down to my breasts, to my nipples poking against the thin fabric of my T-shirt, then back to my eyes. "Was I dreaming, or did we...um...cuddle, this morning?" His cheeks go pink, as if he's embarrassed to use a word like *cuddle*.

I can't help a smile from stealing across my lips. "We did."

He nods. "I'm glad that wasn't just a dream."

"Me too," I whisper.

He's enormously erect, thick and hard, his balls tight against his body, the tip of his cock straining near his belly button. I can't stop looking at it—wanting it. Needing it. Needing James, needing more than we've had so far. Needing to know how it feels to...to be *his*. For him to be mine.

But I'm scared to want that. Scared to reach for—for an *us* that I'm not sure he's capable of giving me.

"Nova..." He clenches his fists, then shakes them out. His eyes close, and then open—the way I do when I'm summoning my courage. "I want..."

I'm not breathing. "What, James?"

"You."

"I want you too, but…" I force the hardest truth out. "But not unless you're all in. Not unless you can give me all of you."

He pushes aside the shower curtain now, so there's nothing between us but steam. "There's a part of me that'll always be…a little broken. Time heals all wounds, but some wounds never heal, not totally."

"I know that. Same for me, but—"

"I can only offer you…me." He wipes water off his face, off his beard. "I'm all in, Nova. If you can accept that I'm…damaged, I guess, then…"

I huff a gentle laugh. "James…" I shake my head. "All of us are damaged. I know you can't give me the part of you that belonged to Renée—I wouldn't want you to try. That's part of you, James." I swallow a massive lump in my throat. "That's part of what I've been falling in love with—you. Just…*you*. All of you. The fact that you understand where I've been more deeply than anyone else ever could…the fact that you've come through what you have, that you're here for your girls."

"I said it last night—I want more than to just to be here. I want more than to just live." He holds up his hands, drops them. "I want that with you, Nova. I've been fighting it, fighting wanting it. Fighting the guilt over everything."

"I can't fight your guilt, James. Nor can I compete with a ghost. I won't try."

He shakes his head. "She's not a ghost, Nova. She's my past. She's there; she'll always be there, but…" A shrug. "I know I was drunk last night, but when I said goodbye to her, I meant it. I hate that I had to get so messed up to be able to say that, to do that, but it was real."

"What about the guilt?"

"It may not go away immediately. Something like that doesn't just vanish. But can you stick with me while I work through it?"

I take a couple of steps forward. Water droplets from the shower spatter against my T-shirt, my face. "What are you saying, James?"

"I'm saying I'm in love with you, and I want *us*. I want this."

"All in?" I ask, my voice a whisper.

"All in," he whispers back.

He reaches for me, picks me up by the waist and lifts me into the shower. Closes the curtain. His back is to the spray, shielding me from most of it, but I'm still getting wet. I don't care. My shirt sticks to my skin, outlining my breasts, my hardened nipples.

I can't help the smile that steals across my face, and I don't try. I want him, but I'm not going to make the first move. Let him show me how he feels, what he wants. I'll follow his lead.

His move is to kiss me. James takes my face in his hands, cups my cheeks. Pulls me close, his eyes intense and wild. His nose angles past mine, and then my eyes close and his lips slant against mine, and I taste him—he tastes clean.

"I found a new toothbrush under your sink," he murmurs, his lips brushing mine. "Hope that's okay."

I smile. "More than okay. Everything is yours. All of me, all I am."

He pulls away, frowning in puzzlement. "How can you say that? How can you just…offer me yourself, just like that?"

"I can't help it, James. That's why I've been so cautious. I've been holding back, trying to keep my heart at least a little objective, but it's futile. I fell for you, hard. If you tell me you're all in, then I can let go. And that means…" I shrug. "It means…here I am, James."

He reaches down and peels my sopping wet T-shirt up and off, drapes it over the shower rod. His eyes stay on mine, even though I'm topless and bare for him. Still staring into my eyes, he tugs my underwear down, pushes them past my hips. They reach my knees, and I wiggle, squirm, and they plop around my feet.

He twists, and places me under the spray—it's

hot, and I gasp at the sudden heat of it, but then melt a little under the warmth. I let my hair get wet, close my eyes and luxuriate for a moment in the stream of hot water. I feel him closing in, but I keep my eyes closed, rake my hands through now heavy wet hair, and let the water stream down my body.

His hands close around my hips. I feel his mouth on my diaphragm. His lips stutter across my skin, skating down my left side, and then over my ribcage, to my right hip. I reach out, eyes closed, and find his head, wet hair and beard.

When I open my eyes, he's kneeling in front of me. Staring up at me. Gazing, his expression open and adoring. Like all the heaviness has faded, like all there is, in this moment at least, are he and I.

"James…" I breathe.

He palms my breasts in his two huge hands, lifting them, caressing. Then he lets them drop heavily, bouncing and swaying, dripping water. Then his thumbs trace over my hip bones, and his palms arc over my thighs. He leans in, and his lips touch my belly just under my navel.

It's a request, an unspoken request for permission to go south.

God, he doesn't need permission.

I laugh, and spread my feet as wide apart as the tub will allow. I stare down at him and wait.

His grin is hungry, and I swallow hard as he closes in, eyes on mine as he brings his mouth to my core. I cup the back of his head with my hands and pull him closer, and I bite my lip and sigh as he flicks his tongue against me.

"James, please…" I whisper. "I need…so much."

"What do you need, Nova?" he murmurs.

"You." I shake my head, letting out a harsh breath as I tug him upward. "I need you."

He stands up, leans in, and kisses me again. And this time, it's not just a momentary kiss, not just a fleeting touching of lips, a taste of him. It's us—losing ourselves. I press up against him, wet skin against wet skin. His erection presses against my thigh and belly, and my breasts crush against his chest. I roam his broad shoulders with my hands and scour his bulging biceps and taste his hungry mouth. I arch my back and moan as he caresses my ass, and I pull away so there's room between us; I grip his length in my fists and whimper at the enormity of him. It takes an eternity for my hands to slide all the way down from tip to root, and another eternity to caress back upward. He groans, and I feel a finger at my core, teasing my clit.

James is the one to pull away.

"Why—" I have to pause for breath, to summon words. "Why'd you stop?"

He reaches past me and turns off the water.

Shoves the shower curtain open, steps out past me without answering my question. There's a clean towel on the rack, and he yanks it free, reaches for me. His touch is gentle as he pats me dry, runs the towel over my hair—which is cute and endearing, but he clearly has no clue how long it takes to dry hair as long and thick as mine. I don't even care, though—not when he uses the towel to scrub himself mostly dry, and then reaches for me.

I take his hand, and he leads me out of the bathroom and into my bedroom. Closes the door. He turns to face me, still holding my hand.

"This is more than messing around in the shower," he says. "No more messing around."

I swallow hard. Step toward him; stare up into his deep brown eyes. "No more messing around."

He steps close to me. We're pressed up against each other—breasts to chest, cock to core. But still, a hesitation. Him? Me? Both of us. We're both hesitant to move past this into...making it real, making it permanent. Even though we both physically want this, it's an emotional decision.

James steps back, raking his hand through his wet hair. "I want you so fucking much, Nova."

"I want you too, James."

"I want this to happen...but I want it to be right. It should be a choice, something that we do together, not just something that happens because we're both here and horny."

I groan. "You're right. I know you're right." I laugh, a bitter, resigned sound. "I want it to be right too, but...*fuck*, James. I *want* you."

He chuckles, gestures downward at the straining evidence of his need. "I definitely get it, Nova."

I clench my hands into fists to keep from reaching for him. "My self-control is...not great right now, James." I drop my eyes to the floor. "I want you, and part of me doesn't care about...god, anything except getting my hands on you." I lift my eyes to his. "Getting my mouth on you. Getting you inside me."

"I'm guessing you don't have any condoms."

I groan a sigh. "No."

He turns away, and he's just as drool-worthy from the back as he is the front. That ass of his—tight as a drum and round and hard and I want to sink my teeth into it, get my hands on it.

God, I'm out of control with desire.

"I'm just trying to do right by us, Nova," James murmurs.

His broad shoulders droop with the weight of this, of shouldering the burden of us.

He's right. Messing around, fooling around, knowing we won't be able to go as far as we want—at least not safely and responsibly...that would be just torturing ourselves.

But I just…gahhh! I've been dreaming of him. I woke up in his arms. I finally have him naked, have him in my home, naked in my bedroom, hard as a rock and begging to be touched.

How can I resist him? How the hell am I supposed to let him put clothes on and walk away from me? I can't.

He braces his palms against my door, head hanging between his shoulders—the war he is waging with himself is obvious in his tortured posture.

"I fuckin' *need* you, Nova," he growls.

I feel myself moving, stepping silently across the room. I stand behind him, hesitating.

"James." I hear myself whisper.

He shakes his head. "We're not clueless kids, Nova."

"I have been careful and responsible my whole fucking life, James," I say. "Even when I was experimenting in nursing school, I kept my heart and my head out of it—it was purely physical. It was nothing but an attempt to bury the way I was feeling—heartbroken and alone."

"That's how I've felt for six years—heartbroken and alone."

I move a little closer, and now I can touch him, but I don't. Not yet. "After that, I did nothing but work.

There's been nothing and no one. Barely even myself, if you want the truth. It was easier to just bury my sexuality than to try to relieve myself, because I only ever ended up feeling more lonely and pathetic."

He nods heavily. "Believe me, I know."

I sigh. "I'm tired of it, James." I watch his broad back heave with his conflicted breath. "I was always careful. Responsible. Even experimenting was a calculated thing. I kind of…I don't know how to put it. I kind of watched myself go through that experimental, promiscuous phase with a mental and emotional detachment. It was never spontaneous. I never let it get beyond my control. It was never passionate, or wild."

He's still—very, very still. "What are you saying, Nova?"

I take another shuffled step closer to him, and now our bodies are so close to touching I can almost feel him—a spark of electricity crackling between us even though we're not actually in contact.

"I can't hold back, James. I don't have any more control. I want more than to be smart and responsible and careful and rational."

I give in. Lean up against him, press my body all along his, lying against his spine. My breasts rest against his back, and I press my core against his buttocks. Resting my cheek on his shoulder blade. I let my arms wrap around him. It's a hug at first, just wrapping him up, holding him. Then I stop trying to hold in my neediness. I let my hands do what they want, go where they want. They dance and trace over his chest, down his abs. Lower and lower.

"Nova…"

I kiss his spine, his shoulder blades. Press up hard against him. Crush my boobs against him. Rub my core against him. "I don't care if it's stupid or irrational, or impetuous. I just want you, James. Right now. However it happens, however I can get you."

I carve my palm down his belly and take him in my hand, stroke his length greedily. He groans, a long low pained sound. He arches his back, head hanging. Moans raggedly, as if my touch is more than he can handle. I palm his buttocks with my other hand, loving the feel of it, caressing and tracing. Then, finally, I use both hands on his erection, slowly exploring his length with twisting plunging strokes of my fists.

"Fuck, Nova," he breathes. "What are you doing to me?"

I kiss his spine again. "I don't even know, James. I just know I can't help it, and don't want to. All I want is us…just us. That's all that matters."

He groans again, hips pushing forward into my touch. "I…oh god, Nova. I'm not gonna last long at this rate."

"I don't care, James. Come—come right now. Come all over my hands. Make a mess, I don't fucking care. I just want us. I don't care if you need time to get hard again. I don't care what happens, I just need you. I need to touch you. I'm done waiting."

He groans, thrusts into my hand.

And then, with shocking suddenness, he wrenches out of my grip, twists in place, and I'm airborne. Lifted, and his mouth is on mine, his lips slamming roughly against mine, and I wrap my legs around his waist and feel his hands clutching my ass. He kisses me, and none of the kisses we've shared can hold a candle to this one.

It's absolutely feral, ravenous. Demanding. His tongue slashes into my mouth and his lips claim mine—it's a kiss that says I've crossed the line—there's no going back from this. Whatever restraint he may have had is gone, and now he's taking what's his—

Me.

My soul soars, my heart flips; my stomach drops out, my voice rises in a long whimper of relief.

He has me, utterly—I'm held up by him, all of me depending on his strength. He has me utterly—whatever he does, next, I want. If he only kisses me, I want that. If he takes me, here and now, I want that. Anything in between, I want.

He pivots and slams my back up against my

door, and I cling to him, fusing my mouth to his. I'm wrapped around him like a koala around a tree: he lifts me higher. I pull my hips back, away from him. Cling to him with one arm and both legs, reaching a hand between us. His hands are on my thighs, lifting me, spreading me open. God, yes. I grasp his cock and nestle the fat, bulbous head to my opening, and he gasps and I groan.

"James," I whisper, my voice ragged and lost.

He flexes his hips, and I whimper as he nudges into me. "Nova. I fucking—I need you. I can't—I need you."

I'm clinging to him, arms around his neck now, holding myself up, his hands on my buttocks clawed tight. I bite his lower lip, and he grunts.

I want to say a billion things, but I have no words. The only response left to me is a physical one: I let go of his neck, let my weight sag. I let go, and he fills me. He growls, a primal sound ripping from his throat, and I cry out, a shrill wail as I am split open and filled in a way I never knew was possible.

"Oh *fuck*, Nova," he breathes.

"James—" I whimper. "James. James."

He slides an arm under my ass to support me, and with the other he cups my cheek—our eyes meet, mine shaky and tear hazed, his wild and tender at once. Deep inside me, he kisses me.

A gentle kiss, at odds with the fact that I'm pinned to the door by his throbbing cock.

A loving kiss, slow and tender and searching.

I have to hold on to him, clutching his neck with my arms and his waist with my legs.

Then, he can't kiss me any longer, because he's out of breath and beyond control. He moves—pushes, thrusts. His thrust is powerful, slow, measured. He drives into me, and I realize that as full of him as I am, I didn't have all of him inside me. He thrusts, and I take more and more and more of him, so much it's impossible, and with each inch I take, the more breathless I become.

So…fucking…*much*.

I don't need to breathe—I clash my mouth against his and sip his breath, a ragged whimper escaping once I have enough oxygen in my lungs.

His hands cup my ass, lift me, pull the cheeks apart as he lifts—and I help, tightening my thighs around him and pushing up with arms and legs, driving him out of me. As if I am weightless, he lifts me, his hips pulling down and back to draw himself out of me, and now our eyes meet, gazes locking in the moment of hesitation, right before the next movement.

"Nova…" He nips at my lip, holding the moment, keeping me up, waiting to push in. "I—I can't be gentle."

I shake my head, dragging words out of my belly. "Please—James. Oh god, please…" I dig my fingers into the ropy cords of muscle along the ridge of his shoulders. I claw at him. "Don't be."

"I don't want to—to hurt you, or scare you." He's speaking through gritted teeth. "I just…I can't—"

I grasp his jaw in fingers shaking with need, gripping *hard*. "Do I seem delicate to you, James?" I breathe, writhing against him.

"No," he gasps, the word a short sharp sound. "No."

"I'm not."

He rolls his hips in a shallow movement, and I whimper at the teasing glide, the too-little thrust of him inside me. "You make me fuckin' crazy, Nova."

"Then give me the crazy," I say. "Stop talking and show me."

He keeps his eyes on mine, hesitating another half second more, and then he drives into me. His hips crash against mine and his cock slams into me, thrusting fully into me.

I can't help but scream, and it's a scream of pleasure like I've never known—pleasure isn't even close to the right word, but there are no other words to encapsulate how I feel in this moment.

He's bare inside me, and I can feel every massive inch of him, splitting me open and pushed so deep.

I have no idea how I'm taking all of him, but I am, and it's absolute bliss, pure heaven. Almost painful, but not quite. A burn, an ache as I stretch around him, pulsing and hot. I reach down between us and trace where we're joined, gasping and whimpering at the hugeness of him inside me. He's plunged so deep inside me there's no further he can go, but there's still more of him. I can almost wrap my hand around his cock at the base, and he's fully inside me.

I almost laugh at the absurdity of it, but then he starts moving, and I can't breathe all over again. All I can do is take him, cling to him, hold on as he draws back and thrusts in. The movement makes me shudder, shake. He groans, head hanging now.

"Nova," he snarls. "Fucking hell, Nova."

I bury my face against him, my lips at his throat. I nibble, and then bite. "Ohhhh god. Oh god—James." That's all the coherency I can muster.

"Is it okay? Are you okay?" So much concern. As if he doesn't realize I need more. So much more.

I nod jerkily, and writhe on him as best I can— but he has me in his control, his hands on my buttocks holding me up. "Yes!" I gasp. "More. More."

He lifts, pulls out of me, and thrusts in while lowering me—he does it slowly, carefully. Gently. "Like that?"

I nod, and kiss his throat, nip at his shoulder,

and then bury my fingers in his beard and try to kiss him with a shuddery mouth as he repeats—lift and pull back, lower and push in. I can't sustain the kiss, because I'm too shaken by what he's doing to me. Keeping my lungs working takes all I have.

I cling to him and whimper.

I try to work with him, move with him. He does his lift and lower routine again, and I find a rhythm in it, move my hips to the rhythm, clinging to his neck with desperate strength, burying my face in his chest, and gasping and nipping until I'm sure he's going to have hickeys and bruises, but I have to find a way to show him that I want more when I can't speak.

I'm too full of him to speak. I ache with such delicious fullness. Throb with it. My clit pulsates, and each time he thrusts in his shaft stutters against it, and I shake with it, shudder with it, toppling toward the edge of a world-ending orgasm.

"Kiss me," James orders, a grunted command.

I kiss him. God, do I kiss him.

Until I can't function or breathe or do anything but shudder as he glides in, slowly, slowly. And then, once I've come down momentarily from the dizziness of accommodating his size inside me, I kiss him again, sipping and nipping at his mouth, nibbling his lower lip, tasting his tongue. When he pushes in once more, I dissolve into shuddering whimpers, writhing helplessly around him.

He pulls his head back to look into my eyes, assessing me. Still so worried—worried he's hurting me. "Say something dammit," he snarls. "I need you to say *something*."

I writhe on him, locking eyes, and claw my fingers into his shoulders and clamp my thighs around him with all my strength. Showing him how strong I am.

I have one word for him. *"More,"* I breathe.

He laughs, disbelieving. A thrust, this time his hands just hold me in place, spreading me open for him as he drives in, not slowly but still with a measured pace. "Like that?"

I shake my head. "No, god—James...please." I find an angle, find leverage, hold on and lift up and sink down around him, whimpering through clenched teeth as I take him and move harder and faster, slamming my hips down hard to take him and take him and take him, showing him how I want him. "Like that."

He snarls, and we're animals together, lost in this primal connection. He matches me, meets me and now I feel him letting go. Feel the wild abandon in the way he claws at my ass to lift me and lets go so I crash down with a slap of meeting bodies.

He staggers in a circle, finds the bed. Drops

forward. I'm on my back now and I don't let go with any part of me. He buries his face in my breasts, and I press my elbows together so my breasts mound up around his face. His hips move in gentle circles, and then he pulls his face out of my cleavage and his mouth finds mine and his tongue slashes and our lips tangle, and we find each other in mutual groaning ragged cries of delirious perfection.

"Nova?" he breathes. "I—ohh god, oh god, fuck—Nova, I can't stop."

I nip at his earlobe. "Why the hell would you stop?"

"We're bare."

I groan. "Fuck!"

"Yeah."

He's still moving, and I'm still caught in the rapture of need. But awareness filters through—I stopped taking any kind of birth control a long time ago—when I knew I wasn't going to be having sex with anyone, I saw no reason to take it.

We have to stop.

I whimper. "James. God, how do we stop? How do we stop?"

"I'm not taking that risk," he murmurs. "We're not covered, are we?"

I shake my head. "No. I'm not on anything."

"*Fuck*," he growls, the word a growled curse

under his breath.

Then, with a violent wrench, he rolls off me, off the bed, and staggers away from me. Struggle is etched in every line of his body. I'm shaky—I was seconds from coming.

So was he.

I can't let it end like this. I get off the bed, my legs not working properly. All I know is I need him, I can't let it be over like that, unsatisfied, in agony, doing the right thing for both of us when I can't even remember my own name.

I push at his shoulder, and he turns, his expression fraught.

"If I so much as look at you, Nova…" he threatens. "You so much as look at me the wrong way, I'll explode."

I have no idea what to do, how to fix this. "James, I…"

He shakes his head. "It's fine. I'm fine. Just…just give me a second."

He's aching, straining. Taut and glistening with my essence. Heavy and thick and leaking.

I drop to my knees, and he shakes his head. "No, Nova. No."

"I want to." I gaze up at him, my hands on his quads. "I'm going to, because I want to."

He shakes his head. "Nova…" I take him in my

hands, and he grunts, tensing. "I'm fuckin' serious, Nova. Don't. I'm fine."

"I'm not fine," I say, and I stroke him. "It's not about that. I know you'd be fine. That's not the point."

He grunts again as I flick my tongue against the tip of him. "Then what's—ohhh *fuck*—then what is the point?"

I grin up at him. "That I want you."

"I want you too. I just want to come *with* you."

I laugh, teasing him with another flick of my tongue up the underside of him. "You will."

"Nova…" he breathes. "Oh god. You don't have to do this."

"I know." I lick him again. I love the taste of him. It's been so, *so* long since I've done this, and I'm glad, because it feels kind of like the first time all over again. New and daring and nerve-racking and exciting. "I want to."

"Why?"

I take him in my mouth and suck around him and he whimpers, a surprisingly small, gentle sound for such a huge, primal man. I don't need to answer that with words. All I need to do is show him. So I do.

He buries his hands in my hair, which is wet and heavy. He holds it in his fists and stares down at me, watching as I wrap my lips around him and slide my mouth down around his cock, lower and lower until

I can't take any more and then back away. He grunts, holding utterly still. I let him fall out of my mouth and lick the tip again, and James flinches.

"Fuck, fuck, fuck, Nova." His hips flex, and I know he's close. He was close before, but now he's holding back. Good—let him try.

I clutch his cock with one hand around the base and cup the other around his heavy sac and massage them, and taste him on my tongue and lick and suck until he's gasping and moving helplessly.

He sighs, tenses, thrusts into my mouth, and I taste him first, and then he floods my mouth with a loud growl and grunt. I stroke him hard and fast and suck and swallow as he spurts and gasps and comes and whimpers, each thrust more helpless than the last.

Finally, he's done, and I'm grinning at the way he staggers backward, catching heavily up against the wall.

"Jesus, Nova."

I stay there, staring up at him, loving how absolutely floored he is, how utterly wrecked. "Hi."

He shakes his head. "Good fucking god, woman."

I grin, pleased with myself and anticipating his response. "You okay?"

He shakes his head. "Not by a long shot, baby." His eyes flare. "I can barely fucking stand up."

He moves for me, and I let him lift me to my feet, let him press me backward to my bed. He tosses me onto my back and levers over me.

I expect him to move down my body, but he doesn't. Instead, he just hovers over me, staring at me hard. "I want to just eat you out until you scream."

I lick my lips, tasting him. "I'd be okay with that."

"Not good enough."

I frown. "No?"

"Nope."

I think he's going to...I don't know. Kiss me. Tease me. Hold me.

Instead, James slides off the bed.

I panic a little. "Where are you going?"

I barely remember doing it, but apparently I washed and dried his jeans, so they're in a laundry basket on my bedroom floor. Shoves his feet into them and buttons them. Stomps into his boots without socks. His T-shirt is on the floor. He snags it and shrugs into it. Now, dressed, he smirks at me.

"There's a little drugstore about half a mile from here, right?" he asks.

I nod, somewhat confused. "Yeah—yes."

"Your truck keys are where?"

"My purse," I say. "But where are you going?"

"I'll be right back."

"You're *leaving*?"

He comes to the side of the bed, leans over me, kisses me. "Yep."

"Why?"

"I'm getting condoms." He backs away.

"How long will you be gone?"

"Five minutes, maybe?"

"What am I supposed to do while you're gone?"

He shrugs. "Five minutes, babe."

The amount of panic I feel is kind of ridiculous. But this is just not how I expected this to go. "James, I…" I shake my head; try to clear away the panic. "Don't go."

He perches on the edge of the bed next to me, pulls me onto his lap. Wraps his arms around me. "I need you more than I can say." He holds my face in his hands. "Messing around with you, kissing you… it's not enough. What you just did—Nova, that shit fuckin'…" He growls. "It wrecked me."

"James, I just wanted to—"

He touches my lips. "This whole thing with you and me…nothing about it is normal. I've never felt this way. Never felt this…*need*. You sucking me off…" His eyes flare. "Fucking amazing. Brand new. Never felt that—not in a long damn time at least. And certainly not after…" He pauses, hunts for words. "After being inside you. Feeling you wrapped around me. You were so fuckin' *tight*, Nova."

I feel him thickening behind his jeans. "I've never felt anything like that either."

"You made me feel like…" He growls, irritated at his inability to find the words. "You made me feel like a god, Nova. Being inside you was—it was the best fuckin' thing I've ever felt."

"Me too," I whisper.

"I need it." He palms my cheeks and brings our mouths close, whispers against my lips. "I *need* that. I need to feel you come while I'm inside you. I need to feel you fuckin' lose it while I'm makin' love to you. I need you so goddamn bad it hurts, and as good as it felt to have your hot little mouth on me, it's not enough. Not for what I want—what I need."

"I just didn't want it to end like that," I whisper.

He kisses me, and yet again he proves to me why I've fallen so hard for him—he can kiss me stupid, kiss me until I'm gaga and breathless and helpless and boneless and absolutely stupid.

"It's never gonna end, Nova," he whispers back.

FOURTEEN

I SIT ON THE BED AND WAIT.

Naked, aching from almost coming but not, needing more of James, racked with irrational fear that he won't come back. I sit on my bed and wait. I run through ridiculous scenarios in my head—he gets in a car accident, he changes his mind, a robber holds up the drugstore while James is there and James tries to play the hero and gets killed…each one more stupid than the last.

He's been gone less than five minutes, but I miss him so bad it hurts—an agony in my chest, a need in my gut…in my core. I taste him in my mouth.

I have a thought, and immediately act on it.

I have a lingerie set in my underwear drawer— brand new, still with the tags on. I had an idea of splurging on lingerie in an attempt to make myself feel sexy, but after trying it on, I just felt dumb. What's the point of lingerie if no one but me will see? So

I find the set and tear the tags off. I put it on, and admire myself in the mirror. Expensive pushup bra, see-through white lace, with matching thong panties. All but naked, just covered enough to be sexy, all my assets on display. *Goddamn*, I do look hot.

I go into the bathroom and rip a brush through my hair until it's smooth and tangle free, running a hair dryer over it until it's less damp and my natural curls pop out a little. Not as good as it can look when I spend forty-five minutes drying and brushing and curling, but not bad for two minutes. Then I put on makeup—minimal, just a touch of eyeliner and lipstick to bring out my eyes and make my lips look pouty and red.

I hear my truck in the driveway, and then James's distinctive heavy tread clomping on the back porch. I feel a thrill sizzle through me, feel a renewed jolt of need as I hear James in the kitchen, then in the hall.

I sit on my bed and try to pose without looking like I'm posing. James halts in the doorway, a giant box of magnum condoms in one hand, and a single red rose in the other. My alarm clock says he's been gone seven minutes.

He looks up as he leans against the doorframe, and when he sees me his eyes widen and his jaw drops open. "Holy motherfucking shit, Nova."

I can't help but actually vibrate with excitement

at his presence, and thrill at the awe in his voice. "Hi,"
I murmur.

He tosses the box of condoms onto the bed and
prowls with wolfish, predatory grace toward me,
thick arms swinging at his sides, stretching the sleeves
of his T-shirt, muddy jeans hanging low on his bare
hips, the zipper straining. His eyes are deep and dark
and afire with need.

"Jesus." His voice is ragged, gravelly. "I musta
died and gone to heaven, 'cause you look like a fuckin'
angel, Nova."

I can only smile. I don't know what to say.

He crooks a finger at me. "C'mere, sweet thing."

I stand up and go to him. Rough, strong hands
close around my face, thumbs ever so gently brushing my cheekbones. His warm brown eyes invite
me to see into his soul, to explore the depths of his
heart. His breath comes in hoarse, shallow gulps,
almost grunts, as if restraining his primal need for
me requires all of his reserves of strength. I gaze up
at him, tangle my fingers in his beard and pull him
closer, taste his breath, steal it for my own. His fingers trace and traipse across my shoulders, down the
serpentine column of my spine, exploring each ver-
tebra in turn, dancing with a fiery, sprightly gentility
over my flesh. I keep my fingers in his beard and nip
at his lips, demanding the ravishing kisses I've come

to expect from him—the dizzying, mind-melting, panty-wetting kisses that make me shiver and shudder and whimper...

Oh, yes. There's the kiss, his mouth slanting across mine, his breath hot and his tongue insistent. One huge hand spreads open and carves over my lower back, fingertips grazing centimeters above the lace of my underwear, and his kisses ravage me, leave me gasping into his mouth, whispering his name in awe of the crackling energy coursing between us, the connection he's opening himself to, finally—letting his heart and soul reach out, blossom and seek mine like the fragile shoots of a flower reaching for the bright heat of the sun. I feel him—his soul tangling and wrapping around mine, in this kiss.

"James," I whisper. "Don't make me wait any longer. Please."

His rumble of laughter is quiet and kind and amused and aroused. "Impatient, are you?"

I push at his shirt, slide my hands over his hard muscles. "Yes, James. I am. I've waited and waited for you. Before I knew it was you, I was waiting for you." I get his shirt off, scour his torso with greedy hands. "We've gotten so close. It's like getting a taste of what you want, and not being able to actually have it."

He cups a breast over the bra. "I know, Nova. God, I fuckin' know." A fingertip brushes the lace over my core. "You don't even know how bad I need you."

I gasp at his teasing touch, and reach for his zipper. "I might have an idea," I say, grinning into his kiss.

He hooks a finger into the waistband of my underwear, and I'm eager for them to be gone, to be bare to his touch. "I've been holding on to a razor's edge of control with you, Nova." He tugs them down. "That shit is *gone*, sweetheart."

"Oh good," I whisper. "Show me."

And, in the instant before his touch finds my wet, waiting core, his phone rings. "Goddammit," he snarls. "Not fuckin' now."

"Normally I'd tell you to answer it," I say. "But this time? Let it ring."

Only, my phone starts ringing, too. James removes his hands from me, reluctantly, as if to do so requires digging deep into a reserve of self-control he isn't sure he has.

"What do you think the chances are of us both getting calls at the exact same time?" he murmurs.

I shake my head. "The odds are against that," I say.

James digs his phone out of his back pocket, and I trot into the kitchen to grab mine out of my purse just as it stops ringing—only to start up again.

The caller ID says it's Audra.

"Audra? What's up?"

"Imogen—" Audra sounds more shaken than I've ever heard her. "She—she went into premature labor."

It takes a moment for the impact of that to hit me. "But she's—she's barely thirty weeks.

Is she at the hospital?"

"On the way now. She called Jesse, and he and Franco raced over and picked her up. Franco called me, and he's calling James too."

"I know. He's with me."

Such is the seriousness of the situation that Audra doesn't comment on this. "Get to the hospital."

"Ten minutes, max."

I hang up, and James is already tucking his phone back into his jeans pocket. His eyes meet mine. "Best get some clothes on," he says. "This ain't good."

The laundry basket full of clean clothes is at the foot of my bed; I throw on the first things I can find: a set of scrubs. James is already dressed, so I shove my bare feet into a pair of tennis shoes and grab my purse. James still has my keys, and I don't even think twice about getting into the passenger seat so he can drive.

We reach the hospital in less than five minutes, reaching the elevator at the same time as Laurel and Ryder. Being in scrubs puts me in a position of authority, subconsciously, and both Laurel and Ryder glance at me as we ride up to the maternity floor.

"Will she be okay?" Laurel asks.

"Thirty weeks is…viable. It depends on why she went into labor so early. She seemed healthy." I shrug. "But I'm not an L-and-D nurse."

The four of us jog from the elevator to the maternity waiting room, where we find Franco and Audra sitting side by side, holding hands, looking identically worried, as are all of us.

I don't even realize until Franco's eyes go to our hands that James and I holding hands. He says nothing, however; his eyes go next to James's face. I follow his gaze, and realize that James is tensed, jaw locked, brow furrowed. His hand is all but crushing mine.

And I remember, then, how his wife died: just like this.

I squeeze his hand. "James." His eyes flick down to mine. "She'll be okay."

"She has to be. He can't lose her the way I lost Renée."

"No one is losing anyone," I say. "It's going to be okay."

He juts his chin in the direction of the nurse's desk. "You work in the hospital. Can you go back and see what's going on?"

That's not really how things work, generally, but

I'm not about to argue with him. It's worth a shot, anyway. I head to the desk, and the nurse behind it is someone I know—I did rounds with her when we both first started here.

"Jeanine," I say. "I'm here about Imogen."

Jeanine is a small, neat, compact, efficient woman with a severe brown bun. "Imogen Irving?"

I nod. "About to be Imogen O'Neill."

Jeanine taps at her computer and reads. "Premature labor—thirty weeks. She's in the OR right now."

"Can I go back? I need to at least check on Jesse—the father."

She hesitates, and then nods. "Just you."

She indicates the door, comes around and swipes her card to let me through. It's not hard to find Jesse—there are four burly security guards surrounding him, trying to reason with him, to keep him out of the operating room. I take one look at the scene and jog back to the doorway.

I open it, wave at James, and he trots over, follows me in. Jeanine is studiously looking the other way; smartly, too—Jesse is causing a god-awful ruckus, and James is probably the only one who might be able to get through to him.

James sees Jesse being restrained by the guards—Jesse is shouting, straining, fighting, and it's taking all

four guards to hold him back. James wades through
the scrum, pushes the guards away.

"Jess, brother. It's me." He grabs Jesse's wrists in
his ham hock fists. "Take a breath, Jess. Cool off."

"She's in there!" Jesse wrestles against James's
hold. "I need—I need—"

"They're doing everything they can, Jess. I promise you. There's nothing you can do in there, brother.
Nothing except get in the way."

Jesse has tears in his eyes, on his cheeks. "Not
her, too. Not her, too."

James yanks Jesse forward into a rib-cracking,
unbreakable bear hug. "I *know*, Jess. But it's going to
be okay. She's going to be okay."

"Not her, too," Jesse repeats. "I can't lose her,
too."

Renée was his sister. Now Imogen, his fiancé, the
mother of his baby, is in a similar situation.

"I have to go in there. I have to see her." Jesse
struggles, but even he is no match for James, who
holds on to him for dear life, keeping Jesse wrapped
up in a hug.

"You can't."

"You were *there*, goddamn you," Jesse rages. "You
got to say goodbye."

"No one is saying goodbye, Jess. Not today. She's
going to be okay."

"You don't fucking know that!"

"I do," I say, catching the attention of both men. "She's thirty weeks, Jesse. Early, but viable. They're *both* going to be okay."

"Promise me?" Jesse whispers, sagging in James's arms. "Promise."

The nurse in me knows better than to promise, but I meet his eyes and hold steady. "She's going to be okay—they both will. Imogen and your baby will be okay."

"Renée," Jesse breathes. "The baby's name is Renée."

James grunts, and I realize it's a barely restrained sob of his own.

The security guards are hovering close by. One of them meets James's eyes while nodding at Jesse. "You got him?"

James nods. "We're good."

"No one's going in there," the security guard says, and his eyes go to me. "Not you either."

I shake my head. "We're staying here with him until we know what's going on."

The four guards cautiously leave, although I notice one of them surreptitiously takes up a spot in a corner down the hall.

Jesse has settled some, and I give him and James a little space. They lean back against the wall and murmur to each other in low tones—a private conversation, about Renée, I'm guessing.

How long we wait, it's hard to tell. Time passes bizarrely in those narrow, fluorescent-lit, antiseptic hallways.

After a tense, awful, measureless amount of time, a doctor comes out, a facemask tugged down around his neck. He scans the hallway and sees us.

"Jesse O'Neill?" he asks, glancing from James to Jesse.

"Yeah," Jesse grunts, steps forward. "How—how is she?"

The doctor smiles, and we all breathe—for the first time, it feels like. "She's okay—they're both okay."

Jesse hesitates. "Both of them?"

The doctor nods. "Your wife lost a good bit of blood, so she's weak, but she'll recover in no time. Your daughter will be on oxygen for a while, but she's looking well. She just needs a little extra help for a while, and then she'll be breathing on her own."

Jesse shakes, goes limp with relief, and James has to hold him up. "Thank god." He lets James hold him up a moment, and then finds his feet. "I need to see them."

The doctor nods. "Of course. You'll need to scrub up, just as a precaution for your daughter's health. This young, their immune systems aren't up to par just yet, so we have to be a little extra cautious for a while." He gestures at the doors he's just exited from. "This way."

Jesse nods, and follows the doctor, pausing in the door to look back at James—the look they exchange is beyond my ability to translate, but it's deep, heavy, and significant.

James nods after a moment. "Go."

Jesse's eyes close briefly, and then open, and he nods at James before vanishing through the doorway.

Once he's gone, James sags against the wall and covers his face with both hands. He breathes deeply, shoulders hunched. I go to him, stand in front of him, gather him toward me. He leans against me, sagging into me, buries his face in my hair. I run my hands in circles over his shoulders, holding him close.

After a moment, his shoulders shake, but silently. I just hold him, saying nothing. What is there to say?

A few minutes pass, and he straightens. "Thank fuck," he growls. "I couldn't have gone through that shit again. Jesse even less so."

"We should go let the others know," I say.

James nods. "Yeah. Let's go."

He takes my hand, twines our fingers together, and it's the most natural thing in the world, holding his hand.

Everyone stands up as we enter the waiting room, all eyes expectantly on us.

"She's okay," James says, without preamble. "Imogen and…and Renée—they're both okay." He stumbles on the second name, voice cracking

Franco and Ryder close in around James, all three of them tangling in a complicated three-way man-hug, heads together. A moment later, all six of us hug one another tightly.

"When can we meet our new niece?" Laurel asks.

"I don't know," I answer. "She's on oxygen and anyone who holds her will have to be scrubbed, so they're going to limit visitors for a while. We may be able to see Imogen at some point soon, though."

In this case, however, "soon" turns out to be more than four hours later. Ryder and Franco left half-way through the wait and came back with carryout food for all of us, and a giant box of coffee.

Finally, a nurse enters the waiting area and tells us we can go back and see Imogen, but only two at a time. Audra and Franco go first, and they're with her for maybe thirty minutes. By unspoken agreement, James and I tell Laurel and Ryder to go next, and we wait another thirty-some minutes. Finally, it's our turn to scrub clean, put on a gown and mask, and go back to the room where Imogen, Jesse, and the new baby are.

Imogen is on her back in a hospital bed, hooked up to an IV, an oxygen cannula in her nose. Jesse is perched on the edge of her bed, holding her hand. An incubator is on one side of the room, and inside is a tiny little blanket-wrapped bundle wired with monitor leads and oxygen tubes.

Imogen is pale, weak looking, and exhausted, but she's gazing at Jesse adoringly. When James comes in, she smiles at him. "I hear you had to hold my man back."

James nods, trying for a smile and not quite making it. "Yeah. He was…well, he was ready to rip the hospital apart to get to you."

"Thank you for being there for him," she says.

James answers her, but his eyes are on Jesse, who is in turn gazing at the incubator. "He's my brother."

Imogen looks at me, at James, at our still-joined hands, and her eyes light up. "You two!"

James looks down at our hands, but doesn't let go. He just shrugs. "Yeah."

"You figured it out?" she says, her voice hopeful.

"Sort of," I say. "We still have some…figuring… to do."

James chuckles, and neither Jesse nor Imogen miss the undertones swirling between us.

Imogen grins. "Did we interrupt something?"

I laugh. "This is pretty much the only thing that could have interrupted us."

"Well, don't let us keep you," Imogen says. "We're not going anywhere anytime soon. Go finish figuring it out!"

James grunts a negative. "You're family."

He lets go of me and crosses to stand over the incubator. He crouches, staring down through the glass at the tiny little sweetie inside. "Hi, Renée. I'm your uncle Jamie." His voice is so quiet, so tender. "Someday, I'll tell you all about your namesake."

I'd be lying if I said that didn't send a twinge through me, but I stand beside James and rest a hand on his thick shoulder. He glances up at me, smiles, and then looks at Jesse and Imogen.

"She looks like you, Imogen." He grins at Jesse. "Fortunately for her."

Imogen smirks. "She's got his nose."

James laughs. "Poor little thing. Maybe she'll grow into it."

Jesse shakes his head. "Don't be a dick, dick."

Imogen whacks him, or tries to. "Watch your language around our daughter, Jesse O'Neill."

Jesse snorts. "She's not even five hours old. I don't think she minds."

Imogen's eyes close, flutter, and shoot back open. James stands up, takes my hand again.

"You should rest," he says. "We'll come back tomorrow."

Imogen nods, but she's already drowsing. Jesse watches her, and then, once she's asleep, he catches my eye and points at the hallway. He and James and I crowd into the hallway outside the room, and Jesse shuffles his feet, and then glances at me.

"This sort of puts a wrench in the wedding plans," he says. "I know you said you're not up for planning it, but I—um, I had an idea, and I was hoping you'd be able to help me with it."

I smile at him, squeeze James's hand, and listen to his plan.

FIFTEEN

TWO DAYS AFTER RENÉE AUDRA O'NEILL IS BORN, ALL eleven of us are gathered—in rather cramped quarters, it must be said—in an unused room in the maternity ward; the bed has been temporarily wheeled out to make room for all of us. There's an eleventh person: a minister—a willowy, silver-haired woman in a lavender dress, a thin leather notebook in her hands.

"Dearly beloved," she says, in a quiet, bell-like voice. "Family, friends...we're together in this place to celebrate the joining of two lives, the marriage of two beautiful souls."

Imogen is in a wheelchair, still connected to an IV and oxygen, but she's in her dress, a veil draped over her shoulders, facing Jesse, eyes on his, reaching up to hold his hands; Jesse is in his tux, hair brushed to a wavy shine and loose around his collar.

James is beside and behind him, also in a tux.

Nina and Ella are on one side of the minister, holding bouquets of fake flowers—real ones were a no-go, in consideration of Imogen's weakened immune system—and Nate is on the other side, solemnly holding a pillow, on which are the rings. The rest of us are lined up as best as possible on either side of the bed, women on the left with Imogen, men on the right with Jesse.

Imogen had resigned herself to having to postpone the wedding, so Jesse's surprise of having me scramble this together means she's still crying with pure happiness. She hadn't suspected a thing—when Audra, Laurel, and I had shown up with her dress, she'd been puzzled, and hadn't believed us when we promised her she was marrying Jesse now, today, here in the hospital. We had to FaceTime Jesse so he could reassure her himself and then, once she believed it was real, she promptly lost her mind. She'd alternated between sobs of happiness and panic at trying to look her best, given that she's been in the hospital for two days and was still so weak she could only stand up for short periods of time. The three of us had worked with the nursing staff to get Imogen showered and dressed, get her hair brushed and dried and curled, all without disturbing her IV or oxygen lines.

Now, here we are, gathered in a tiny hospital room, breathing each other's air, with half the maternity ward staff and patients clustered outside the open door, watching the proceedings.

"I've done weddings in a lot of unusual places," the minister says. "In churches of all kinds, in more than a few bars and restaurants, in courthouses, in fields, in barns, even in a cemetery, once. I've even done weddings in this very hospital—in oncology wards, usually. This is the first time I've performed a wedding in a maternity ward, however, and I have to say this is by far my favorite place to do a wedding."

She turns to look at the iPad resting on Imogen's knees: it shows a real-time feed of little Renée, sleeping in her incubator. The doctors said it was too early for her to be around this many people, so we'd had to improvise a way to have her be a part of the wedding.

"Love knows no boundaries, and I can't think of a better place to marry you than a place where we can see, very literally, love come to fruition in the form of sweet, innocent babies." She pauses, glancing from Jesse to Imogen. "I'll keep this brief, and to the point. Love brought you together. Love will bind you through whatever comes your way—especially if you remember that love is a choice—an action, not just an emotion. Me marrying you two is nothing more than a symbol, and a civil, legal formality. You are, truly, wedded the moment you commit yourselves to each other to live your lives as one. All I'm doing is broadcasting that commitment to your family and friends."

"Family," Jesse puts in. "We're family, all of us."

"To your family, then," she says, smiling. "So. On to the fun part." She looks at Imogen. "Imogen—you've written your vows, I understand?"

Imogen nods, sniffles tearfully, and pulls a folded piece of paper tucked into the side of the wheelchair. She tugs on Jesse's hands, and he holds tight as she shakily pulls herself to her feet. Audra and James both hover at either side of her, ready to help her stay on her feet. Imogen wavers, and then visibly draws on a reserve of strength, stiffening her spine and locking her legs, holding on to one of Jesse's hands, clutching the paper in the other.

"I wrote this in about fifteen minutes," she says, her voice quavering. "So…it's not gonna be Shakespeare."

Jesse chuckles. "Because I'm known for my eloquence," he says. "From the heart, baby. That's all that matters."

Imogen nods, smiles, and takes a shaky breath. The paper shakes as she reads from it. "Jesse—from the moment I first met you, I knew. You showed up that day to fix a window that mysteriously broke… all by itself." Everyone laughs, especially Jesse and James, who know the real story. "You didn't just fix the window, that day—you fixed *me*. You repaired my heart. And every single day since then, you've made me a better person. You make my life better just by existing. You make me happy just by being you. Even if you do sometimes forget to take your stupid big muddy boots off on the porch."

She pauses, sniffles, smiles at Jesse, brightly, lovingly, adoringly, and she continues.

"There's nothing in this world that could make me happier than to be your wife. To share life with you. To be Imogen Catherine O'Neill." She smiles down at the iPad, at Renée, who snuffles, whines in her tiny baby voice, and then quiets again. "You've given me everything—more than everything. I love you more than I know how to say, so I promise to spend every moment of every day for the rest of our lives trying to show that love to you."

Jesse clears his throat, gruff and hesitant. "Well, shit. How am I supposed to match that?" He glances at the minister. "Sorry. Shoot, I mean."

The minister just laughs. "I'm here to marry you, not judge you."

Jesse clears his throat again. "Anyway. Imogen, I'm—you know me, and you know I'm not much for making pretty speeches. I didn't even write anything down. I just…I figure the best thing is to just tell you what's in my heart."

He pauses, closes his eyes for a minute, and then opens them—he's visibly emotional, but his voice is strong and steady. "You say that I didn't just fix your window, I fixed your heart. Well, I may be good at building things and fixing things but, until you, I didn't know the first thing about..." He waves a hand vaguely, hunting for a word to finish the thought. "Life. Love. Anything, really. I didn't know anything about anything except building houses. You've opened my eyes, my heart, and my whole world to things I didn't know existed." He looks down at the live stream of Renée, one room over. "I don't know the first damn thing about being a husband, much less a daddy, but I do know one thing—and that's that as long as I have you, I can figure it out. With you at my side, Imogen, I can take on the world. I love you more than...more than fu—friggin' anything I can even imagine, and I'm honored beyond words to be your husband, and to raise this amazing, miraculous, beautiful little girl together with you."

James slaps him on the shoulder. "Good job, brother."

The minister smiles again. "Indeed. Beautiful words, both of you." She turns and glances at Nate. "You have the rings, sweetie?"

Nate nods, his expression serious. "Yes ma'am. Right here." He lifts the little velvet pillow.

She takes the larger of the rings and hands it to Imogen. "Imogen, echo me, if you would."

Imogen nods, and places the ring on the tip of Jesse's finger, but doesn't slide it down yet, and repeats the minister's words. "Jesse—this ring is a symbol of my love. It represents the eternal bond, forged in this moment, before these witnesses. This ring represents my vow to love you, cherish you, and honor you all our lives, in sickness and in health, come what may. With this ring, I vow my eternal love for you."

And then, with a tearful gulp, she slides the ring onto Jesse's finger. He's equally moved as he repeats the same vow to Imogen, and places the ring on her finger.

There's a moment of silence, then, as Jesse and Imogen stare at each other.

"Well?" The minister glances at them both in turn, expectantly. "Don't wait for me—seal it with a kiss!"

Jesse gently gathers Imogen in his arms and kisses her thoroughly, but delicately, and then, mouths just barely parted, they laugh together.

"And with that scorcher of a kiss," the minister says, laughing and pretending to fan herself, "I now pronounce you married, in the eyes of the State of Illinois, in the eyes of God, and, most importantly, in the eyes of these, your gathered family. What this marriage has joined, let nothing ever separate."

There's applause, then, not just from us in the room, but from the fairly sizable crowd outside—not just hospital staff anymore, but expectant fathers, soon-to-be mothers in wheelchairs grimacing between contractions, doctors, friends, families of other patients.

One of the things that joins all of us as a family is that we're all each of us has—for a myriad of reasons, we're all the family any of us has, by choice or by loss. So, to share this, surrounded by our family, the family we've chosen? It's everything.

Imogen gratefully and exhaustedly lowers herself, with Jesse's help, into the wheelchair, and a nurse excuses herself as she weaves between the crowd to enter the room, carefully carrying a sheet cake—she's followed by another nurse with paper plates and plastic cutlery.

The celebration that follows is makeshift, occurring in the overcrowded room, barely enough space to move let alone eat cake or mingle, but it's a joyful one.

It ends when Renée begins to fuss. Imogen gives hugs and kisses to everyone, and then Jesse wheels her to the room next door, so she can feed their daughter. That's when we all begin to filter out, heading for the elevator as a group.

Two hours later, the rest of us have dined together at a nearby Italian place, said our temporary goodbyes, and parted.

Twenty minutes later, James and I are sitting in his truck, in his driveway, a thick, expectant silence between us.

The girls are with James's parents for the night.

And he and I are finally alone,

SIXTEEEN

JAMES SHUTS OFF HIS TRUCK, AND OPENS HIS DOOR, BUT doesn't get out just yet; he sits with his foot on the step, one hand on his knee, and the other draped over the steering wheel. He's staring into space thoughtfully, one finger tapping restlessly on the steering wheel.

I wait silently, knowing he'll speak when he's ready.

After several minutes of silence, he lets out a slow breath. "That emergency delivery the other day was scary." His voice is a deep, quiet rumble.

I reach out and massage the rock-hard round bulge of his shoulder. "Yeah, it was."

"I keep having flashbacks." His voice is so strained, so tense. Stretched taut, tightly controlled.

It's late evening, a pink-red-orange sunset stains the sky and the long, ropy wisps of clouds. I open my door. "Let's go for a walk."

James glances at me, brow furrowed. "We're finally alone, though. Not sure when that'll happen again."

I shake my head and smile. "We have all the time in the world, James. Let's just go for a walk."

He nods, and hops down from his truck. The doors slam with twin thunks, and I round the hood of the truck, meet him by the driver's door, and take his hand.

We walk in a slow stroll, hand in hand, down the side of the rural dirt road, the sun setting in front of us.

"You're probably sick of hearing about this shit," James says.

"No, James. I'm not interested in burying this stuff anymore. We've both spent years burying it. Repressing it. Refusing to talk about it. Pretending it's fine. We both need to let it all out."

He rakes his free hand through his hair. "I've spent the last couple months talking it all out with Dr. Richard. It's helped. I think, by and large, I've made good progress at putting the past in the past. Letting Renée just be…part of me, part of who I am and who I've been, but not letting the tragedy of losing her define me anymore."

"That's hard work."

He scoffs. "Ain't that the truth. I've had to let

myself think about her, when I've spent these years since her death trying to *not* think about her. Doc Rich says I can only move on by accepting the thoughts, living in them, and moving through them." He laughs. "It took me a couple weeks' worth of sessions with him to not dismiss trite, gooey shit talk like that, to be honest. It just sounds like stereotypical shrink babble." He speaks in a mocking whine. *"You have to live in the painful thoughts, James. Live in the thought, let it flow through you, be in you, and then let it move past you. If you don't learn to do this, you'll always be stuck in the past, and your personal tragedy will always consume you."*

I can't help a laugh. "He really talks like that?"

James nods. "Oh yeah. It took some getting used to. I almost stopped going, and I actually did see a couple other therapists, but in the end, as goofy as he sometimes sounds, he has good shit to say, and I feel like he's actually listening to me. Like he understands, and actually has the tools to teach me how to be better." He shrugs. "The others just made me feel like they were sitting there, hearing me speak, diagnosing, and waiting to charge me for their time. Doc Rich is the only one who I feel gets me, and actually cares."

I smile. "I'm really glad you found him, and that you're talking to him."

He glances at me. "Have you ever spoken to anyone?"

I laugh, nod and shrug. "Yeah, sort of. A colleague of mine at the hospital is a psychiatrist, and I've had a few sessions with her."

"Not the same. I don't want to sound like I'm the expert, or like I'm trying to tell you what to do, but I know for me, I've been stuck in my shit for six years. I had to talk to someone objective, who doesn't know me at all, to help me get out of my own way."

I sigh. "I know. I just…" I shrug, finding it hard to capture my feelings on the subject.

"Don't want to have to admit you need help?"

I can't help but laugh again. "Yeah, that's a big part of it."

He makes a sound somewhere between a sigh, a scoff, and a laugh. "I get that more than you know. I'm a red-blooded American male. I'm a builder. I fix things professionally. I can take apart a car and put it together, I can build a house from scratch with my bare hands. I can look at a building that's falling apart and know exactly what to do to fix it. One look at a roof and I know exactly how many years are left on it and how much it'll cost to fix it. I've been building and fixing literally my entire life." He holds up his hands. "There is very little I can't do with these." He drops his hands again, takes mine in his once more, and scoffs, shaking his head. "I can't fix me with them, though. As a man raised to be tough, to be strong, to be a doer, a fixer, an alpha male without emotions or weakness, admitting even to myself that I needed help was…fucking hard, Nova. It meant admitting my head is fucked up, that my heart is fucked up. That I have emotions I don't know how to deal with. Growing up, if I showed weakness around my dad, I got whooped. Get hurt playing ball? *Suck it up, son.* Take it like a man. Get teased, bullied, and made fun of? *Kick their asses, Jamie.* Show 'em you're tougher than they are, and they'll leave you alone."

He walks in silence for a while, and then speaks again. "Renée and I got in a huge blow-out fight when I fucked up my knee in that car wreck. My football career was over, and I couldn't admit it. I was determined to rehab my knee and go for the combine. I was gonna get drafted by the Bears. That was my sole focus in life. Renée was pissed. She knew I loved football, knew I was really, really good. She knew I had a real shot at going pro, which is like…the chances of that are like winning the lottery, pretty much, and I had scouts and agents telling me I was a shoo-in. Not to toot my own horn, but I was one of the best offensive linemen in the country." He pauses, sighs. "Then I wrecked my knee, and it was over. Renée wanted me to think about life beyond football. Rehab my knee, certainly, so I'd have full mobility, still be able to work out and all that, but just admit my career playing competitive ball was done. I couldn't, wouldn't. I got pissed, she got pissed, and we blew up at each other while I was in the damn hospital. Cleared the floor, just about. I've never lost my temper like that, before or since."

Another pause, a long silence.

"Renée left me. Broke up with me. Said she couldn't and wouldn't be with a man who was so stuck on himself that he couldn't admit when something was beyond his control—and that the fact that I was so angry about it—at her, for even suggesting I let go of playing ball—meant I was weak and pathetic. Those were her words to me. Weak and pathetic." He scoffs. "You know how deep that cut? I could squat six hundred pounds. Deadlift eight hundred. Bench over four hundred. Run the hundred-yard dash faster than half the defensive ends at the combine. And I was pathetic and weak? God, that hurt. She didn't come back, either. Broke up with me in the hospital—walked the fuck out on me. Her parting words to me are something I'll never forget. 'Jamie,' she said, 'the only person, the only force in this entire goddamn world that will ever be able to stop you is *you*. You are too damn stupid and stubborn to get out of your own way, and I cannot and will not stand by and watch you keep hurting yourself. I love you, Jamie. I love you more than life, and I always will, but I won't be with you if you can't get over yourself.'"

I shake my head. "Damn. Takes real balls to say that to the man you love."

"At twenty years old, too. She was the wisest and most self-aware person I've ever known." He walks in silence for a while. "So I thought about it, and what she said. Took me weeks, but I realized she was right. The point is, though, that she left me. Broke up with me. Wouldn't answer my calls, wouldn't come back to the hospital. Nothing. I wrote her letters, sent them to her through Jess. Nothing. I was in so much pain, physically and emotionally, and my dad was just... *suck it up, son.* Play hurt. Toughen up. Get over her—she's just a girl."

"Jesus. What an asshole."

"It's how he was raised, so it's how he raised me. It's taken me this long to de-condition myself from all that, and sometimes I think I'll never quite totally beat that mentality."

"Seems to me like you have," I say.

He shrugs. "To some degree, yes."

"I will go see someone," I say, at length. "Craig is still inside me, down deep. Being with you still makes me feel guilty, sometimes, and I can stubborn my way past it for the most part, but..."

James shakes his head. "That's what Doc Rich has had to drill into me these past few months—you can't stubborn your way past this shit. You're just burying it, not dealing with it."

"You're right, James. I know you are."

"These past few days, though?" He shakes his head. "Seeing Jess like that?"

I gaze up at him. "Brought it all back?"

He nods. "Yeah. Hard-core." We reach the end of his street that ends in a T-junction at a huge fenced-in field, scattered with cows munching on grass. We stand at the fence line and watch the cows amble this way and that. "I was there again, for a minute. In that hospital, in that very fucking hallway. I remember it like—like it was yesterday. Jess was with the girls—my folks were in Florida, and hers were at their lake house. So it was just Jess there to watch Nina and Ella while I took Renée to the hospital. So I was alone. Totally alone. Pacing that hallway, trying not to panic. But I—I *knew*. I knew something was wrong. It all happened so fast—one second she was fine, the next she was…bleeding, having these crazy contractions. Twenty-six weeks, she was. Too soon, and we both knew it. I knew, I fucking *knew* something was seriously wrong, and nobody was telling me anything. The more time that passed the more I just knew in my fucking guts that it was wrong, all wrong. Eventually, I just…snapped. Just like Jesse did, only there wasn't anyone to hold me back. There was one security guard, but he was this fat old dude, and he didn't stand a chance. I shoved him through the fucking wall, literally. I shoved my way into the OR, and she was..." He blinks hard, coughs, clears his throat, keeps going. "There were these blue sheets covering her—the doctors, surgeons, nurses. Blood everywhere. She was opened up, and I—I fuck—I fucking *saw*. Saw her opened up, bleeding out, trying to save her and the baby. They couldn't put her under—they had to do an emergency C-section, and she was awake, and alone. They were trying to save her, and the baby, but they—they couldn't. And she knew it. And she was fucking alone."

"Good god, James."

He goes on, as if he didn't hear me. "I grabbed her hand, and she looked at me, and I knew she knew. It was in her eyes. 'Take care of the girls.'" He whispers this. The way she probably did. "I couldn't say a damn thing, I was crying so hard. It's okay, she said. It's going to be okay. Take care of the girls." A long pause. "'Don't stay alone forever, Jamie.' She squeezed my hand so fucking hard when she said that. 'Promise me, Jamie. Promise me you'll find someone to take care of you.'"

I'm crying, because there's no other logical response.

"I promised her." He clears his throat, dashes a

wrist against his eyes. "But until now, I had no concept of what it meant to be able to actually keep that promise. I made the promise in the moment, and it's stuck with me, but...how do you do that? I couldn't figure it out. I'm still working on it."

What do I say? I just hold his hand tightly, and lean my head against his shoulder.

He glances down at me. "Doc Rich says I have PTSD from it. That people often go untreated, because there's this idea that only combat veterans, or people who go through, like, something like 9/11, or whatever, can get PTSD. But anything super traumatic can cause it, and it's a spectrum, you know? Varying degrees of severity and it shows up in different ways with each individual."

"Makes sense," I say.

"So, it's not something I'm going to just *get over*."

I look up at him. "Of course not. I don't expect that."

He lets out a breath, staring out over the field again. "I just want you to understand that I'm working on it. That I...I'm working on moving on. On being a better father to Nina and Ella—more present, more involved, more...how did Doc Rich put it? More emotionally available to them." He fiddles with the barbed wire, rubbing the pad of his thumb over one of the barbs. "And for you. I want...us. I want you—not just sex, but life with you. I want to love you."

I feel my heart swell. "James…" I pull him around to face me.

I have a million things to say, but they're all jumbled and tangled and stuck behind the lump in my throat. And sometimes, the only thing to say is nothing—the only way to say what you need to say is with a kiss.

So, I kiss him.

And kiss him.

And kiss him.

Until we're both breathless and I'm gasping and he's rumbling in his chest, breathing hard and staring down at me with awe in his eyes. "Jesus, Nova."

I smile against his lips. "Now you know how you make me feel when you kiss me like that."

"I got one more thing I need to say. And it may come out kind of…messy."

I cling to his shoulders and nod up at him. "Okay, I'm listening."

"You're not going to have to compete with her ghost, Nova. I'm gonna love you, and it's…it's a different kind of love. I don't love you the same way I loved Renée. Don't mean it's…less, or not as strong, or…or not as real or whatever. Just that it's…*different*. You're you, and the way we are together is just a whole different thing than the way she and I were. So...you're not competing. I'm not comparing. It's like...well, at the risk of sounding like a typical construction dude, you're a hammer and she was a screwdriver. Different tools, and you can't compare them to each other. They're different."

"Thank you for saying that," I whisper. "I needed to know that."

"I needed you to know that." He brushes my lips with his thumb. "You're you, exactly you—and I'm in love with you. You make me feel like a kid again, sometimes. Like I just fuckin' want you so bad it feels crazy. A good kind of crazy."

I smile up at him, a mischievous grin. "How about you be the hammer, and I'll be a nail, and you can pound me?"

He cackles. "God, Nova. Only you could make a dirty joke out of that."

I rub my hands over his broad hard chest. "Who was joking?"

He doesn't say anything—just stares down at me for a moment, and then hauls me into a fast walk back toward his house. We reach his front door, and he's unlocking it, but pauses in the act of turning the key.

I glance at him. "What's the issue?"

He palms the back of his neck. "The, um...the

condoms are at your house. I don't have any here."

I laugh. "Then I guess we go to my house."

We make the drive in record time—I wouldn't say he drove recklessly, but this was an occasion when it was fortunate that he knew the back roads as well as he did.

Finally, finally—we're standing in my kitchen, closing the door behind us, and James is gazing down at me.

I reach for him. "James?"

He rubs that thumb over my lips again. "Nova?"

"I have one quick, random question for you."

"Okay."

"We all call you James, exclusively, but I heard Jesse call you Jamie once, and you said, 'I'm your uncle Jamie' to little baby Renée." I pause, and try to put this tactfully. "Is that a nickname you don't go by anymore?"

He considers his response for a moment. "Growing up, I was Jim to my parents, which I hated, and Jimmy at school, which I hated even more."

I frown, make a disgusted face. "God, no. You're not a Jim or a Jimmy."

He laughs. "That's how I feel. In junior high, I tried to get people to just call me Bod, which kind of stuck, and I refused to answer my parents until they stopped calling me anything except James, which is how I sort of ended up as James to pretty much everyone, and that's the name I generally prefer. I absolutely *hate* being called Jim or Jimmy. Makes me feel like I'm in third grade again, dressing out in pads for the first time, getting yelled at by my dad to quit bitching about my sprained ankle and play fucking football like a goddamn man."

I wince in sympathy. "That happened?"

He nods. "Oh yeah. He was a real hard-ass." He laughs. "Well, Renée is the one who started calling me Jamie."

I scoff. "All roads lead back to her, huh?"

He nods seriously. "Yep, pretty much." He rolls a shoulder. "She knew I hated short versions and nicknames, but she felt like calling me James was too formal, as she put it. She actually tried Jamesy for a while."

I cackle. "Jamesy?"

He laughs, nodding. "That morphed into Jamie, and that's all she called me after that. Jess used to use it sometimes." He goes serious. "Haven't been called that since she passed, though."

"James it is, then."

He scratches the back of his head. "I actually considered going by Jamie professionally, but she nixed that idea."

"I think she was right. James is professional,

Jamie is personal."

He tucks a strand of hair behind my ear. "I've been thinking about that lately, as a matter of fact. This whole therapy thing, moving on—rebuilding myself, in some ways…I was thinking it may be time to change it up. Go by something other than James to those close to me. It's why I used Jamie with baby Renée. I want to be Uncle Jamie to her."

I pass my hand through his hair, thinking. "I don't know. To me, you're just…James."

He leans down, kisses me. "I actually like that." He frowns in thought. "It feels like…I'm not sure how to put it. The way you say it, it feels kind of like a mental or emotional version of an affectionate caress."

I cup his cheek, rub his cheekbone, and scratch my fingers through his beard. "Like that?"

He breathes out softly, eyes shuddering closed at my touch, nuzzling his cheek into my hand. "Yeah," he murmurs. "A lot like that."

I whisper a laugh. "Like a little puppy," I say, grinning as I caress his face and beard. "If you had a tail, it'd be wagging, I bet."

His eyes flick open, suddenly on fire. "Oh, something's wagging all right, it's just not a tail."

I lift up, touch my lips gently to his in a feather-soft, whisper-quick kiss. "Take me to bed and make love to me, Jamie."

His only answer is to pull me by the hand down the hallway to my room. He leads me into the center of my bedroom and stares down at me, and I feel him weighing something.

"What is it?" I ask.

"I want to ask you for something, but I don't want to seem…shallow, or…greedy. Not sure how to put it."

I peel his shirt off, toss it aside, and roam his huge hard torso greedily. "Ask me for anything, James."

"I wish we could pick up where we left off, last time." His eyes are wild and raging with need. "You, in that sexy lingerie."

The grin that slides across my face is pleased, eager, and amused. "Oh, but we can."

"Yeah?"

I nod. "When I woke up this morning and got dressed for Jesse and Imogen's wedding, I did so hoping you and I might find some time alone."

He arches an eyebrow, and I see eager hope in his expression—it's adorable and erotic at the same time, somehow. "I woke up hoping the same thing."

I smile up at him, put all my desire, all my nascent and growing love, all my need, all my long-denied arousal into that smile. "So, I guess you might say I have a little present for you."

I gesture at myself—I'm wearing a sleek green dress, one that's tight enough to be sexy, but not so revealing as to be inappropriate for a wedding, especially one in a hospital maternity ward.

"You just have to unwrap it."

SEVENTEEN

I STAND STILL AND WAIT FOR HIM.

I don't have to wait long—he reaches for me, pulls me close. Bends over me, kisses me into incoherent stupidity in that way he has. And this time, while he's kissing me, his fingers find the zipper tab at the back of my dress and tug it down from between my shoulder blades to the small of my back. My dress sags open, and I press my palms against his chest, round my shoulders to let the barely there straps slide down my arms. James helps, fingers grazing along my biceps, pulling the top of the dress away from my body.

He steps away, breaks the kiss. Instead of letting the dress fall to the floor, he keeps hold of the bodice and slowly lowers it down my front—revealing my cleavage in slow increments, then my belly, then my hips, then my thighs; as he lowers the dress, he sinks to his knees, and his mouth plies my flesh with kisses on the way down. Each kiss leaves me more breathless than the one before.

At long last, he's on his knees in front of me, and I'm staring down at his love-struck eyes, blazing with desire and awe—for me. I caress his hair, stroke it back from his face. He kisses my belly, gazing up at me. His lips touch and dance and flicker to the side, to my hip bone, and his hands carve around my waist, fingertips clawing down my back. Another kiss, and another, just above the waistband of my underwear, from navel to hip bone, and then the other way. His hands follow the line of my spine upward, and his eyes remain on mine. I don't dare look away, I cannot.

I palm his cheeks, the nape of his neck. He finds the clasp of my bra, and I suck in a breath, hold it and wait. He leans back, and his eyes leave mine, but only to rake over my body, hungrily soaking up the vision of me in the white lace.

"God, Nova—you are…so fucking beautiful." His voice is a ragged whisper.

"When you look at me that way…I feel beautiful."

"I feel like the luckiest man in the world, getting to see you like this."

"You're about to get a whole lot luckier," I say, smirking down at him.

"Oh, I know. I just…I want to savor this." He

growls then, and opens my bra with a deft movement.

I chuckle. "That was fast. I thought you were savoring?"

He tugs my bra off and tosses it aside, feasting on the sight of my naked breasts. "I did. But I'm getting impatient. I'll savor more later." His hands grip my buttocks, fingers gently pinching the flesh, and then slide up my back and carve around my diaphragm, twist to cup and lift my breasts. "Plus, I'm hoping I'll be able to convince you to wear that for me again."

I would laugh, but I'm too breathless from the fire of his touch. "James, baby—with the way you look at me, I'll wear it all the time. Just try and stop me." I gasp as he tweaks my nipples, sending a thrill of pleasure through me. "I'll spend a fortune on lingerie if it means you'll look at me that way."

"Babe, I'll buy it for you, if it means I get to see you in lingerie. You are the sexiest woman in the world."

He uses his mouth for other, more worthy endeavors than talking, then his lips close over my nipple and his tongue flicks, and then he kisses the underside, around my wide pale areola. His hands, meanwhile, set fire to my skin on their journey down to my hips, where his fingers hook into the lace and continue downward, clawing down my thighs. My panties slide off, and I step out of them, and now I'm naked and his mouth laves kisses to my other breast, and he's exploring my ass and the tender silk of my inner thighs. I bury my fingers in his hair and focus on breathing, sucking in the bliss of his kiss, his touch, his loving mouth and hands.

Lips and tongue flick and slide down my belly, around my navel, and over my core. His tongue flits down my seam and I need to breathe, need to gasp, but I can't. I have no breath and no capacity to remember how. I am nothing but the wild explosion of sensation as he parts my flesh with his tongue, and then drags a single thick finger over me and slides it into me and smears my clit with my juices, and then delves back in, curling to find it wet and hot and clenching already. His tongue circles and swipes, flicks and licks. I arch my back and push my hips forward, shamelessly begging more of this, whispering *yes, yes—don't stop, please*, in a rhythmic chant.

My knees shake and tremble, and I'm forced to hold on to his shoulders for balance, for support, lest my legs give way and I fall. There's no teasing, no playing—only his pursuit of my pleasure. He follows the clues of my gasps, the way I arch my back when he uses his tongue this way, flicks his fingers inside me that way, or when he speeds up or slows down. He builds me up and drives me to the edge and in the seconds before I lose all control, he looks up at me, pausing ever so briefly. Smiles, and then resumes.

I explode, crying out and nearly ripping out his hair, writhing against his mouth.

My legs do give out, then, and I collapse.

Into his waiting arms.

He lifts me, carries me to my bed, lays me down with chivalrous gentility. As if I weigh nothing. I'm still trembling and whimpering when he crawls up from the foot of the bed, spreading my thighs wide with his broad shoulders—I drape my knees over his shoulders and bite my lip as he stares up at me. There's no need for words, then, just the need in his eyes and the erotic glisten of my essence on his beard and lips, nothing but the ravenous way he laps at me, French-kissing my core with all the dizzying fury he kisses my mouth, all lips and tongue, delving and demanding. I writhe and gasp, and ride his mouth, grinding against him and reaching back to clutch my pillow, and scrabble at my headboard. My spine arches off the bed and I can't help but scream through a second climax.

He shows no sign of pausing, but I can't take any more. He's nuzzling my thighs and licking greedily at my pussy when I tug at his beard, haul him by his hair and his shoulders up to me. I wipe at his face with my hands, and then bring his mouth to mine.

"You taste like me," I whisper, grinning.

He braces his weight with one fist and caresses my breasts with the other. "I love the taste of you. I love the sounds you make, and the way you try not to scream."

He begins to slide back down, but I catch at him. "No, James. No more."

He smirks. "I want more."

I reach down between us and fumble at his dress pants. "And believe me, you can have all you want, whenever you want. But right now, I need *this*." I manage to rip open the button and zipper, dipping my hand under his underwear, grasping his erection.

He growls. "I feel like I owe you a couple more. The scales aren't even."

I stroke his length. "Who's keeping track?"

"I am."

"Well, I'm not." I caress him, twisting my fist around the plump round head, and then plunging down to the root. "I just want you. I don't care if I come once or a hundred times—I just want you inside me. I need you, James. That's all I care about."

He huffs, growls, bowing his spine upward and flexing his hips to push into my hands, and then yanking away. He flops onto his back and fights to get his pants off, but he's impatient and clumsy, and he still has his shoes and socks on.

I laugh, and roll to lean over him. I take his big

beautiful cock in one hand and untie his shoes with the other, slide them off, tug his socks off, and then his pants and his underwear—and then, finally, we're naked together, and he's groaning at my touch.

He grabs at my wrist. "Stop, Nova—you have to stop for a second."

I laugh. "Getting close, are you?"

He huffs. "Fucking right I am. The way you touch me, it feels so fuckin' good I won't last another goddamn second if you don't give me a chance to get control."

"I don't want *control*, James," I snap impatiently. "I want the opposite."

He laughs. "I just mean I'm not about to let go before I get a chance to be inside you, so you gotta back off a second. I'm out of practice and don't last as long as I used to."

"Oh." I frown at him. "I couldn't care less how long you last. I just need you inside me, *now*."

He moves to his knees. "Condoms?"

I point at the middle drawer of my bedside table. "In there."

He takes out the box, opens it, and rips open a square. Levered up on one elbow, I watch as he rolls it on. His eyes lock on mine, and my breath catches.

It's a wild, fraught moment—I was caught up in the sexuality of it all, momentarily distracted by chemical need, by physiological desire. In that moment, I remember what this is all about—us.

He rolls into me, and his arm curls under my neck—I let him take me to my back, and I wrap my arms around his neck, bury my hands in the hair at his nape and pull him closer. He kisses me—leaves me delirious as only he can, and we kiss and there's no stopping, nothing between us, nothing holding us back.

I breathe him, and feel him above me—a sheltering, powerful presence, his hard body pressed against mine, his shoulders blocking out the world, so there's only him, only us. He kisses me, and I'm lost in it, my lungs and lips and brain and heart and soul fuse to his, wrap around him, tangle with him. His kiss, his murmur of need—I hear it and feel it all through me.

We move together, writhing and tangling hands, touching, exploring. I whimper, and he echoes it with a groan. His arm is curled under my neck, supporting me—his bicep is my pillow; his other hand is all over me, scouring my flesh, my breasts, my core, cupping my hips and palming my breasts. I roam his shoulders and claw at his buttocks, and then reach between us and find his condom-sheathed length. I guide him to my opening as I cup his balls and caress them as he nudges between the tight, throbbing lips of my core.

He moans my name, a whispered plea: "Nova…"

I nip at his ear and breathe my response: "James—oh god, James, please."

I clasp his face between my breasts and cry out loud as he pushes into me, arching my back as he fills me. How can anything feel this good, this perfect? I didn't know it could be like this—that this exquisite ache of accepting him inside me could feel so incredible, that I could burn and throb from the way his thick, pulsing erection splits me apart and stretches me; I cry out, not just a wail of pleasure, but an actual sob—his name, always his name on my lips.

He coils over me, thrusting fully into me and curling his body down, contracting his torso, hands trailing down my breasts. His groan is a long, drawn-out snarl of relief, pleasure, and pent-up need.

"Nova—" he murmurs, and withdraws.

I hook my ankles around his flexed taut buttocks, draping my thighs open to take him deeper, pushing up against him as he begins to move. Slowly, dragging out of me and plundering back in, he leans over me to stutter his lips down my chest, tongue flicking with haphazard desperation against my nipples.

"Oh fuck, Nova." He groans, and I feel his abs tense. "God, Nova. My Nova."

I clutch at his face and nip at his earlobe, bite down on his shoulder as his slow, powerful thrusts wreck me, again and again and again, driving me to weakness, to gasps of burgeoning climax—within minutes. How long? No clue, and I couldn't care any less how long, because each second is absolute heaven.

He writhes with helpless desperation against me, his sighs becoming groans, his groans becoming growls, his growls becoming a chanted pleading of my name.

"Nova—Nova—*Nova*..." He drags a kiss over my cheek, seeking my lips.

I palm his face, take his mouth and show him what a kiss is—ragged and wild and manic. I sob into the kiss, because I'm lost, I'm on fire, I'm exploding.

"I don't want it to stop," he whispers.

"Me neither."

"But I can't—god, god*dammit*, oh god, Nova—I can't—I can't stop. I can't..." He bites down on my lip, hard, and I squeal in surprise, and then return the nip, the bite.

"Don't—don't, James." I breathe into his ear, urging him to move by clawing at his flexing buttocks, by driving against him, demanding more from him, begging for more every way I know how. "Don't stop, don't you fucking dare stop."

"I want it to last forever," he pants, "it's too soon, but I can't fuckin'—oh god, oh fuck, Nova, god, my love...you feel too good, and I can't help it."

I palm the hard-tensed round flexing muscle of his buttocks and move against him, panting in unison with him. "James, please—" I plead, my voice too broken for anything but a sobbed whisper. "Now, James. Come with me—I can't wait."

And, indeed, I can't. I don't try. I explode around him, my core clamping down so hard I feel every inch of him as he throbs and thrusts inside me. I cry, I wail, I bury my face in his throat and let myself scream out loud, a half sob, half scream, a breathless shriek that deafens even me, an orgasm detonating deep inside me and spreading like wildfire, like an atomic bomb is rippling outward from my core.

As I come, James roars, thrusting into me with wild, rough, careless, ravaging power, and I take it all and meet him thrust for thrust. I feel him come. I'm clenching around him in wave after wave of climax, and with each clench I feel him throb thicker and harder, and I feel him push deep, feel him tense, falter, and then his forehead rests against mine and his voice is breaking, hoarse as he grunts through clenched teeth.

There is not a single vestige of control left in him, now, and I treasure down to my very molecules the crazed abandon in the way he moves with me; we meet each other in climax, his snarls matching my screams, his slamming grinding slapping thrusts mirroring my furiously gyrating hips. There is only us, only this, our voices and our bodies and our love become something neither of us knew could be possible.

Finally, after a singularly too-brief eternity, we both go still, sweating, gasping.

James collapses against me, and I cradle him to my breast, both of us panting in unison.

Buried inside me, slackening, his breath on my chest, his hair tickling my nose, he tries to move off me.

I cling tight. "Don't you dare move, James Bod."

He laughs. "I'll crush you."

"Then I'll die a happy woman." I scratch his back, his buttocks, and his shoulders. "There's nowhere I'd rather be than under you."

He lifts his head up, grins down at me. "What about on top of me?"

I squeeze around him. "Get hard again and I'll show you."

A few minutes of blissful, companionable silence later, I let him roll off me, and he goes into the bathroom, cleans up, and returns. "I gotta make this master suite happen," he says.

I laugh. "No kidding."

He flops to the bed beside me and extends his arm. I eagerly nuzzle into the crook of his arm, and we drowse in sated silence for a while.

"I love having you here," I say. "It's only ever been just me in this house, and I…I just like you here. In my home, in my bed." James's silence is oddly tense, and I wait through it uncomfortably. Finally, I crane my neck to look up at him. "What? You don't like being here with me?"

He frowns down at me, wrinkling his nose. "What? No. That's stupid—of course I do."

I trace patterns in the dusting of chest hair. "Then what? I tell you I love having you here, and you clam up."

He chuckles. "You just assumed the opposite. I guess I love being here with you more than I…more than I should, probably."

I frown even harder at that. "More than you should? Now who's being stupid? We just consummated our relationship with mind-blowing sex, or, rather, lovemaking, I should say, because even though that's a cliché and a sorta cringey term, it's the truth. I love you, James, and I love having you here." I rest my head back on his chest and continue idly tracing designs in his chest hair. "I want you here all the time, if I'm being honest. If I could have my way, I'd never let you leave."

"Nova, I—"

"I know, I know. You have your own home, and

it's the girls' home, too. That's an element of this whole thing we're going to have to sort out, eventually, because at some point we're going to want to live together, but I love my home and we're just now getting it to where I super sparkly hearts love it, and I don't think I'll want to sell it anytime soon, but I know you and the girls have your home, where they—where you—" I tear up abruptly, my emotions running at high octane from the intensity of what we just shared. "Sorry. I'm being stupid. I just—"

He shuts me up with a kiss, curling his arm to crowd me up against him, lips fusing to mine tongue slicing away my words, and my breath. "Yeah, you are being stupid." He laughs. "You didn't let me finish."

I don't bother trying to stem the tears—which aren't sadness, I'm just…overwhelmed by the suddenness and intensity of all this. "Okay. So finish."

"The reason I feel like I love being here more than I should is because I don't want to have to leave either. And this is *your* home. And this thing between us is, like, brand new. And I don't get to invite myself here, or become too fully involved in your life before you're ready."

I scoff at that. "I'm in your life, James. I'm in it as fully as I can be."

"The girls are a lot to consider. They'll be confused at first."

I laugh. "Oh, I don't know. I think they'll welcome the idea of us."

He frowns at me. "Why do you say that?"

"Because when Imogen had us all at the spa for the baby announcement shower thing, Nina told me she knew you liked me, and gave me permission to date you. She said she hoped that if we dated, it'd make you less cranky, because you're a butt all the time, and, I quote, *'it's super annoying.'*"

James laughs. "She said that?"

I nod. "And that was back when Imogen first knew she was pregnant. I'm sure she's picked up on some of the, um, changes."

He sighs. "She's a perceptive little devil, that one."

"It's up to you how you introduce the idea of us to them, obviously. I just want you to know that you, and they, are welcome here. My home is yours, and theirs." I swallow hard. "I'd love having you all here. I could turn the extra room into a girly paradise for them."

James groans, scrubbing his face with his free hand. "I want to say something, but I'm worried it's too much too soon."

I drape my thigh over his and twist to look up at him. "No such thing, James."

He blinks down at me. "Fine." He sighs. "Okay,

so—even since before you and I started getting seri-ous, I've been contemplating the idea of selling my place."

I'm floored. "You…what? Why?"

"I guess it's part of moving on. There are so many memories there, you know? Too many. Doc Rich said it may be worth thinking about, in the name of moving on. Renée and I picked that place together, you know? It's where she and I built a life together. There're good memories, obviously, but…painful ones, too. I just don't want to yank them from the only home they've ever known willy-nilly, you know? If we move, I want it to be…for a reason. Somewhere specific, for a specific reason. And that place is cool, with the pool and the barn and the big yard and all that."

He's angling at something that makes my heart thump so hard in my chest that it hurts. "James, what are you saying?"

He won't quite look at me, and I palm his cheek, using his beard to tug his face down so he has to look at me. "Just…that, um—I guess, that I do plan on moving, selling the place and…and moving some-where. So, what you said, about us wanting to be to-gether—it wouldn't necessarily be that big of an issue. If you, um. If you were—"

I can't help the giddy, excited, happy grin from

spreading across my face. "Say it, James. Don't be shy."

He looks down at me and chuckles wryly. "You're getting a kick out of this, aren't you?"

I nod. "Oh yeah." I wriggle against him like an excited puppy. "I'm all in, James. I've been doing my damnedest to hold my emotions in check. To stay even a little objective. But, that day at your pool party, I—I fucking fell for you then. I was scared about how strongly I felt for you within seconds of just...*seeing* you. And then we kissed, and I...god, James, I *knew*."

"You knew?"

I nod. "I was ready to go all in back then, except for being scared to death of falling in love again. It took this long just to accept that it was happening, that I couldn't stop it—that there was not a damned thing I could do to stop myself from falling in love with you, totally and completely." I sigh. "I was just in denial. The guilt of feeling like I was betraying Craig plus, the fact that I knew you were in no way ready to know how hard I was falling...it was all too much, and I sort of retreated from it, mentally and emotionally. Tried to bury it, hold it back, or—or pretend it wasn't real, wasn't there."

James is swallowing hard, eyes dancing as they search my face.

"I can't hold it back anymore, James." I move astride him—it's both sexual and something else: I need him, I want him, I need to be closer to him—as close as I can physically get, sexually and emotionally and physically and spiritually. "I just can't. I hope you're buckled up, baby, because I'm about to get super fucking clingy and needy and demanding."

He weaves his fingers into my hair, massaging my scalp, pulling my face to his. "How the fuck do I deserve you, Nova?"

I shake my head. "There's no deserving—that's not a thing."

He swallows hard, and when he speaks his voice is cracked and hoarse. "I—I thought my heart was…dead. Broken. I thought I'd never—never feel this again. I didn't think I *wanted* to. I didn't think I *could*." He shakes his head, too full of emotion to speak, for a moment. "I'm alive with you in a way I…in a way I thought was impossible."

"So, what were you trying to say about selling your house?" I say, prompting him.

He laughs. "I was saying that once this place is finished, and once we've had some time to get the girls used to us being together, that if you're open to the idea, we could…be here. With you. Together."

"What about your pole barn?" I ask. "All your tools and workout equipment and all that." I gesture at my backyard—which, while sizable, is in no way going to accommodate all that. "It's not happening out there—sorry, babe, but that pole barn of yours is bigger than my whole yard."

He shrugs. "I dunno. I've been running the company out of my garage up till now. But I was thinking of expanding, taking on a few more guys so Jess, Ryder, and Franco have time to pursue their own projects here and there. And to expand I'd need a separate facility for a fleet of trucks, a warehouse for tools and building materials. I kind of want to focus more on new builds, which would mean a couple different crews. I've taken a look at a few possible industrial properties that may work. Point is, all that shit would go there."

I plant my palms on his shoulders. "I like this plan." I frown. "I wonder if you may need to do that addition Franco mentioned. Another bedroom or two, another bathroom, bigger garage…a pool."

"You do, huh?" His eyes follow the pendulous swaying of my breasts, and I know the conversation is close to over. "You wouldn't mind me and the girls moving in with you?"

I shake my head, nuzzle my nose against his. "No, James. Not only would I not mind it, I can't think of anything that would make me happier." I sigh, and feather my lips against his.

James cups a breast, palms my buttock. "No? Nothing?"

I reach down between my thighs, and find him waiting for me, hard and thick and hot and incredible—and incredibly mine. I stroke him slowly—more of a sweet caress than a greedy clutch.

"Actually..." I writhe against him, sliding his thickness between the damp lips of my core. "I can think of *one* thing."

He reaches out, rips open a condom—I take it from him and take my time rolling it on, making a pleasurable game of it, making it take as long as I possibly can. Once it's on, rolled to the root, I nestle the very tip of him inside me and writhe my hips in a slow, teasing undulation.

He groans, moves, and tries to thrust. I take his hands and tangle our fingers, pressing his palms to the pillow over his head.

I continue teasing him with quick, shallow movements. "Want it?" I whisper.

"Fuck, Nova—yes! I want it. I need it."

I crash my mouth against his and kiss him with all the need inside me, while continuing the teasing roll of my hips.

He snarls like the grizzly bear he resembles, and breaks my grip, sits upright, and slams up into me. I laugh even as I cry out, snaking my arms around his neck and clinging to him, thrashing up and down on him—taking all of him, hard and fast. He's feral, then—primal. All mad passion, taking me with everything he is, everything he has.

He wraps my long red hair around a fist and pulls me closer, kissing me while his other arm curls around my waist to clutch my opposite hip. He bites my lower lip and moans; I cling to his neck and shoulders and let my voice ring out. He grips my ass and parts me to drive deeper, and deeper, and I feel myself clenching, spasming around him as he thrusts into me, kissing me and tugging me wider.

I bury my face in his neck, whimpering through my climax, and the moment I begin to orgasm, he cries out pushing deep, groaning, snarling.

And every sound I make, then, is his name... every sigh, every grunt, every snarl from his lips is mine.

He presses our foreheads together. "Look at me," he murmurs; my eyes snap open. "I love you, Nova. I love you—I love you, I love you..." This, to the rhythm of our joining.

I find the rhythm, match it, echoing him, responding: "Love you—I love you—god, James, James—I love you!"

When neither of us has anything left, no breath in our lungs, no climax left in our bodies, we flop back on the bed, me on top of him again, and this time I'm cradled in his arms, heedless of the mess going cold and sticky against my thigh, content to breathe him, hold him, be held by him, to feel his breath on my hair and his arms around me and his hands roaming my skin as if he just can't get enough of touching all of me.

"Can we just do this forever?" I whisper.

He rumbles a laugh. "We may have to leave the house eventually."

"Nah. There's delivery. All we need is food and condoms, and the occasional nap."

James sighs happily, contentedly. "I guess you're right."

I nuzzle against his beard. "At the very least, we can stay up all night fucking like we're sixteen again."

He rumbles, somewhere between aroused and amused. "Keeping up with you is gonna be fun, isn't it?"

I pat his chest. "You can try. You've awakened a very needy creature inside me, James. I hope you've got your A game ready."

"More than ready. Bring it, babe." He slaps my butt. "Got anything to eat? Or should I call the afore-mentioned delivery?"

I wriggle. "I've got something for you to eat, all right."

He grumbles a laugh. "You really are insatiable,

aren't you?"

"You have *no* idea."

"Maybe not, but I'm sure as hell looking for-ward to finding out."

"So am I," I whisper, as he begins to do dirty and thrilling things to me. "So am I."

THE END

EPILOGUE

Three years later

I'M SITTING IN A ROCKING CHAIR ON THE FRONT PORCH OF Ryder and Laurel's farmhouse. On my lap is little Renée Audra—she's three years old, sassy, too smart for her own good, rambunctious, a brown-haired, brown-eyed beauty with the most infectious laugh in the world. Right now, however, she's sleepy. Not quite asleep, but close. It's almost six in the evening, and it's been a full day; she usually takes a nap around eleven or noon, but today she didn't get one, being too busy helping me, her auntie Nova, get ready.

I married James today. Here, in Ryder and Laurel's front yard. Nina, thirteen, and Ella, ten and a half, were bridesmaids, along with Laurel and Audra, of course. Imogen was my maid of honor, and Renée was the flower girl—a duty she took with such seriousness it became comical.

Renée has a younger brother: JJ—for Jesse James,

but no one has ever called him that since the day he was born, two years ago. JJ was another surprise for Jesse and Imogen, and arrived after an all-too-easy pregnancy and complication-free birth. At two, he's a hellion of the highest order, a troublemaking, back-talking, mischievous, manically energetic little boy with a curiosity and compulsion to tinker that's bound to get him in as much trouble as it does bring him success—he's a spitting image of Jesse, with shaggy, curly brown hair and expressive brown eyes that he can use at will to charm just about anyone out of just about anything. Currently, he's trying to ride Ryder and Laurel's Great Pyrenees, Goblin, who is patiently allowing JJ to climb all over her without so much as an irritated look.

Helping JJ in his quest to ride the dog is Colin, Audra and Franco's son—also two years old. Adopted by Audra and Franco at birth, Colin is black, with an untamable explosion of thick, tightly curled hair that Audra refuses to cut; he's the quietest of the bunch, but just as much of a troublemaker—he's actually the ringleader, he just isn't loud about it. Audra was unable to conceive, and after almost a year of trying, she and Franco decided to adopt rather than pursue fertility treatments or in vitro; it took a few months of searching and a few months more of background checks and home studies, but exactly two years ago today, as a matter of fact, a young woman gave birth in a downtown Chicago hospital, kissed her baby once on the cheek, and then, tearfully, handed him to Audra. The young woman, Maeve, was seventeen at the time, and struggling to finish high school; now, she's about to graduate from a community college with an associate's degree in liberal arts, and plans to transfer to Northwestern to pursue journalism; Colin's adoption was open, and she makes the trip to the suburbs once a month to play at the park with Colin and visit with Audra and Franco, who have, unofficially, somewhat adopted her as well. They've helped her with college tuition, helped her find scholarships and grants, and often make surprise visits to Chicago to bring her food and clean laundry.

Laurel and Ryder are in rocking chairs beside me; Laurel is breastfeeding her six-month-old girl, Natalie, who was yet another unexpected but welcome surprise—apparently James and I are the only ones in the group who know how birth control works. James actually got a vasectomy last year, as we, after months of discussion, decided more children weren't in our future. My maternal instincts are totally fulfilled by being a stepmother to Nina and Ella. They both called me Nova up until last year, and then, abruptly, Ella started calling me Mom, which made me cry tears of happiness and sent James out to the garage to hide his own emotional reaction—we all followed him, though, and surrounded him with girly hugs and refused to let him get away with his macho "I'm not crying, I just have dust in my eye" routine. Once Ella started, Nina wasn't far behind; she resisted for about two weeks, and then "slipped," as she put it. She remembered her mother more than Ella, and it was much harder for her to make the transition to seeing me as Mom, and not just Dad's girlfriend, but once Ella started calling me Mom, it was easier for Nina to get on board.

"Auntie Nova?" Renée murmurs, her head against my chest.

"Yeah, pumpkin?"

"I'm not sleepy."

I laugh. "Okay, sure—whatever you say, honey."

"I'm not!" She's fading, even as she protests. "I'm just watching a movie in my head."

I laugh again. "Not sure what that means, but okay."

"Can I have more cake?"

"Maybe later. You'll have to ask your mom and dad. I think, for now, you should just let me cuddle you. Keep watching that movie in your head."

"Are you and Unc'a Jamie gonna have a baby now that you're married?"

I shake my head. "No, pumpkin. We're not."

"Why not?"

"Just…because."

"Because it's too complicated to explain to little kids?"

I laugh at that. "Pretty much, honey." I scratch her back with my fingernails. "Just rest, Renée."

"Fine. But I'm not sleepy."

"I believe you," I murmur.

And then, just like that, she's out.

James clomps loudly up the steps at that moment. "Where's my little bugaboo?" he growls playfully.

I shush him, widening my eyes and glancing significantly down at the sleeping bundle on my lap.

James makes an "oops" face, and kneels quietly at my side. "Oh, sorry."

Renée doesn't stir, but she mumbles sleepily, "Hush, Unc'a Jamie. I'm resting."

James laughs, kissing her on the temple. "Sorry, pumpkin. Keep resting."

I shake my head at him and he winces, before settling his butt on the porch. Together, we watch JJ and Colin in their tireless quest to get Goblin to let them ride her; Nate is on the tire swing not far away, watching them with amusement.

Nina comes out of the house at that moment, letting the screen door slam with a loud bang that startles Natalie, who snuffles at Laurel's breast, whimpers, and then goes back to nursing.

"Mom?" She gestures with her cell phone. "Josh is being a jerk."

I eye her over Renée's head. "Ignore him."

"He wants me to come over, but I said I couldn't because I have a family thing going on today. I was gonna tell him you and Dad were getting married, but then I'd have to explain things and that's just annoying, so I didn't. He keeps texting me about coming over to do homework with him, even though I know all he's doing is playing that dumb video game of his. He just wants me to do his math for him."

Josh is her best friend—or, as we call him, her "friend-boy" because they've "liked" each other since fifth grade and are already making plans for announcing that they're officially dating—which James has decreed won't be allowed until they're at least fifteen. Until then, they can like each other all they want, have all the feelings they want, but they're not allowed to date, to say they're dating, to refer to each other as boyfriend/girlfriend, or anything of the sort, because, as James says—there's no such thing as being in love in middle school.

It is cute, though, how they are with each other. They text and talk all the time, and when they can't hang out at our house or Josh's, they're FaceTiming and helping each other with homework…which usually means Nina doing most of Josh's for him, because while he's plenty smart, he's a little lazy with the schoolwork, and Nina is an overachiever with a little mama instinct a mile wide and a mile deep, and will do it for him if he procrastinates long enough. In turn, though, he carries her backpack for her in the hallways, helps her with her chores around the house, and helps her study in the one subject she's hopeless in—social studies.

Ella finds the whole thing amusing and gross at the same time, and gets a ridiculous amount of amusement out of tagging along with them just to annoy Nina, even though Josh thinks of Ella as his own little sister and doesn't mind when she tags along on their teenage adventures.

Dad Bod Construction became Dad Bod Homes a year and a half ago—Franco, Ryder, and Jesse each bought a full quarter share of a new company the four of them now own, building custom homes together. James is the architect and project manager, Jesse is in charge of framing, Ryder handles the electrical installation and oversees the plumbing as well, Franco does the interior finishes, and each of them has their own crew under them. The business is a booming success—James's designs are cozy, open, and attractive, and with Jesse handling the interior design—along with Imogen and Laurel, who now both work for the company in various capacities—the waitlist for a Dad Bod house is over eighteen months. They are able to construct the homes in short order as well, since James and Jesse work together to break ground and start construction on a new home while Franco and Ryder work on finishing the previous one, and then Jesse circles back to put on the finishing touches while Ryder and Franco start on the next one.

I went back to school during these past three years, got my MD, and I'm now in the process of completing my residency at the hospital here in town. I plan on continuing my education, specializing in neuroscience—my time as head assistant to the lead neurologist piqued my interest in the subject and, in a couple more years, I'll be a licensed neurologist myself.

James takes my hand and squeezes it; I don't have to even look at him to know what he's thinking: the girls love nothing more than to be allowed to stay over here and help Laurel with the baby—and by help, I mean spoil rotten. Laurel loves having them over, because Nate, as loving as he is as an older brother, is a clueless teenager when it comes to caring for a baby, so having girls around who *want* to change diapers and make bottles and rock and play means she gets to have a little breather and enjoy some semi-free baby downtime.

Which means, with the girls staying here tonight, we'll have the house to ourselves; we all live in my house, and have for a couple of years now, since the remodel was completed. That took a bit longer than expected, because we expanded pretty significantly, adding two bedrooms and another full Jack-and-Jill bathroom, enlarging the garage by more than double, with a den/home office for James above it, and an in-ground pool out back. My house is in the same school district as they'd been in, so it was an easy transition for them, and we all started feeling like a family right away.

Although, James and I had to learn to be sneaky about our sexual escapades.

"I was thinking we could watch that movie about the *cowgirl*," James says, emphasizing the word.

I chuckle. "Isn't that the one where the roles get *reversed*?" I say.

This is a little game we play; we plan out which positions we want to have sex in later, but doing so in conversation around other people. Our little exchange just now means he wants cowgirl, and I added to make it reverse cowgirl.

James doesn't answer, but the way he shifts tells me he's already imagining it.

Ryder snorts. "You two are not subtle, you know that?"

James glances at him. "What do you mean?"

Ryder gestures at us. "You two, and your cute little coded conversations. Do you really think none of us have ever cottoned on to what you're doing?"

"I don't have a single clue what you mean, Ryder," James says.

Ryder cackles. "Right. And I'm the Queen of England."

James eyes him. "You're too ugly to be the queen."

"Drag queen, maybe," Jesse adds, coming up to the porch with four beer bottles in his hands.

Franco is behind him, carrying Colin over his shoulder like a potato sack. "Nah, he's too ugly even to be a drag queen. Although, his man-boobs are big enough that he wouldn't need to stuff his bra."

Ryder glances down at his chest. "I do *not* have man-boobs, you dumb twink." He flexes his pecs, alternating them. "These are a hundred percent solid muscle, sonny. Something you and your sissy little CrossFit-nancy friends would know nothing about."

Oh god, here we go. Not this conversation again. "Can you guys not argue CrossFit versus powerlifting again?" I groan. "It's getting old."

"What's getting old is Franco," Ryder says. "All that high impact cardio is making his joints creak like a geriatric with arthritic knees."

"At least I can *see* my knees past my belly," Franco says, putting Colin down and poking Ryder in the stomach.

"Hey, asshat, that's solid muscle too." He pokes his own belly. "Just...it's hidden beneath a layer of softness. Makes me approachable to women and children. You just scare them with your veiny, six percent body fat scarecrow look."

"You look like Tim Allen in *The Santa Clause*, when he dyes his beard red in an attempt to not look like Santa," Franco says. "And watch your language around my kid, you tubby bitch."

James and I half sigh, half laugh at the banter between the guys. Colin has escaped Franco's notice and is back out in the yard, trying to get Nate to push him on the tire swing, but he wants to swing on it upside down, hanging underneath it like a monkey, and Nate is trying to convince him why it's a bad idea. JJ is digging in the dirt under a juniper bush near the side of the house, Goblin the dog is finally napping now that the boys have left her alone. Baby Renée is sleeping, Natalie is resting on Ryder's chest and being burped, Ella is watching a Disney movie inside, Nina is text-fighting with Josh and sitting on James's knee... it's a beautiful summer evening, and I'm officially Nova Bod, James's wife, and the happiest woman on earth.

Although, judging by the matching blissed-out expressions on Laurel, Audra, and Imogen's faces as they each find a comfortable position on or near their husbands, they may each be thinking the same thing:

How did we get so lucky?

Life is bliss, in this big, happy family, and I wouldn't change a single thing..

Jasinda Wilder

Visit me at my website: **www.jasindawilder.com**
Email me: **jasindawilder@gmail.com**

If you enjoyed this book, you can help others enjoy it as well by recommending it to friends and family, or by mentioning it in reading and discussion groups and online forums. You can also review it on the site from which you purchased it. But, whether you recommend it to anyone else or not, thank you *so much* for taking the time to read my book! Your support means the world to me!

My other titles:

The Preacher's Son:
Unbound
Unleashed
Unbroken

Biker Billionaire:
Wild Ride

Big Girls Do It:

Better (#1), Wetter (#2), Wilder (#3), On Top (#4)

Married (#5)

On Christmas (#5.5)

Pregnant (#6)

Boxed Set

Rock Stars Do It:

Harder

Dirty

Forever

Boxed Set

From the world of *Big Girls* and *Rock Stars*:

Big Love Abroad

Delilah's Diary:

A Sexy Journey

La Vita Sexy

A Sexy Surrender

The Falling Series:

Falling Into You

Falling Into Us

Falling Under

Falling Away

Falling for Colton

The Ever Trilogy:
Forever & Always
After Forever
Saving Forever

The world of *Alpha*:
Alpha
Beta
Omega
Harris: Alpha One Security Book 1
Thresh: Alpha One Security Book 2
Duke: Alpha One Security Book 3
Puck: Alpha One Security Book 4

The world of Stripped:
Stripped
Trashed

The world of *Wounded*:
Wounded
Captured

The Houri Legends:
Jack and Djinn
Djinn and Tonic

The Black Room
(With Jade London):
Door One

Door Two

Door Three

Door Four

Door Five

Door Six

Door Seven

Door Eight

Deleted Door

Standalone titles:
Yours

Non-Fiction titles:
You Can Do It

You Can Do It: Strength

You Can Do It: Fasting

You Can Do It: Cookbook

Jack Wilder Titles:
The Missionary

To be informed of new releases and special offers,
sign up for
Jasinda's email newsletter.

www.ingramcontent.com/pod-product-compliance
Lightning Source LLC
Chambersburg PA
CBHW050535260626
47157CB00002B/310

* 9 7 8 1 9 4 8 4 4 5 2 2 1 *